Praise for the novels of RaeAnne Thayne

"A heartfelt tale of sorrow, redemption and new beginnings that will touch readers."
—*RT Book Reviews* on *Sweet Laurel Falls*

"Plenty of tenderness and Colorado sunshine flavor this pleasant escape."
—*Publishers Weekly* on *Woodrose Mountain*

"Thayne, once again, delivers a heartfelt story of a caring community and a caring romance between adults who have triumphed over tragedies."
—*Booklist* on *Woodrose Mountain*

"Readers will love this novel for the cast of characters and its endearing plotline… A thoroughly enjoyable read."
—*RT Book Reviews* on *Woodrose Mountain*

"Thayne's series starter introduces the Colorado town of Hope's Crossing in what can be described as a cozy romance… [A] gentle, easy read."
—*Publishers Weekly* on *Blackberry Summer*

"Thayne's depiction of a small Colorado mountain town is subtle but evocative. Readers who love romance but not explicit sexual details will delight in this heartfelt tale of healing and hope."
—*Booklist* on *Blackberry Summer*

Also by RaeAnne Thayne

Look for RaeAnne Thayne's next novel
The December Market
available soon from Canary Street Press.

For a complete list of books by RaeAnne Thayne,
please visit raeannethayne.com.

RaeAnne Thayne

WILLOWLEAF LANE

CANARY STREET PRESS

CANARY
STREET
PRESS™

Recycling programs
for this product may
not exist in your area.

ISBN-13: 978-1-335-00863-3

Willowleaf Lane

First published in 2013. This edition published in 2024.

Canary Street Press
22 Adelaide St. West, 41st Floor
Toronto, Ontario M5H 4E3, Canada
CanaryStPress.com

Printed in U.S.A.

To my wonderful sisters-in-law,
Karla Freebairn, Melanie Child, Sherri Robinson
and Rose Robinson. I love the four sisters I was born with
but I'm so grateful I gained four more from my husband
and through my brothers' wise choices.

CHAPTER ONE

Charlotte Caine considered herself a pretty good judge of character.

Being morbidly obese most of her life, until the serious changes she had made the past year and a half, had given her an interesting insight into human nature. She wanted to think she had seen the best and the worst in people. Some people pretended she was invisible; others had been visibly disgusted as if afraid being fat might rub off on them, while still others treated her with true kindness.

Given her skills in that particular arena, she liked to play a game with herself, trying to guess the candy preferences of the customers coming into her store. Jawbreakers? Lemon drops? Or some of her heavenly fudge? Which would they pick?

When Sugar Rush was slow, like right now on a lazy July day late in the afternoon, it made a pleasant way to pass the time.

By the looks of the skinny preteen with the too-heavy eye makeup, Charlotte guessed she would pick a couple packs of chewing gum and maybe a handful of the sour balls the kids seemed to love for some reason Charlotte didn't understand.

But she could be wrong.

"Is there something I can help you with?" she finally

asked with a smile when the girl appeared to dither in front of the long counter that held the hand-dipped chocolates.

The girl shrugged without meeting her eye. With all that makeup, the dark hair, the pale features, Charlotte was reminded of a curious little raccoon.

"Don't know yet," she answered. "I haven't decided."

She stopped in front of the fudge, her gaze going back and forth between items inside the display.

"The blackberry fudge is particularly delicious today, if I do say so myself," Charlotte said helpfully after a moment. "It's one of my better batches."

The girl looked from the silky fudge to Charlotte. "You made it? For real?"

Charlotte had to smile at the disbelief in her voice. "Cross my heart. The brand-name candy in my store comes from a distributor, but Sugar Rush produced everything in this display case."

She didn't try to keep the pride out of her voice. She had every reason to be happy at the success of Sugar Rush. She had built up the gourmet candy store from nothing to become one of the busiest establishments in the resort town of Hope's Crossing, Colorado. She had two other full-time employees and four part-time and might have to expand that in the future, given the rapid growth in her online orders.

"Wow. That looks like a ton of work."

"It can be." She loved the candy-making part but hated the inevitable accounting required in running a small business. "It's interesting work, though. Have you ever seen anybody dip chocolates by hand?"

Her young customer shook her head even as an older couple came into the store. They had probably come from the big RV she could see parked in a miraculously open spot. She smiled at them as they migrated instantly to the boxed jelly beans displayed against the far wall.

"It's pretty cool. My crew usually starts early in the morning and wraps it up by about noon, when it starts to get too warm for things to set up."

When she first opened the store, Charlotte had made everything herself but she inevitably ran out of inventory by the end of each day. Now she had three people who came to her back kitchen before 6:00 a.m. to hand-dip the sweets. She still made most of the fudge herself, prepared in the traditional copper pots with wooden spoons.

"You're welcome to come watch," she said. "Are you staying in town long?"

"I really hope not," the girl muttered fervently, her expression dark.

"Oh, ouch." Charlotte smiled. "Some of us actually choose to live in Hope's Crossing, you know. We like it here."

The girl fiddled with the strap on her messenger bag adorned with buttons and pins. "Sorry," she mumbled. "I'm sure it's a nice town and all. But nobody asked me if I wanted to move here. Nobody cares what I think about anything."

Sympathy welled up inside Charlotte. She knew very well what it was like to be this age, feeling as if her life was spinning completely out of her control.

Who was she kidding? She had spent most of her life feeling out of control.

"So you're moving here. Welcome! You know, you might discover you really like it. Stranger things have happened."

"I doubt that."

"Give it some time. Talk to me again after you've been in town a few weeks. I'm Charlotte, by the way. Charlotte Caine."

"Peyton," the girl offered and Charlotte had the strange feeling the omission of her last name had been quite deliberate. The fairly unusual first name struck a chord somewhere in her subconscious but she couldn't quite place where she might have heard it before.

"Would you like to sample a couple flavors so you can choose?"

"Is that okay?"

"Sure. We give customers sample tastes all the time. It's quite sneaky, actually. One taste and I've generally hooked them."

Small pieces of the different variations of fudge were arranged in a covered glass cake tray on the countertop. She removed the lid and after a moment's scrutiny, separated a few flavors onto one of the pretty plastic filigree sample plates she kept for that purpose then handed it to the girl.

"These are our three most popular flavors. Blackberry, peanut butter and white chocolate."

She waited while the girl tried them and had to smile when her eyes glazed a little with pleasure after each taste. She loved watching people enjoy her creations, even though she hardly tried them herself anymore except to test for flavor mixes.

"These are *so* good! Wow."

"Thanks. I'm glad you like it."

"No. *Seriously* good! I don't know which to choose. It's all so yummy."

"See why the samples are a sneaky idea?"

"Yeah. Totally. Okay, I guess I'll take a pound of the blackberry and a pound of the peanut butter."

"Good choices." Two pounds of fudge was a large amount, but maybe Peyton had a big family to share it with.

"Oh, and I'll take a pound of the cinnamon bears. I love cinnamon."

Charlotte smiled. "Same here. Cinnamon is my favorite."

She enjoyed finding yet another point of commonality between them. Maybe that explained her sympathy for the girl, who appeared so lost and unhappy.

While Charlotte hadn't been uprooted at this tender age to a new community, she might as well have been. Her entire world, her whole perspective, had undergone a dramatic continental shift at losing her mother. She had felt like she was living in a new world, one where nobody else could possibly understand her pain.

While Charlotte cut, weighed and wrapped the fudge, Peyton wandered around the store looking at some of the Colorado souvenirs Charlotte stocked.

The husband half of the older couple clutched a bag with saltwater taffy while his wife had several boxes of jelly beans in her arms. The two of them moved to the chocolate display and started debating the merits of dipped cashews versus cherries.

Charlotte smiled politely, waiting for the argument to play out. When Peyton approached the cash register, Charlotte held out the bag of sweets.

"Here you go," she said.

"Thanks." Instead of taking it immediately, Peyton reached into her bag and retrieved a hard-sided snap wallet with splashy pink flowers on a black background.

She pulled out a credit card and Charlotte spied several more inside the wallet.

She felt a moment's disquiet. Why would a girl barely on the brink of adolescence need multiple credit cards? Had she stolen them? Charlotte wondered fleetingly, but discarded the idea just as quickly.

She had certainly been wrong about people before. She would be delusional to believe her instincts were foolproof. History would certainly bear that out. She had instinctively liked Peyton, though, and didn't want to believe her a thief.

She probably had self-absorbed, indulgent parents— divorced, more than likely—who thought throwing another credit card at her would fix any heartbreak or trauma.

Charlotte slid the card back across the clear counter. "Tell you what. No charge. Why don't you consider this a welcome-to-Hope's-Crossing sort of thing?"

Peyton's mouth dropped open a little and she stared at Charlotte, obviously astonished by the simple kindness. "Seriously?"

"Sure. It's a gift for you and your family."

At her words, the look in Peyton's dark eyes shifted from incredulity to a quiet sort of despair before she veiled her expression.

"I don't have a family," she declared, her voice small but with a hint of defiance.

Was she a runaway? Charlotte considered. Should she be alerting Riley McKnight, the police chief of Hope's Crossing, so he could help reunite her with whomever she had escaped? With the vague idea of keeping the girl talking so she could glean as much information as possible, she glanced at the other couple and saw they were busy sampling every variety of fudge.

"Nobody at all?" she asked.

Peyton shrugged, the movement barely rippling her thin shoulders inside the T-shirt that looked a size or two too large. "I had a mom but she died last year."

Ah. Maybe that explained Charlotte's instant empathy, that subtle connection she felt for the girl.

"I'm sorry. My mom died when I was about your age, too. Sucks, doesn't it?"

Peyton made a sound that could have been a snort or a rough laugh. "You could say that."

"So who do you live with, then?" she asked with studied casualness.

"My stupid dad," Peyton said and Charlotte felt herself relax. Okay. The girl had a dad. One she wasn't crazy about, apparently. No need to jump to conclusions because she said she had no family.

"Where is your dad?"

She pointed out the door. "He stopped to take a phone call. I got bored waiting around so I came in here."

"No brothers or sisters?"

"No. Just me."

"So you and your dad are moving to Hope's Crossing together?"

"Yeah." Her mouth tightened. "He took a job here even though I told him I didn't want to move. I had to leave all my friends in Portland, my best friend, Victoria, this boy I like, Carson, and the mall and everything. This dumb town doesn't have any good stores."

Charlotte, for one, had hated clothes shopping when she was Peyton's age. Even before her mom died, she had been pudgy, with plenty of baby fat that stubbornly clung on. Afterward, the pounds just piled on until she couldn't find a single thing that fit in any store except what she had considered the fat old lady stores.

Now her favorite thing was to go into a clothing store and actually have choices.

"We have a pretty decent bookstore and a couple nice boutiques that specifically cater to teens. And a killer candy store," she added with a smile.

Peyton didn't look thrilled about any of those offerings. "Yeah. I guess. It's not the same as Portland. I could buy *anything* there."

Charlotte wasn't sure the shopping options were the measure of what made a good town, but she decided not to offer that particular opinion.

"The good news is, as long as you've got an internet connection, you can still find everything you like. And Denver's only a few hours' drive."

"I guess that's true."

Peyton still didn't look convinced of the wonders of Hope's Crossing. Charlotte couldn't blame her. Change could be tough for anyone, especially a young girl who had no control over her own circumstances.

"Thanks for the fudge," Peyton said.

"You're welcome. Come back anytime. Next time maybe I'll have cinnamon fudge for you."

"You make that? Really?"

"Sure. It's generally something I have only around the holidays but I'll see about a special order."

The small cowbell hanging on the door rang out. Charlotte looked up from Peyton, donning her customary friendly smile of greeting—then the smile and everything else inside her froze when she caught sight of the man who'd just walked through.

Oh, crap.

Her stomach dived like the time she accidentally wandered into a black-diamond ski run when her older brother Dylan took her up to the resort once.

"There you are." The man was gorgeous, with a square jawline, a slim elegant nose and hazel eyes fringed by long lashes.

Smokin' Hot Spencer Gregory. The cameras and sports magazines had loved him, once upon a time.

"Why didn't you tell me you wanted to leave? One minute you were there, the next I turned around and you were gone."

The curious girl who had tasted Charlotte's fudge with such appreciation disappeared, replaced by a sullen, angry creature who glowered at the man.

"I did," she muttered. "I said I wanted to come in here. I said it like three times. I guess you were too busy with your phone call to notice."

He frowned. "Pey, you can't just wander off. I was worried about you."

"What did you think was going to happen in this stupid town? I was going to die of boredom or something?"

Right now, Charlotte would give anything to be wearing something sultry and sleek. Black, skintight, with some strategically placed bling, maybe. Instead, after all these years she had to face him with little makeup and her hair yanked back into a ponytail, wearing jeans and a simple blue T-shirt, covered by an apron that had Sugar Rush emblazoned across the chest.

At least she wasn't wearing the ridiculous hairnet required while making fudge. Small favors, right?

She had barely registered the thought when the full

implications of the moment washed over her like molten chocolate.

Peyton. *Peyton.* Why hadn't she figured it out? That's why the name had seemed familiar—somewhere in the recesses of her brain, in the file marked Spencer Gregory that she had purposely buried as deeply as she could over the years, she suddenly remembered Spence had a twelve-year-old daughter. Named Peyton.

And the said Peyton had just mentioned that her father had taken a job in Hope's Crossing and they were moving to town.

Oh. My. Fudge.

Spencer Gregory, the only person on the planet she could honestly say she despised, was back in Hope's Crossing. Permanently.

Why on *earth* hadn't anybody bothered to tell her this particular juicy rumor? She had to think that, by some miracle, the news hadn't made the rounds yet. Otherwise it would have been the topic of conversation everywhere she went.

The bag with its silvery Sugar Rush logo still lay on the countertop. She picked it up and held it out.

"Here you go," she said to Peyton. Her voice came out cold and small and she widened her smile to compensate.

"Um. Thanks. Thanks a lot." The girl finally reached out and grabbed it and shoved it into her messenger bag.

"How much does she owe you?" Spence reached into his wallet with what one of the women's magazines had once declared the sexiest smile in sports.

If she had known Spence Gregory would be eating some of her fudge, she might have had second thoughts about tossing it around indiscriminately.

"She said I didn't owe her anything. It's a gift to welcome us to town," Peyton stated.

Spence looked just as stunned by the gesture as his daughter had. "Wow. Thanks."

He *should* be astonished. Charlotte sincerely doubted anybody in town would be standing with open arms to welcome back their native son. As far as many people were concerned, Spence Gregory had taken the clean, charming image of Hope's Crossing and, as her brothers might have said, hawked a loogie all over it.

"Wow. Thank you. That's very kind of you."

"You're welcome," she lied gruffly.

His smile deepened as he gazed at her without a trace of recognition. There was a certain light in those hazel eyes, something bright and warm and almost… appreciative.

The nerves in her stomach sizzled. Oh, how she would have loved to be the recipient of that kind of look from him when she was fifteen. Back then—okay, even as recently as a year ago—she never would have dreamed it was ever within the realm of possibility.

Instead of making her giddy, having Spence Gregory smile at her *now,* after all this time, only infuriated her.

She deliberately turned away from him to his daughter. "Peyton, come back anytime. I'll see what I can do about the cinnamon fudge."

The girl gave her a hesitant smile that meant far more than her father's well-practiced one. As she did, Charlotte became aware that the browsing couple that had been in her store for what felt like hours was in the middle of a whispered argument.

Finally the husband stepped forward. "You're Smoke Gregory, aren't you?"

Spence stiffened, his friendly smile melting away. "Yeah," he said tersely.

"I knew it. Didn't I tell you I knew it?" he crowed to his wife. "And you said he wouldn't dare show his face in public!"

"Darwin, hush!" she said, her face turning scarlet.

Spence had gone completely rigid, a hard, solid block of granite in the middle of her store.

"Well, I just want you to know, we're big baseball fans. We love the Pioneers. We live in Pendleton and drove to Portland several times just to watch you play."

"Did you?"

"Yeah. You were a darn good ballplayer. Shame about everything else."

"Isn't it?" he bit out.

"And for what it's worth," the woman said, her face still red, "we don't think you killed your wife."

Charlotte could only stare at the couple, appalled, as what little color was left in Peyton's pale features seeped away like spring runoff.

Fury sparked in Spence's gaze and Charlotte shivered at the heat of it. He placed a big hand on Peyton's shoulder, who went taut.

"Good to know," he said coldly.

"Could we have your autograph?" the woman asked in a rush. "Our grandson followed your whole career. Had a poster on his bedroom wall and everything, right up until…" Her voice trailed off at something she saw in Spence's dark features.

After a moment, he seemed to take a deep breath. He lifted his hand from Peyton's shoulder. To Charlotte's astonishment, he managed to look almost calm.

"Do you have anything for me to sign?"

After an awkward pause, the husband of the couple grabbed one of Charlotte's printed Sugar Rush napkins and thrust it at him, along with one of the pens she kept by the register in a pretty beaded canister she had made.

Spence used the countertop to sign the napkin with a flourish. From her vantage point, she managed to read the message upside down. Generic and succinct. *Best wishes. Spencer Gregory.* Along with the number forty-two he had famously worn through more than a decade as a starting pitcher for the Portland Pioneers.

The wife gripped the napkin and Charlotte realized they had dropped all their purchases atop a bin full of root beer barrels. They left the store without buying anything, leaving behind a vast, echoing silence in the store.

Charlotte never expected she would have a moment's sympathy for Spence Gregory, not after everything, but in light of that painful encounter, she couldn't help a little tingle of dismay. Was it like that for him everywhere he went?

"Are you ready to go?" he asked his daughter.

She nodded and headed for the door.

"Thanks again," Spence said. He cocked his head, his gaze narrowed. "You look familiar. I have a feeling I'm going to be saying that a lot now I'm back in Hope's Crossing. Did I know you when I lived here before?"

For a horrifying moment, Charlotte didn't know how to answer him. He didn't recognize her. How could she tell him they'd sat across from each other a couple nights a week at her dad's café for years? That she spent night after night helping him with his English homework?

That he had once broken her heart into a million tiny glass shards?

She had to say something, even though she knew perfectly well what his reaction would be.

"Yes," she muttered.

He scrutinized her harder, obviously trying to place her. "I'm sorry. I'm afraid you're going to have to help me out."

She didn't *have* to do anything. Just for a moment, she wished one of her older brothers was around to politely encourage him to leave her store. They were just as big, just as tough as Spence Gregory. In fact, she thought Jamie might even be bigger.

"Charlotte Caine," she finally murmured.

Just as she expected, his eyes widened with disbelief first and then astonishment.

"Char... Of course. Wow. You look fantastic!"

"Thanks," she said, her voice clipped.

"Really fantastic. I wouldn't have recognized you."

"You didn't." She pointed out the obvious.

"True enough."

"I have to admit, I'm surprised to see you. Somehow I hadn't heard you were coming back."

"You mean nobody has started a petition yet to keep me away?" He said the words in a joking tone but both of them knew it wasn't far from the truth.

"Not that I've signed yet."

Though his mouth quirked up with amusement at her pointed reply, she thought she saw just a hint of bleakness in his gaze. Again, she felt that flutter of unexpected sympathy.

"Harry Lange brought me in to be the director of

the new recreation center in town," he answered. "I'm starting tomorrow."

Of course. She should have known Harry Lange was somehow involved. The town's richest citizen didn't seem happy unless he was stirring up trouble somewhere. Still, this seemed a bold move, even for him. Why would he select a man for the job who had, by the skin of his teeth, just barely avoided going to prison for supplying steroids and prescription drugs to his teammates? And whose wife died under mysterious circumstances the very day those charges were thrown out?

"I suppose getting engaged at seventy years old can make a man lose a few brain cells," she answered.

The words tasted ugly on her tongue and she wanted to call them back. Usually she liked to give people the benefit of the doubt, but she just didn't have it in her to be objective when it came to Spence Gregory.

His mouth tightened and he looked almost hurt, though she knew that couldn't be true. What did he care if she welcomed him with somewhat less-than-open arms?

"Apparently," he murmured. "Yet here I am. For the next six months, anyway. It's a temporary position."

That was something, anyway. She could endure anything for six months, even having him back in the same zip code.

"Let's go, Peyton."

"Okay."

Peyton looked subdued instead of angry now and Charlotte directed her sympathy where it rightfully belonged—to a young girl who had lost her mother far too young and spent her days under the cloud of her father's scandal.

Having to live with the man many considered responsible for her mother's death couldn't be an easy situation for a young girl.

She gave her a warm smile. "See you around, Peyton. It was really nice to meet you. Enjoy the fudge."

"I'm sure I will," she mumbled. She pushed open the door and walked out into the summer afternoon.

Spence hesitated, looking as if he wanted to say something else, but he finally lifted a hand in a wave and followed his daughter.

After the door closed behind them, Charlotte pressed a hand to her stomach, fighting the urge to rush over and flip the sign to Closed, lock the door and sag against the counter.

She liked to think she was a pretty good person most of the time. She volunteered at the animal shelter, she always paid her taxes on time, she tried to throw a little extra into the collection plate at church on Sundays.

She didn't consider herself petty or vindictive. She was friendly with just about everyone in town, even the cliquey girls who had once made her life so painfully hard at school and had grown into cliquey women with the same prejudices.

But a small acrid, angry corner of her heart despised Spence Gregory with a vitriol that unsettled her.

What was Harry Lange *thinking?* She had to wonder if Mary Ella knew what her fiancé was up to, bringing back the man who had once been the darling of Hope's Crossing but was now considered a pariah.

Maybe it was one of Harry's twisted schemes. The man appeared to have been turning over a new leaf in the past year since reconnecting with his son Jack and the granddaughter he didn't know existed, but maybe it was all for show. Maybe Harry *wanted* the recreation center he had basically financed to fail so he could sweep in and somehow make money off it for his own purposes, perhaps as a tax write-off for a business loss.

Whatever the reason, she couldn't believe she would be the only one in town upset at this new development, though she had very personal reasons to be angry about the return of Spence Gregory.

The cowbell clanked suddenly and, for an instant, fear spiked that she would have to deal with him again, while she was still trying to come to terms with his return.

Seeing Alex McKnight rush in, her long blond curls flying behind her, was a sweet relief.

"Hi, Alex." She even managed a smile, envious, as always, at Alex's effortless confidence. She was smart and sexy and a brilliant chef—and was comfortable enough in her own skin that none of it mattered to her except the chef part, of which she was fiercely proud.

"Guess who I just saw walking Front Street?" Alex said, her green eyes wide.

"Spencer Gregory," she answered dully.

"Wow. You are *good*." Alex looked surprised and a little amused.

"Not really. He just left the store."

"Can you believe it? The guy must have balls as big as ostrich eggs to show up back in town like nothing ever happened."

"Take it up with your stepfather-to-be. Apparently he hired Spence to run the new rec center."

Alex's eyes widened for an instant and then she shook her head. "The man is insane sometimes. What goes on inside Harry's head?"

Charlotte didn't know. And right now she didn't want to talk about either Harry Lange or Spence Gregory.

"Can I get you anything?"

"Actually, I came in to ask you a huge favor." With a cheerful grin, Alex let herself be distracted. She seemed so happy lately since she had started seeing Sam Delgado, a new contractor in town.

Charlotte was thrilled for her, she really was, but sometimes she couldn't help an insidious little niggle of envy. While Charlotte found their developing relationship wonderful for the two of them—especially since she knew firsthand how deeply Sam cared for Alex—Charlotte had once entertained hopes herself toward the man when Sam had first come to town.

He had endeared himself to Charlotte forever by reaching out to help her troubled brother Dylan, offering him a job with Sam's construction company despite Dylan's new limitations. Her brother had refused—no big surprise there—but Charlotte wanted to think the offer had meant something to Dylan. It had certainly meant something to her—so much that she had asked Sam to go to the town's annual Giving Hope Day gala.

She had hoped the two of them might hit it off and that he might ask her out again. Sam was new in town. He hadn't even known her before the changes of the past year and a half and she had hoped that might give her a slight advantage, but it had become obvious fairly quickly that Sam was completely tangled up over Alex.

During these past few weeks since the two of them had come together, it was transparent to all they were crazy about each other. Alex gave every appearance of a woman deeply in love.

"I'm glad to help," Charlotte said now, pushing down that spurt of envy. "What can I do?"

"You don't even know what it is, and you're already agreeing to help. That's one of the things I love most about you, Char."

She cherished all her friends who had supported her on her recent journey toward reinvention, in no small part because they had loved her just as generously eighty pounds ago. "You know I'll help in any way I can. Unless you need me to rob a bank or taste test one of your new fattening dessert recipes."

Alex grinned. "Nope. This one is easy. A friend of Sam's has been in town helping him with all the work coming his way. He's thinking about making his temporary stay in our fair little hamlet a permanent thing. He's a single guy, really sweet but a little lonely, I think."

Charlotte braced herself, guessing what was coming next. Her friends seemed to feel a compelling need to set her up on dates with eligible men lately. First Claire McKnight just happened to know a new police officer in her husband Riley's department she thought would be perfect for Charlotte, then Evie Thorne had wanted her to go out with a business associate of her husband, Brodie.

She was beginning to wonder if she had subconsciously started sending out some secret bat signal that she was single and desperate. Which so didn't describe her at all. Okay, she was single. But she hadn't yet descended into desperation.

"I don't know." She stalled for time.

"Come on. It will be fun. Sam was thinking we could take him out to dinner to celebrate his move here. Maybe go up to Le Passe Montagne."

"Not Brazen?" Charlotte asked, surprised.

"Well, obviously that's the best restaurant in town but Sam knows how hard it is to get a reservation there."

"Even when a guy is sleeping with the chef?"

Alex grinned, looking completely pleased with the world. "Even then. If you want the truth, I did suggest we just meet there but Sam seems to think I don't relax when I'm eating in my own restaurant. Imagine that."

Charlotte laughed, despite the lingering disquiet over Spence's reappearance. It was hard not to laugh around Alex, who deserved every bit of the success her new restaurant was enjoying.

"I think I can picture it. He knows you well, doesn't he?"

Her friend made a face. "So we were thinking next week sometime, maybe Saturday. I'm giving you plenty of advance notice. Will that work?"

"I'm not really crazy about blind dates," she said, which was a rather monumental understatement.

"Don't think of it as a blind date. Just a few friends getting together."

"Two of whom happen to be seeing each other."

"Well, yes. Come on, Char. He's really a nice guy and we want to make sure he feels like he has a few connections in town besides us."

She swallowed a sigh, imagining how awkward it would be to go on a double date with Alex and Sam Delgado, considering her prior interest in Sam.

She opened her mouth to politely decline but clamped it shut again. Just the night before while she had been eating her Healthy Choice dinner for one, she had promised herself she would try to get out more. She had no real reason to say no, other than a little embarrassment at unrealized dreams. And heaven knows, she had enough of those lying around to fill a darn auditorium.

An image of Spence Gregory, lean and dark and muscled, filled her head but she shoved it aside.

"Sure," she said quickly before she could talk herself out of it. "Dinner would be lovely. Thank you for the invitation."

"Perfect. We can talk next week but let's tentatively plan on a week from Saturday, about seven. Does that work?"

"Yes."

"You're going to love Garrett, I promise."

"I'm sure I will," she lied as Alex gave a cheery wave and left the store.

Customers came in right behind her and Charlotte was grateful for the distraction they provided. She didn't need to think about blind dates or old hurts or how, after only a few minutes with Spencer Gregory, she once more felt fifteen years old—fat, awkward, shy— and desperately in love with a boy who barely knew she was alive.

CHAPTER TWO

A FEW HOURS after leaving the candy store, Spence decided house hunting had to rank about dead last on his list of favorite activities. Even behind the IRS audit he had once endured.

"I've got several more houses to show you but I'm not sure we even need to see them," the perky real estate agent flashed her extremely white teeth at him as they pulled up to the address she indicated, in a neighborhood he remembered delivering papers to.

"Given what you've told me you're looking for, I think you'll really love this house," Jill Sellers went on. "The location is fantastic, close to the mouth of Silver Strike Canyon and the recreation center but within walking distance of the downtown restaurant scene. The house comes fully furnished, which I know you want. The interior is beautifully designed in a contemporary style for the discriminating renter."

Was that what he was? Since when? As far as he was concerned, a couple beds and a working kitchen just about covered his needs.

She beamed at him, which he found more than a little unsettling. He certainly didn't remember her being this helpful when they went to school together, at least in their earlier years. By the time he had reached high school, he had started to excel in sports and the same girls—who the year before had turned up their nose when he walked past in his ripped jeans and too-small jacket—had suddenly seemed to look at him with new eyes.

He supposed he should be grateful he wasn't a complete leper in town.

"I'm sure we'll love it," he answered.

"Or not," Peyton muttered.

She hadn't liked any of the rental properties Jill had showed them in the past two hours—and made no secret of it. Several houses later, he was sick of her attitude and tired of trying to find something she might like, when he knew in his bones she wasn't going to be happy with anything.

Nothing in Hope's Crossing would please her. She was quite determined to hate everything about the community, which ought to make for an interesting six months.

He sighed, wondering again if he had made a huge mistake taking this job at the recreation center. It had seemed like an ideal opportunity when Harry Lange had called him—far better than sitting around working on his golf handicap, dabbling in a few investment interests he had held on to and waiting for offers he knew were never coming.

He had also had some vague idea that perhaps this might be an opportunity for him to reconnect with the daughter who had turned into a baffling, surly stranger.

"You're going to have to at least take a look inside before I'll let you tell me how much you hate it," he said to Peyton.

"Whatever."

She followed the two of them into the house. Though

moderately sized from the outside, the inside seemed to open up, probably because of the soaring windows of the two-story great room that looked out behind the house at Silver Strike Canyon. From the front, the house would have a pretty view of town.

The decor, while fine, seemed a little impersonal. What else could he expect in a property that was mainly used as an executive rental?

The master bedroom was huge with an oversize shower in the attached bath that featured multiple showerheads. The second bedroom also had an attached bath and he saw Peyton's eyes light up at the jetted tub, though she quickly veiled her expression.

The best feature of the house, as far as he was concerned, was the completely glass solarium with a small but adequate lap pool.

"This one works for me," he said when they returned to the gourmet kitchen for another look, after Jill Sellers had led them through the house, her speech punctuated with exclamation points and capital letters. "We'll take it."

"I just knew you'd *love* it!"

She touched his arm in a way he definitely recognized as flirtatious. He glanced down at her hand against his sleeve, the nails pink, sharp and glossy. Unbidden, he had a sudden image of Charlotte Caine's hands, competent, a little callused, with her nails short and unpainted.

She had made all the fudge in the store. Peyton had told him as much when she had rather grudgingly shared a couple samples with him.

He forced away thoughts of Charlotte. "You must have good instincts," he said in reply to Jill.

"I hope so. Without good instincts, I wouldn't be able to do my job, would I?"

He didn't know a blasted thing about being a real estate agent and had no desire to learn. Of course, he didn't know the first damn thing about being the director of a community recreation center either, yet here he was, preparing to take on the job.

"Can you see if they'll consider a short-term lease? I only want six months. And how soon can we move in?"

He wasn't even sure if he—or Peyton—would make it that long, but he had committed to six months and intended to stick to his contract with Harry.

"I'll speak to the owner, see if I can negotiate a little, and bring you back a lease agreement to sign in a few hours. You could be in this little gem by bedtime."

"I still don't see what's wrong with staying at the lodge," Peyton muttered.

What he wouldn't give to have her carry on a halfway civil conversation with him. Of course she preferred the luxurious accommodations at the Silver Strike Lodge. But he had a feeling Harry wouldn't be too thrilled about extending their stay indefinitely in rooms that generally went for several hundred dollars a night.

"We're not spending the next six months in a hotel. We need a real house."

"We have a real house. In Portland."

By the time those six months were up, she was going to make him crazy. "Which will still be there when we're finished here in Hope's Crossing. Meantime, we need a kitchen, outdoor space, room for a housekeeper."

"Babysitter, you mean."

This was another argument he didn't want to debate with her again so he decided to ignore the comment for now. "This works better than any of the others we looked at, don't you think?"

"I guess."

That was as ringing an endorsement as he was likely to get from her. "We're in," he said to Jill. "Give me a call after you talk to the property management company."

"I will. I have your number. And you have mine, right?"

"I'm sure I can find it somewhere." He managed a polite smile and hoped she understood he didn't intend to call her about anything but his real estate needs—which, after signing this lease, would be nonexistent.

He ushered Peyton out to the Range Rover he had picked up to replace the sports car he drove in Oregon. As he backed out of the driveway and turned in the direction of the canyon mouth, he was struck by the charming view—the colorful houses nestled in trees as they climbed the foothills, the picturesque downtown with its historic architecture, the grand rugged mountains standing sentinel over the valley.

He certainly didn't remember Hope's Crossing ever being so appealing when he was living with his mother in that tiny dilapidated house a few blocks off Main Street that probably hadn't been painted since his grandfather had died twenty years before Spence was born.

Kids could certainly be self-absorbed and he had been no different. Like Peyton, he had spent his days in a cloud of discontent, hating just about everything in his life except football and baseball. The town and its inhabitants had been part of that. He had convinced himself he couldn't wait to leave, but when he looked back now, he realized he had never really hated Hope's Crossing.

For every snobby cheerleader mom who thought he was going to impregnate her daughter just by looking at her, there had been others who had seen beyond the mended clothes, the threadbare shoes, the haircut he usually tried to manage himself—until he took a job in high school to pay for little luxuries like a decent razor and a letterman's jacket.

Dermot Caine, for instance.

He smiled as he drove back toward the canyon, though it was tinged with a shadow of guilt. Now there was someone he should have remained in contact with over the years. Dermot had always been kind. Hell, he had given Billie Gregory a job when no one else would and had kept her on even when she showed up half the time blitzed, when she bothered to show up at all.

Thinking of Dermot inevitably led his thoughts to Charlotte. He remembered again that shock when she had identified herself at the candy store.

Charlotte Caine. He couldn't get over how she had changed. All that gold hair shot through with hints of red, the big blue eyes, the sexy, curvy figure he could see beneath the apron she wore.

Was she anything at all like he remembered?

When he had known her before, she had been more than a little overweight and had hidden those stunning eyes behind big thick-framed glasses. While she could have moments of quick wit and she was as kind as her father, she could also be painfully shy.

If he remembered correctly, she had been a couple or three years behind him in school though she was four years younger. She had been ahead a grade and he had been behind because of the dark time after his father had died when he was eight, when Billie had gone off the deep end and dragged him aimlessly around the country from flophouse to homeless shelter to the backseat of her car.

He had hated being older than everybody else but still struggled in school—with English class, especially. He had never been a very big reader until long road trips with the Pioneers when he had little else to do. Charlotte, on the other hand, could have been an English teacher herself, even at twelve. She knew her stuff and he had been savvy enough to take advantage of the generous help she offered him.

He would venture to say, Charlotte Caine had been the only reason he had been able to keep his grades up high enough to allow him to participate in school sports.

In a roundabout way, he supposed he had her to thank for his whole career with the Pioneers—which didn't explain the instant attraction that had been simmering in his gut since the moment he had walked into that candy store and saw her standing behind the counter looking fresh and lovely.

What was wrong with him? He didn't have time for this. Harry Lange had offered him one chance at redemption, one chance to move beyond the demoralizing isolation of the past year and prove he was more than lousy headlines.

He couldn't screw this up. He needed to focus on repairing his damaged reputation, not on Charlotte Caine, no matter how much she had changed.

THIS WAS THE hardest thing she had to face.

Other people had their Rubicons, their Pikes Peaks. She had her dad's café.

As she walked from Sugar Rush down the street and

around the corner to Center of Hope Café after work, her stomach rumbled in anticipation. She swore she could already smell delicious things sidling through the air, tempting and seductive.

Yeah, she worked all day in a candy store, surrounded by chocolates and caramels and toffee, but there she could resist temptation. It was her business and she certainly wanted to produce a delicious product but she supposed it was a little like being the teetotaling owner of a distillery. She didn't mind a little fudge in moderation once in a while but she never had a desire to stuff herself until she was sick.

This, though. The gnawing craving for some of her father's comfort food sometimes kept her up at night.

Gooey rich macaroni and cheese. Shepherd's pie, with thick roast beef and creamy mashed potatoes coating the top like a hard snowfall on the surrounding mountains. Cinnamon-laced apple pie with Pop's famous homemade vanilla ice cream.

Her dad's café specialized in the kind of food that numbed and sedated, that soothed hunger pangs and heartache in equal measure.

Despite eighteen months of struggling to change a lifelong addiction to it, whenever she stumbled over one of life's inevitable bumpy patches, she still craved a hit of Pop's cooking like a junkie needed crack cocaine.

She knew why. She knew the food at the café represented more than just butter-laden calories. It was her mother waiting for her with a warm towel fresh from the dryer at the end of a rainy walk home from the school bus. It was Pop snuggling her on his lap for a bedtime story, his whiskers tickling her neck. It was summer nights spent sleeping in the tree house with her brothers behind their home while crickets and frogs filled the night with song.

Pop's food was like home, or at least the home she remembered before the winter she turned ten, when everything changed forever.

On days like this, with her emotions in chaos, she wanted nothing more than to be snugged up against the counter at the diner, burying every concern and feeling of inadequacy under calories.

Drat Spencer Gregory anyway. He had no business coming back to town and leaving her so shaken, filled with dismay and memories and the echo of old pain.

Lasagna. Wouldn't a big plate of lasagna, dripping with cheese, hit the spot right about now? She bet Pop had some hot and ready. She only had to say the word.

She sighed, increasing her pace. She wouldn't ask for lasagna. She was stronger than the craving. She only had to remember how hard she had worked the past eighteen months to reshape her life. No matter how provoking her day might be, she couldn't go back to old habits, the well-traveled pathways in her brain that would inevitably lead her to a destination she no longer wanted.

Instead, she had a chicken breast at home in the refrigerator, soaking in her favorite low-fat marinade of lemon juice, tarragon and a splash of olive oil. As soon as she finished a few errands, she would throw it on the grill along with some vegetables and be far better off.

She pushed open the door and the familiar rich scents surged through her bloodstream like a solid jolt of high-octane caffeine.

"Hey, girl." Della Pine, who had been waitressing at the Center of Hope as long as Charlotte could remember, greeted her with a wide smile on her wrinkled cheeks. She tottered toward Charlotte in the painfully high heels she always wore, even when she had to spend all day on her feet.

Despite the extra inches, the woman still barely reached Charlotte's chin, except for her hair, which towered over both of them in all its teased glory.

Charlotte leaned in and kissed the waitress's cheek, smiling at the familiar olfactory concoction of hair spray, cold cream and lavender powder.

The café was busy, as usual, hopping with the dinner rush. The clientele was generally a healthy mix of tourists and locals. She recognized a few of the latter and raised a hand in greeting.

"Is Pop around?" she asked when Della grabbed a couple menus off the counter by the door for a pair who had come in after Charlotte.

Della jerked her head toward the back. "Check the office. We had some trouble with one of the beef suppliers. Last I checked, he was still trying to iron it out."

"Thanks."

She headed toward the office, fighting through the temptation to stop and order a few things off the menu on her way.

Chicken-fried steak, maybe, with a big side of garlic mashed potatoes.

Pop was wonderful at running the Center of Hope Café. Over the years, she had learned more from watching him than any of her business classes in college. She had learned by example how to be a responsible, caring employer, how to be kind to customers and workers alike, how to treat everyone with dignity and respect.

And he cooked one heck of a pork chop.

She sighed as she walked into the office, tucked in behind the kitchen.

This place was as familiar to her as her own childhood on Winterberry Road.

Heaven knows, she had spent enough time here when she was a kid. Even before her mother died, she had loved coming to Center of Hope, hanging out at a table and doing homework while she listened to the sounds of life around her.

During the hard, ugly two years Margaret Caine fought cancer, coming to the diner had been an escape from the fear, from the pain and sickness that seemed to seep through the walls of their home like black mold.

She had avoided that toxic sludge as much as possible. Her mother mostly wanted to sleep anyway, and Charlotte had hated being there. Maybe she should have tried harder to help but that was a heavy burden for a young girl. She had felt like she was coping alone, for the most part.

By then, her only sibling still home had been her next oldest brother, Dylan. At sixteen, he had been too busy with friends and sports and school to offer much help.

She couldn't deny she had found undeniable comfort in coming to the café after school to do her schoolwork, where Pop would invariably give her a nice chocolate milk shake and a slice of pizza.

Was it any wonder she weighed nearly a hundred eighty pounds by seventh grade?

She paused outside the office door, reminding herself sharply that she was doing her best to become something else. Though she still craved the pizza, the milk shake, she could have her father's love without it.

She pushed open the door and smiled at the familiar

voice uttering a few tasteful swear words at the telephone he had just returned to the cradle.

Her father was still good-looking in a distinguished way, with a shock of thick white hair and the blue, blue eyes she had inherited. His features were tanned and weathered from all the time he spent out in the garden he tended zealously.

"Problem?"

He looked up as she came in and she wanted to smile at the way his eyes always lit up at the sight of her.

"If it isn't my darling girl, come to see her old da." Though he had left the green hills of Galway behind when he was a boy of six, sometimes the brogue slipped through anyway.

"Hi, Pop."

She hugged him from behind, smelling Old Spice and a hint of garlic.

"And how was your day, my dear?"

She thought of that strange encounter in her store a few hours earlier and the wild chaos of her thoughts ever since.

"Interesting. Did you know Spencer Gregory was back in Hope's Crossing?"

Dermot swiveled around in his office chair and folded weathered hands over his still-lean belly. "Well, now, you know, I did hear something to that effect. About a dozen customers had to tell me they saw him around town."

She could only imagine how the café must have buzzed with the news. People would be talking about this for some time to come.

"Well, nobody had the courtesy to warn me. I just about fell over when he walked in. I still can't believe it. How can he return to town like nothing's happened? Does he expect us to just throw out the red carpet like this town has always done for him?"

"Now, Charley…"

She perched on the edge of the desk. "I'm serious. He gives Hope's Crossing a bad name. I can't believe people can't see that. Now he's back and he's going to dredge everything up all over again."

"I think you're exaggerating a wee bit." Dermot gave her a chiding sort of look, the same one he used to wear when she didn't finish her orange juice in the morning or when she chose to stay home and study instead of go to social activities at school. "A man shouldn't have to pay the rest of his life because of a few poor decisions."

"Poor decisions? I'd call it more than that. He was a drug dealer! He ran a steroid and prescription drug ring out of the team locker room."

"The charges against him were dropped, remember?"

"Because of a technicality in the evidence. He's never once denied it."

She didn't want to admit to her father that she had followed coverage of the case religiously, though she had a feeling Dermot might already know. He seemed to have uncanny insight when it came to her, as much as she might try to be obscure and mysterious.

Spencer's situation was one of those fall-from-grace scandals the media seemed to relish voraciously. He had been a much-admired sports celebrity with a huge paycheck and a slew of endorsements—a kid from nowhere with fierce talent and extraordinary good looks who had made it big early in the game and continued to produce stunning wins for the Pioneers for the next decade.

She couldn't lie to herself. She had also followed Spence's career with the same interest as she did the scandal later. Despite past betrayals, she had celebrated his success, happy for him that he had attained every goal he set out for himself as a driven, angry teen. His nickname, Smokin' Hot Gregory—Smoke—referred not just to his stunning good looks but also his wicked fastball that had once been clocked at over a hundred miles an hour.

Then three years ago, everything changed. In one horrible game against the Oakland Athletics, he suffered what turned out to be a career-ending injury. Months later, after he had tried to come back, she had caught the press conference when he admitted to a problem with prescription drugs following his injury and that he had gone into rehab for it.

With other Pioneers fans, she had celebrated when he returned to the program as a pitching coach—and then, like the rest of Hope's Crossing, she had felt personally betrayed when accusations were leveled against him. Someone had been supplying prescription drugs and steroids to his teammates and the evidence against Spence was overwhelming, including a large shipment found in his vehicle parked in the team lot.

Then, in another stunning development, the judge threw out the charges just days before he was supposed to go to trial. Not that the court of public opinion shifted its vote so readily.

While Spence never went to prison, he lost his career, his endorsements, his reputation—and when his stunning former supermodel of a wife was found floating facedown in their pool the very afternoon the charges were dropped, most people blamed him for that, too.

Through it all, Dermot had only seen the good. It was a particularly exasperating failing of her father's, particularly in Spence's case.

"Say what you want about him, but he was always a good boy," her father said now, quite predictably, with that same admonishing look. "You know he had no sort of home life at all, what with his father dying young and his mother tippling away anything she could earn here. My heart fair ached for the lad."

For some reason, at her father's words, she pictured Peyton, pale and thin and troubled.

"He has a girl. A daughter. Skinny as a pike. She could use a little of your good apple pie, if you ask me."

"Or your fudge."

"I gave her some."

She smiled a little, remembering the girl's stunned expression at the simple act of kindness, as if nobody had ever done anything spontaneously nice for her before, then her features had shifted back to truculence when her father found her in Sugar Rush.

"I don't think she likes it here much."

"Oh, the poor lamb."

Predictably, her father was easily distracted by a sad case, and she decided to push yet another even more tender button to avoid further discussion of Spence Gregory.

"Sorry. I didn't come in to talk about Spence or his daughter. I wanted to let you know I'm heading out to drive up Snowflake Canyon tonight to check on Dylan. Do you have anything you want me to take to him?"

Dermot's features softened with worry even as he stood up from his chair a little gingerly, as if his bones ached.

"Excellent idea." He draped an arm over her shoulder and they headed out of the office toward the kitchen. "You're a grand sister, you are. The meat loaf is good today. He always favors that. And I'm sure I could find a bit of soup and perhaps some leftover fried chicken. Another of his favorites."

"Perfect. Those should keep him going for a while."

"That boy. What are we to do with him?"

She leaned her head against Pop's shoulder. "I wish I knew. He can't go on like this. I think he's lost an extra twenty pounds just since he's been home."

She didn't need to add that Dylan hadn't any spare poundage to lose, not after the severe injuries and then resulting infection that had nearly killed him.

"You're a sweet girl to worry so for your brother. Someday he'll thank you for it. You'll see."

She wasn't so sure of that. Though he had come home several weeks ago, he felt even more distant than when he had been back east receiving treatment.

She just kept hoping that if she tried hard enough, she could find the key to helping her brother.

As she helped Pop package up several meals for Dylan, along with some cookies and a nice slice of cake, she reminded herself her brother was a worthwhile thing to fret about, not the sudden reappearance in her life of a man she had long ago vowed that she despised.

CHAPTER THREE

ON A JULY EVENING, Hope's Crossing was a lovely, serene place, far removed from the bustle and craziness of the winter season, when the streets would be clogged with traffic and long lines of bundled-up customers would stretch out of all the better restaurants.

Though the town had plenty of summer visitors, for some reason they didn't seem as pervasive, maybe because so many of them were out enjoying the backcountry.

She drove past the ball diamonds and saw what looked like a Little League game in full swing. It dredged up memories of late spring evenings when she would perch on the bleachers while Hope's Crossing High played—ostensibly to watch her brother but she spent plenty of time checking out the boy who usually occupied the pitcher's mound.

She had been pathetic. Really. Just a few yards shy of creepy Stalkerville.

With a sigh, she turned her attention back to the road and turned up Silver Strike Canyon, where the trees bowed over the road, heavy with summer growth, and the river gleamed bright in the sweet golden light.

After only a mile or so, she took the turn up the box canyon known as Snowflake Canyon. The road rose steeply here, winding in hairpins up the backside of the mountains that enfolded the town, and it took all her concentration to drive here.

This was a sparsely populated area, just pockets of houses here and there. No developer had stepped in to make it a subdivision, probably because the cost of delivering water and other utilities to these houses was prohibitive.

For the life of her, she couldn't imagine why Dylan wanted to live in the tall timbers, isolated and alone. After fifteen minutes, she turned onto his driveway and finally parked in front of his small log home. Though the inside had nice amenities, with a well-outfitted kitchen and comfortable bathroom and bedroom, the outside looked more like a backwoods shack, complete with chickens pecking the gravel. For all she knew, Dylan had a moonshine still in the barn.

True to form, when she pulled up, Dylan was sitting on the porch, his feet resting on the railing. Beside him lounged his big black and tan coonhound, Tucker, who had lived with her and Pop during Dylan's deployments and the long months of his recovery.

Tucker lifted his head when she drove to a stop, then rested it on his paws again, apparently disinterested.

Dylan didn't look any more enthusiastic at her visit. He watched her step down from her SUV out of hooded eyes, and she didn't miss the way he set a bottle of whiskey on a little table beside him.

Though it was hard—so hard—she pasted on a smile as she approached the porch. "Hey, there."

She could tell instantly this wasn't one of his good days. His mouth tightened from what she guessed was pain, and he glowered at her. Hurt pinched just under her breastbone at his deliberate lack of welcome.

Why couldn't he let her in a little? Before his injury, she would have said she and Dylan had been close. Though he was four years older, the same as Spence, he had been her closest sibling in age. As children, he had always been patient and sweet to her, far more than most older brothers would have been to pesky little sisters. As adults, their relationship had shifted to good friends. She sent him care packages every week he was deployed and he emailed her funny little stories about interesting things he saw or whatever military experiences he was free to share, which weren't that many.

Since he had been wounded, he had closed in around himself, shutting her out just like everybody else.

She walked up the porch with one hand clutching the handles of the brown paper bag with *Center of Hope Café* printed on the side. Though he was still handsome, like all her brothers, with chiseled features, full lips and the blue eyes they shared, he looked as if he hadn't shaved in a few days and his eye patch gave him a dark, menacing air, despite the weight he had lost.

He wasn't wearing his prosthetic, she saw, and the stump of his arm just below his elbow looked red and scarred.

"What brings you up this way?" he asked, his voice more of a growl.

No *Hello,* no friendly *How's my baby sister?* Terse and trenchant. That's about the best she could get out of him these days.

She leaned in and kissed his cheek just under the eye patch, catching a strong whiff of booze that broke her heart.

"Brought you some of Pop's food. I figured it might

hit the spot. Have you had anything today but John-
nie Walker?"

He eased away from her and rested his remaining
hand—the one she was quite sure wanted to reach for
the bottle—on his thigh. "I made a grilled cheese sandwich at lunch."

Did you eat any of it, though? She bit her tongue to
keep from asking the question. "Do you care if I put
these in the refrigerator?" she asked instead.

He gestured to the door, and she pulled open the
screen and walked inside.

One might have expected the inside to reflect the
same general air of neglect the house showed on the
outside. Instead, it was almost freakishly neat, with no
dirty dishes in the sink, no scatter of magazines or junk
mail on the countertop.

To her, it always seemed like an empty vacation
rental, as if nobody really lived here to give it heart.
The house seemed bleak and unhappy to her and she
couldn't understand how he could tolerate it for more
than a minute.

She opened the steel late-model refrigerator and
found only two twelve-packs of Budweiser, a small brick
of cheese that had something growing on one corner and
a half-gallon milk container with barely a splash left.

She put the food containers away, her own hunger
completely forgotten.

"Do you need me to go grocery shopping for you
again?" she asked when she returned to the porch.

"Shopping is one of the few things I can manage. I
can still push a cart with one hand."

She frowned. "Then why don't you have anything

in the refrigerator except beer and what I brought you from Pop?"

"I just haven't had time. I'll get to it."

"I don't mind," she offered again. At least if she went shopping, she could be certain he had a few more fruits and vegetables in the refrigerator and a little less alcohol. "I know you don't like going into town."

He made a face. "I don't like going to the doctor as well, but sometimes you can't avoid it."

Except he didn't do that as often as he should, either. She again clamped down on the words, knowing he wouldn't welcome them.

Since he had been back in Hope's Crossing, she had tried nagging, cajoling and bribery to convince him he had to take better care of himself. What was the point of going through the months of medical treatment that had saved his life after his injury and the resulting infections if he was only going to waste it sitting around here?

Nothing appeared to work. If anything, he was only digging in his heels harder.

She had never told him that his near brush with death had been her own impetus for change.

She could remember sitting by his bedside right after he had been flown stateside from Germany. At the time, she had weighed more than two hundred pounds and had felt nauseous and exhausted from the long day of travel and the poor food choices she had made on the airplane.

He had been in and out of consciousness and not really aware of her and Pop sitting there beside him, both of them scared to their bones that he wouldn't make it through the evening.

It had been a long night of prayer and reflection. As

she watched her brother cling to life, she had thought about the years of diets she had tried, the weight she would lose and then regain, the frustrating, demoralizing cycle she couldn't seem to shake.

She had just about accepted she would spend the rest of her life in that state. But now her brother had nearly died in service for his country. He was fighting to survive, barely hanging on, each moment a hard, painful slog.

Meanwhile, she was slowly killing herself, fighting high blood pressure and prediabetes at not even thirty years old. She had been alone and fat and miserable.

It had been an epiphany, a realization that she couldn't keep going on that cycle. She had made a vow that this time would be different. She owed it to herself and she owed it to her brother to show a tiny measure of the same courage and strength he had.

The irony was, right now, she felt better about herself than since she was a young girl. She looked better, she was stronger, she was certainly healthier and no longer needed any medication. Through a healthy diet and an intense exercise regimen, she had lost almost half her body weight.

Dylan, meanwhile, had won the fight to stay alive, at least physically, but the emotional toll his injuries and new limitations had taken on a once-tough, vibrant soldier had been brutal.

He was broody and angry and she knew she couldn't fix this for him, no matter how many grocery bags or plates of food she brought over.

"Want me to heat something up for you?" she asked him now.

"No. I'll grab something later."

"Promise?"

"Yeah, *Mom*."

If their mom were still alive, Margie Caine would drag Dylan down this mountainside by his ear and throw him back into life, whether he liked it or not.

"No hot date tonight?" he asked.

She gave a short laugh, fighting down the fierce wish she could channel a little of their mother right now. "You know me. I've got them lined up around the block."

Despite all the changes, dating was one area she still hadn't really ventured out into. She had never learned to flirt when she was a teenager.

"You ought to," he said gruffly. "Have them lined up around the block, I mean. You just need to put a little effort into it."

If she had been able to find it at all amusing, she would have laughed at the irony of her brother giving her advice on dating when he had become a virtual hermit.

"Thanks for the vote of encouragement. Since I'm up here, I was thinking about grabbing fifteen minutes of cardio before I go home. Do you and Tucker want to come for a walk with me?"

The dog lifted his head, perking up as much as his droopy ears and morose eyes allowed. He gave his musical wooo-wooo bark and clambered to his feet, obviously understanding the magic *w*-word.

Dylan, not so much. He curled that hand on his thigh again, clear reluctance shifting across his features.

"What about my dinner?"

"You can eat it later." She ignored the growl of her stomach. A few endorphins would take care of that until she could get home to her chicken breast. "Come on. We won't go far."

After another moment of hesitation, Dylan slowly rose to his feet and she felt a surge of elation that was probably completely unwarranted for such a small victory. She would take it anyway. A little fresh air and movement could only be good for her brother, though she knew he puttered around the barn and attached wood shop a little.

She walked off the porch, grateful for the old tennis shoes she kept in the back of her SUV for spontaneous exercise opportunities like this one.

She and Tucker had taken a few walks up here before, usually without Dylan, so she had a passing familiarity with some of the trails that crisscrossed the mountainside among the pines and aspens. She headed toward one she liked that wended beside a small pretty creek and, after a pause, Dylan followed her.

Tucker ambled ahead, his hound dog nose sniffing the ground for the scent of any interesting creature he might encounter.

They walked in silence for a time, accompanied by the annoyed chattering of squirrels high above them and the occasional birdsong.

She breathed in deeply of the high, clear mountain air, sweet with wildflowers and pine, feeling some of the tension of her day begin to seep away. "I can't tell you how badly I needed this today," she said.

"Glad I could help." Dylan's dry tone surprised a laugh out of her.

"It's beautiful up here, I'll give you that. Remote but beautiful."

"Nothing wrong with a little seclusion," he answered.

"I suppose."

Dylan had always been so social, always in the middle of the action. She missed that about him.

Because of the time, only an hour or so from true sunset, and because neither of them had eaten, she decided not to push too hard. After about ten minutes, they reached a small glacial lake that blazed with reflected color from the changing sky.

"Let me take your picture," she ordered, pulling out her camera phone.

He frowned but stood obediently enough, his hand resting on the dog's head.

"Perfect," she said, snapping several before he could move away. She didn't bother asking him to smile.

Behind him, the surface of the lake popped and hissed like Pop's cheese sauce bubbling in the pan. "Looks like the fish are jumping. Do you ever come up here and cast a line?"

She regretted the words as soon as she said them, when he shrugged his left shoulder, rippling the empty sleeve.

"Yet another skill I haven't quite mastered with one hand and one eye."

He could do plenty of things if he would only wear the prosthesis. She knew most of his rehab had been aimed at helping him adapt to his new reality. Since his return to Hope's Crossing, he seemed to have resorted to only figuring out how to open another whiskey bottle.

"You will," she answered calmly.

He didn't answer, just gazed out at the water.

Her stomach grumbled again and she sighed. "We should probably head back."

"Yeah. Before the mosquitoes eat us alive. It's a little

tough for me to scratch these days. Hey, how do you get a one-armed man out of a tree?"

He didn't wait for her to answer. "You wave at him."

He seemed to think that was hilarious and was still giving that hard-sounding laugh as he turned down the trail toward his house.

CHAPTER FOUR

THE NEXT MORNING, the sun was barely a pink rim along the black silhouette of the mountains when Charlotte laced up her tennis shoes in her entryway.

Every morning it was the same. She had to force herself out of bed when what she really wanted was to curl up under her nice warm blankets, hit the Snooze on her alarm clock and capture a few more moments of bliss.

Instead, here she was in her oh-so-flattering reflective performance capris and T-shirt, no makeup, her hair yanked back into a ponytail.

She rotated her head a few times, then her shoulders to work out some of the kinks before opening the door and pushing herself outside.

Rain or shine she ran, either here or on her treadmill at home or, when she really needed motivation, at the gym.

She felt no small amount of pride at how far she had come. Even walking had felt like torture when she first started on this journey more than a year ago. With all the extra pounds she had been packing around, it had taken all her strength and will to complete a mile and a half in an hour. She had finished with twitching thigh muscles, achy calves and complete exhaustion.

After about three months of making herself walk an hour a day and increasing her pace so she was covering three to four miles, she had begun to add intervals to her workout using her cell phone as a timer, one minute of running for every two minutes she walked at a regular pace, until eventually she was jogging most of the time.

Together with a far healthier diet than the fast food and her father's café delights she had existed on, the numbers started dropping on her scale and her clothes began to hang much looser.

After the first few moments, she discovered she actually enjoyed working out. She enjoyed being in the fresh air and the wind, and she liked taking a moment to ponder and meditate as she jogged through her beautiful surroundings. She especially savored the feeling of knowing she was doing something good and right for herself, that she was trying to repair bad habits of a lifetime.

It wasn't yet 6:00 a.m. and most of Hope's Crossing still slept. Here and there, a few lights were on and she could see glimpses of people moving behind curtains, the flicker of a television screen at one house, a car backing out of a driveway at another.

Even in July, the high altitude air was crisp. Tourists in her store often remarked at the temperature span. It could be mid-eighties in the afternoon but drop to just above freezing in the hours before dawn. That was good chocolate-dipping temperature. In a short time, her employees would be busy creating delicious things to sell at Sugar Rush.

She ran down the hill, past Alex's restaurant in a renovated old fire station, then took a side street and circled around back up toward Sweet Laurel Falls.

By the time she finished the first mile, she forgot about how badly she hated working out. Who wouldn't love this surge of endorphins, the invigorating wind in her face?

She waved to a few people she knew: Lori Kaplan, who worked the early shift in the housekeeping department at the hotel; Errol Angelo, who drove a delivery truck to Denver every morning; Linda Ng, working in her garden early. She was either trying to beat the heat of the day later or trying to get in some work before her four young children awoke and ran her ragged.

By the time Charlotte headed toward home an hour later, many more houses glowed with warm light and the sun was cresting the mountains. She would have to hurry to make it to work on time. That almond fudge wasn't going to make itself.

Finally, muscles humming pleasantly, she turned onto Willowleaf Lane, still three blocks from her house.

Another early morning jogger ran ahead of her. He must have turned from the other direction, coming down from the bruising route up Woodrose Mountain where steep trails crisscrossed beautiful alpine terrain and offered a splendid view of the valley below.

While she did run there when she had a lot more time and energy, she preferred taking her mountain bike for those trails to cover more terrain.

She didn't recognize the guy from the back, which wasn't unusual. While she would venture to say she knew most of the locals, besides the ever-present tourists, Hope's Crossing had many vacation homes and condos owned by people who only visited a few weeks a year. It was tough to build a community under those circumstances but somehow the town managed it.

She lifted the water bottle she carried at the small

of her back and took a sip, her eyes on the fine physical display a half block ahead of her.

The guy was built. His legs were corded with muscle, she could tell even from here, and the soft gray T-shirt he wore molded to wide shoulders, a slim waist, tight butt....

The tingle of awareness disconcerted her, even though she had to admit she enjoyed the little spice of pleasure it gave her in the gorgeous morning.

Still, she really needed to start dating more if she could ogle a stranger jogging down the street.

It was all she could do to keep pace with him, though she was a hundred feet behind, and she was breathing hard by the time they reached her block. To her surprise, the guy headed into a house on the corner.

He must be renting the Telford place. Good. It would be nice to see someone living there again. Empty houses were never good for a neighborhood and the house had sat vacant for six months. Likely due to the soft long-term luxury rental market she had heard Jill Sellers complain about a few weeks earlier when she had stopped into Sugar Rush for more of the custom-wrapped chocolates she handed out to her clients.

As she approached the edge of the property, she noticed the man had stopped near the porch steps for some after-run stretching. She wondered idly if there was a Mrs. Studly Jogger. Not that it was any of her business.

Just as she reached the mailbox, he turned his face in her direction and she felt as if one of those early morning gardeners had just swung a shovel hard into her stomach.

Spence Gregory. Here. On Willowleaf Lane, in all his sweaty, muscled glory.

That thought barely had time to register—along with the far more horrifying realization that he must be the one renting the Telford house—before her feet became as tangled up as her brain.

She wasn't quite sure how it happened, only that she hadn't been paying a bit of attention to where she was running. She must have stepped off the curb or something. How fitting. One moment she was running along minding her own business, admiring a well-built man who just happened to cross her path, the next she was lying in the gutter.

Pain exploded from her ankle, racing up her leg with hot, angry ferocity, but it was nothing compared to the sheer, raw humiliation of tripping over her two feet, right in front of Spencer Gregory.

She wanted to die. She wanted to slither down that storm grate and just disappear.

Spence.

Of all people.

Fudge.

She could only pray he hadn't noticed the idiot woman who had just made a fool of herself in front of him. That fleeting forlorn hope was dashed when she spied him trotting toward her, concern on his features.

"Oh, wow. Are you okay? That was quite a tumble."

No, she wasn't okay. She was mortified. Even worse, this was far from the first time she had ever made a fool of herself around him. The reminder of all her other little humiliations seemed to parade across her memory in all their delightful glory.

How many times had she tripped up the stairs at Hope's Crossing High School when he said hello to her on his way down the other way? Or spilled her drink when he slid into the booth across from her at Center of Hope Café?

Once, she had ridden her bicycle into a fence just because he had happened to drive past and wave at her.

She wasn't normally a graceless person. Witness that she'd been working out for more than a year without incident until this morning.

Now Spence had only to look at her and she was twelve again, dropping her ice cream cone down her shirt when he had smiled at her at the county fair.

Apparently, her old habits didn't just die hard, they went down kicking and screaming and then resurrected themselves at the least opportune moment.

"Charlotte!" he exclaimed when he came close enough to recognize her. "I thought that was you but I wasn't sure."

She could feel her face heat. "Oh, it's me," she muttered.

"Are you okay? What happened?"

You. You happened.

"I'm not sure. I think I just came down on the edge of the curb and lost my balance."

"I'm so sorry. Here. Let's get you back on your feet."

He held a hand out and she eyed it balefully, even though she knew she didn't have a choice but to accept his help. She gripped his hand and told herself she was completely imagining the spark arcing between them.

He reached his other hand beneath her elbow and helped her up. When she put weight on her ankle, that pain roared through her again and she would have slid back to the ground if not for his supporting hold.

"Ow," she said in a small voice, when what she really wanted to do was burst out into tears. Having six older brothers had taught her early to man up and hide her tears until she was in the safety of her bedroom or they would freak out and not let her play with them anymore.

"Did you break something?"

Wouldn't that just be her luck? "I don't think so. I just twisted my ankle."

"That scrape looks nasty."

The pain from the ankle had been so overwhelming, she had hardly noticed the abrasion on her palm but now she could see blood was beginning to seep around the edges of the tiny embedded pebbles. She must have thrown out a hand to catch herself as she went down.

Stirring fudge would certainly be more of a challenge with a big, ungainly bandage on her hand.

"Let me help you inside, and I can take a better look at that ankle and clean off the scrape. I have no idea where the bandages might be in the house but I can probably find something."

"That's not necessary. My house is just there."

She pointed to her whimsical little cottage, tucked amid the trees.

"Great house. I noticed it when we were house shopping yesterday."

"I like it." *Until you moved in down the street, anyway.*

"This seems like a pretty nice neighborhood."

Again, until you moved in. "It is. There's a good mix of vacation homes and year-round residents."

She couldn't believe she was standing here calmly talking real estate with Spence while her ankle breathed fire up her leg and her palm sizzled along with it.

She was beginning to feel a little light-headed.

"The town has certainly changed since I lived here,"

he went on. "I barely recognized some of these neighborhoods when the agent was taking us around yesterday."

"It's grown, hasn't it. Will you excuse me?"

Hoping she didn't pass out, she shifted in the direction of her house. The thirty feet between them seemed insurmountable, as tough as the 10K she ran with Alex in the spring.

She took a step away from him but made it no farther and would have fallen again if he hadn't rushed forward and absorbed her weight into his solid bulk.

"You need to see a doctor for that."

He was warm. Incredibly warm. And how was it possible he still smelled good after jogging? She caught a hint of laundry soap from his T-shirt and some kind of sexy citrus and musk aftershave.

"I only twisted an ankle. Not the first time. Once I ice it and take some weight off, it will be fine."

She hoped. She did *not* have time for this. She managed to extricate herself from his arms and hobbled another step. By sheer force of will, she managed to remain upright, though it took every ounce of strength.

She made it maybe four steps before she heard a muffled curse.

"You're as stubborn as ever, aren't you?"

"I don't know what you're talking about," she said stiffly.

"I'm talking about the girl who once insisted on going on a six-mile bike ride with Dylan and me, not once mentioning she had walking pneumonia."

"I don't remember that," she lied.

"Funny, I have a vivid memory of it. You just about passed out before the end of it."

"I'm sorry I don't have time to stand around reminiscing with you but I've got to change and get to work. See you later."

She gave what she hoped looked like a jaunty wave and not a dyspeptic robotic one and started toward her house, willing down the pain with every step and trying to figure out how she would squeeze in an appointment with Dr. Harris that morning.

After just a few more steps, her ankle gave out, and she had to grab hold of a convenient aspen sapling for support.

Next moment, Spence swore again under his breath—a surprisingly mild oath for a man who had spent ten years as a professional athlete. Suddenly her feet were swept out from under her, and she was lifted into the air quite effortlessly.

Oh, fudge. She couldn't seem to catch her breath, cradled tight between hard arms and an even more solid chest, but she did her best to gather the scattered corners of her brain.

"Put me down! This is ridiculous. I can walk."

"Maybe. But I would hate to see you do more damage to that ankle by putting weight on it if you've seriously injured it."

He wasn't even breathing hard. Eighty pounds ago, he probably would have needed a couple teammates to help carry her down the street.

"I'm not going to hurt my ankle. Please. Put me down."

He smelled even better up close. Some small, stupid part of her wanted to lean her head on his shoulder and just inhale his warm neck, right there below his rugged jawline.

"You're tight as a drum. Relax. I'm not going to drop you."

"So you say," she muttered. Her insides seemed to flutter and dance and everything girlie inside her hummed to life.

How could she possibly be attracted to him, after everything? It completely belied logic. It was only situational attraction, she told herself. He was big and muscled and she couldn't help being aware of the heat and scent of him.

Nobody except her brothers had ever lifted her up, and even they hadn't done it in years.

"How long have you lived here?" he asked in a conversational tone, as if they were sitting on counter stools at the café passing the time.

She really, really hoped none of her neighbors were awake and gazing out their window at the morning view. This wouldn't exactly be easy to explain, how she found herself in the arms of the town's most notorious former denizen.

On the other hand, she would look even more foolish if she put up a fuss and tried to wriggle out of his arms, onto legs she wasn't entirely certain would support her.

Only two more houses to go and then she would be home.

"Three years," she finally answered.

She ought to leave it at that—her life was none of his concern, thank you very much—but with nerves bubbling through her like fine champagne, she couldn't seem to keep from jabbering.

Maybe it was the way the sunlight glinted gold in his hair or the play of those muscles against her, but her voice sounded husky and strained.

"After I graduated from Colorado State, I came back to town with a degree in business and a master plan of taking over the café from my dad eventually. I tried working as his manager but he wasn't in a big rush to retire, and I discovered I wanted to build something of my own."

"You have," he answered. "I had a piece of your peanut butter fudge last night. It was just about the best thing that's ever crossed my lips."

She knew perfectly well she shouldn't have this little burst of pride at his words. What did she care what Spence thought of her store and her product?

Oh, why did her house feel like it was so far away, like they were swimming through miles and miles of melted chocolate to get there?

"Pop always told me that, when you find something you're good at, you should throw your whole heart into it."

A corner of his mouth lifted. "Good man, your dad."

She had a vivid memory of sitting at a corner booth at the café with Spencer doing homework. She had probably been twelve, he had been sixteen, and his mom had showed up drunk for the dinner shift, as usual. This time, she started talking smack to one of the customers who complained she got his order wrong and then had turned on Dermot when he stepped in to help.

Instead of firing her, like he probably should have done years earlier, Dermot had, in his quiet, effortless way, calmed the situation with the customer, directed Billie to his office and brought her a big pot of coffee and a grilled cheese sandwich.

Meanwhile, Spence had sat at their booth, his head almost buried in the book he was supposed to be writing a report about, but she hadn't missed his red ears and the tension in his shoulders.

Her father had adored Spence like one of his own boys. Just a few months after his mother had died of acute liver poisoning, Spence had signed with the Pioneers, and Dermot had been as proud and excited as if Spence *were* his son.

And when Spence had been embroiled in scandal and controversy, Dermot had followed the news with a baffled, hurt sort of disbelief that had broken her heart, though he had clung to baseless faith.

If she hadn't already despised Spence by that time, she would have hated him for that alone.

The reminder helped her rein in her wayward hormones. "Okay," she said abruptly, the moment he crossed from the sidewalk in front of her neighbor's property to her own. "We're here. You can put me down anytime now."

He gave a short laugh, enough to make his chest move against her shoulder, but kept walking up the path to her porch. "Is your house locked? I can help you inside."

She could hear a car approaching at the other end of the street, and she just wanted this to be over before someone saw. "I'm fine. Please put me down now."

It must have been the *please* that finally did the trick. He carried her up the steps then lowered her gingerly to her feet. She braced one hand on the wall and with the other pulled the key out of its zippered pocket of her capris.

"Thank you," she said shortly. She should say something more but for the life of her she couldn't come up with anything that didn't sound ridiculous.

"You're welcome. Consider it my neighborly duty. Are you sure you don't need me to help you inside, maybe tape it up for you?"

Oh, she could just imagine him kneeling at her feet, his big hands warm on her bare skin as he wrapped it. "I should be fine."

He looked big, muscular. Gorgeous.

"Give me a call if you need a ride to the doctor. I guess you know where I live."

"I'll do that," she lied as if she didn't have a dozen friends and family members she could call, people she would be far more likely to turn to in times of trouble than Smoke Gregory.

He stood and watched as she fumbled through unlocking the door. Already, the acute pain of her ankle injury had begun to fade to a dull, insistent throb. She figured that was a good thing but it still made it a challenge to enter her house with any degree of dignity.

When she made it through the doorway, she turned around and gave him a little one-finger wave then closed the door firmly.

When she knew she was out of sight, she sank onto the conveniently placed bench in her entry and pressed a hand to her foolish heart.

Of all the rental properties in Hope's Crossing, why on earth did he have to pick the one just a few hundred feet from hers? She would be aware of him all the time now. Every time she drove down the street and passed his house, she would wonder if he was home, what he was doing, how he smelled....

If she wasn't careful, she was afraid she would turn

into that fifteen-year-old again, a crazy stalker girl with a crush on the sexiest boy in town.

No problem. She would just have to make sure she was very, very careful.

CHAPTER FIVE

Spence walked back down the steps of Charlotte Caine's house, off balance by the tangle of emotions.

Charlotte Caine.

He still couldn't get over it. Whoever would have guessed she could have such a lithe, curvy body now? He was still having a hard time reconciling the girl he had known to the sexy armful he had carried to her house.

She had always had pretty-colored hair, he remembered, blond shot through with gold and red streaks. When she was a girl, though, she had worn it long, her bangs hanging in her eyes and around those big thick-framed glasses.

He supposed he had changed, too. What did she see when she looked at him now? He was no longer that cocky kid blessed with uncommon ability who thought the world was his to conquer.

Life had a funny way of knocking guys who needed it back down to size.

How had the years treated Charlotte, beyond the physical changes? Her store seemed to be doing well. Did she have someone special in her life? Had she been married? Engaged? He hadn't noticed a ring on her finger but he had certainly learned a little piece of jewelry didn't always mean anything.

So far, he knew she had come home to Hope's Crossing with a business degree but their few moments of conversation while she had been in his arms hadn't exactly unlocked her life story for him.

He pulled out his key and let himself into the rental.

After one night here, he hadn't made up his mind yet whether he liked the place or not. The house was meticulously and expensively decorated, but compared to the glimpse into Charlotte's charming little cottage he'd caught when she had opened the door—plump pillows, bright textiles, bookshelves overflowing—the furnishings here seemed cold, almost sterile.

He wasn't sure if he would be here long enough to redecorate. He and Pey had only packed a few suitcases between them for the drive. The rest of their belongings still filled their Portland house. He hadn't decided yet how much to haul down here.

He would have to see how things went first with the job before he made a decision about that.

He heard noises coming from the kitchen and headed in that direction. When he walked in, he found Pey seated at the breakfast bar, a huge bowl of cereal in front of her, looking at something on her phone.

"Good morning. Did you sleep well?" he asked, then cursed the stiff politeness in his tone. This was his daughter. He shouldn't sound like he was on a business trip, bumping into an associate in the hotel's free buffet line.

She shrugged, a spoonful of cereal almost to her mouth. "Okay, I guess. I need a fan or something. It was too quiet."

"We can probably find you something. Was the bed comfortable?"

"I don't know. I guess. It was a bed. I slept."

She took another bite of cereal and he opened the refrigerator and pulled out a water bottle and a yogurt, grateful he had taken a moment to order groceries the night before. It took him a few tries to find the silverware drawer for a spoon before he leaned back against the counter adjacent to her.

"We can change anything you don't like in your room."

"Can you transport it back to Portland?"

He bit down his frustration at her continual refrain. *This* was why he walked on eggshells around her, because she was prickly and moody all the damn time.

"Nope. Can't do that. How's your cereal?"

"Fine." She poured a little Cinnamon Toast Crunch into her milk. Where did she put all the food she ate sometimes? he had to wonder. She was skinny as can be, like her mother had been.

Once he had found that attractive. He must have. Hadn't he been enamored with Jade at first and thought her the most perfect creature on earth?

Of course, he had been only nineteen and in his rookie year with the Pioneers, starry-eyed and heady with the success that had come far more quickly than a dirt-poor kid who had spent his life watching over a drunk of a mother could either comprehend or cope with.

When a gorgeous supermodel like Jade Howell, three years older and infinitely exciting, wanted to date him, what teenage boy would have refused?

Not him, even though he was pretty sure now she had been more drawn to all those new zeros in his portfolio from his record-breaking contract than she had been to a naive nineteen-year-old kid.

At the time he had been too caught up in the high life of instant fame—fast cars, magazine covers, avid fans—to see that she was a troubled, damaged soul constantly in need of reassurance. Or maybe subconsciously, he *had* seen it and had in some twisted way thought that, if he could make things work with Jade, in some way he might be able to scab over all those open sores from his childhood.

A therapist would probably tell him he had a pretty severe case of knight-in-shining-armor complex from all those years he had tried to look out for his mother. Even so, after six months, he had grown tired of Jade's moods and her petty piques and probably would have ended things if she hadn't gotten pregnant with Peyton.

He didn't like thinking about Jade or the way their hasty marriage had disintegrated before Peyton was even in preschool. Though his wife had certainly loved the creature comforts his income provided, she had hated everything about his career—the traveling, the fame, the fans—and had constantly accused him of cheating.

He took a spoonful of yogurt. It had been a miserable marriage. If not for his daughter, he would have walked away but Jade had threatened to tie him up in court so he would never see Peyton again. He had known she wouldn't have been able to win but the energy in fighting her would only have hurt their daughter.

As poor a father as he had been, he had been raised the only child of a bitter, lost, addicted soul, and he couldn't condemn his child to that same fate.

Eventually, he and Jade had worked out an arrangement of sorts. They lived virtually separate lives in the same house, joined only by their shared love for their daughter. Jade did her thing, he did his and they tried to stay out of each other's way—until she made that impossible by dragging him into the complicated mess her life had become.

Jade had been all sharp edges and angles. Charlotte Caine, on the other hand, had those soft curves that a man wanted to spend days, weeks, months exploring....

"So why were you carrying the fudge lady?" Peyton asked.

He flushed, remembering that surge of unexpected heat when she was in his arms. "You saw that, did you?"

She pointed to the window over the sink, which he realized provided a fine view out into the street.

"I guess I startled her this morning when I said hello as she was jogging past. She lost her balance and ended up twisting her ankle."

"Oh, way to go, Dad."

At her caustic tone, he jumped immediately to the defensive. "Yeah. It was totally on purpose. I like to lie in wait, then jump out of the bushes when unsuspecting joggers appear. Makes a fun ending to my own workout."

She rolled her eyes. "Whatever."

He would like to wring the neck of *whatever* idiot invented that word that was wielded so freely by his daughter.

"It was totally accidental, I promise. I was just being friendly when I saw her go past. I figured she would have seen me. Turns out, she lives up the street in that little white cottage with the blue shutters and the ivy."

"And you had to carry her home."

"Didn't have to, no. But I didn't want her putting weight on her ankle."

Peyton raised a skeptical eyebrow, always looking for the worst in him, and he waited for the dreaded *w*-word. To his surprise, she must have decided to demur.

"You knew her when you lived here before, didn't you?" she asked instead, in almost a civil tone. Charlotte must have made quite an impression with her kindness. Peyton had seemed genuinely touched at her welcome gift.

"Yes," he answered, weighing how much to tell her. He had been fairly closemouthed about his life here in Hope's Crossing, figuring his childhood wasn't exactly much to brag about. She hadn't showed much interest but when she did ask, he evaded and dissembled.

He had spent most of his adult life trying to forget his beginnings here. Off the top of his head, he couldn't remember ever having a conversation with Pey about those hardscrabble times, the weekends when he would eat ramen noodles for three meals each day because that's all they had in the house and about all he knew how to fix.

Another reason he had loved the café, because Dermot would always make sure he went home with something in his stomach and usually a doggie bag of food he could heat the next day.

That was one of his worries about being home, actually. Peyton already thought the worst of him. What would she think once she discovered how much everybody likely hated him here?

On the other hand, he wouldn't exactly win any popularity contests in Portland, especially since the Pioneers had struggled the past few years without him. He knew things had been rough for Peyton at school, enduring taunts and ridicule about her drug-dealing asshole of a father, but at least she also had a core of loyal friends there.

He wondered again if he was doing the right thing, dragging her away from what little she had left. He had to cling to the idea that, if he could make things work here in Hope's Crossing, he might be able to open other options for them both in the future.

"Charlotte's family was always kind to me," he finally said, which was a bit of an understatement. "I was good friends with her older brothers. My mom was a waitress and I washed dishes at her dad's diner in town. The Center of Hope Café."

"You washed dishes? Seriously?"

"Yeah. And I swept the floor at the hardware store after school. And delivered papers at 5:00 a.m. every day from the time I was twelve."

He had figured out early that if he and his mother were going to be able to afford to keep the utilities turned on in the house she had inherited from her mother, one of them was going to have to work to make it happen.

"Newspaper delivery boy. Really?"

He had no regrets, at least about the paper delivery job. As miserable as it might have been riding his secondhand bike around the hilly streets of Hope's Crossing, especially on bitter January mornings, he gave that job a lot of the credit for his throwing arm that *Sports Illustrated* once called supersonic.

"Yeah. Really. It taught me a lot, that job. Maybe you ought to think about picking up a route."

She snorted. "Right."

Her phone bleeped with a text and that apparently was the end of their conversation. She turned her attention to the device and started thumbing a message, probably about her idiot of a father.

"After I shower, I need you to get dressed and grab your laptop or whatever other gadgetry you want to take." He tried for a firm paternal tone. "I'm heading into the recreation center today. Until I can hire a housekeeper, I guess you'll have to come with me."

She stared at him. "You can't be serious."

"Why can't I be serious?"

Her eyebrows nearly reached her fringe of bangs. "I'm almost thirteen. I don't need a babysitter! I'm old enough to *be* a babysitter, for heaven's sake."

Yeah, how many nights had he spent on his own? After his grandma had died when he was nine, Billie sometimes wouldn't come home for a couple days at a time. Of course, she didn't spare a thought for the child she only remembered half the time.

A vivid memory flitted through his mind, the first time she had decided to stay at the bar all night until closing and then go home with somebody who bought her a few drinks. He remembered locking the front door and huddling in his bed, missing his grandmother like crazy. He hadn't slept at all that night and had been so bleary-eyed, he had ended up in detention for dozing off in class, where he was warm and safe.

He hadn't thought about these things much in years. He wasn't sure he liked the way the memories had started to bubble up to the surface since his return, like some geothermal hot spot reinvigorated by volcanic activity deep beneath the crust of the earth.

Peyton probably was old enough to stay by herself but the idea didn't sit well with him, for reasons he couldn't fully explain.

"I have no problem with you being on your own for a few hours. Even three or four," he said. "But this is all day long. I just don't feel good about leaving you in a strange house by yourself when you don't know anybody in town yet that you could call in case of an emergency."

"I don't want to sit around a stupid, boring recreation center all day!"

He licked the last bit of yogurt from his spoon and tossed it in the sink and the empty container into the trash. "It's a recreation center," he reminded her. "By its very definition, you should find plenty to do. Swimming, racquetball, mountain biking. You won't be bored unless you want to be, trust me on that, ladybug."

"Would you stop calling me that? I'm not five years old anymore, and I'm so tired of you treating me that way. I don't want to spend all day at your stupid job!"

He should have known she would dig her heels in about this, as she did about every other damn thing in their lives.

"This isn't negotiable," he said, trying not to grind his teeth. "Get dressed. I can give you half an hour."

She stared at him for a long moment and apparently seemed to know he had drawn a line he wouldn't let her cross.

"I hate you and I hate this stupid town!" she exploded. "Why couldn't I have stayed in Portland with one of my friends or with Mrs. Sanchez?"

"You think Mrs. Sanchez would have extended the retirement she had been planning for a year in order to stay with you?"

"If you paid her enough, she would have! You just didn't want to."

A bleak sense of futility seemed to settle in his gut.

His daughter would have preferred staying with their housekeeper to moving here and having a new adventure with him. She said she hated him. For all he knew, she meant the words.

Like the rest of the world, she blamed him for her mother's death. He wanted to believe she didn't think he was literally responsible for Jade's drowning, that he had held her head underwater or something, but Peyton seemed to think he should have done more to help Jade when her addictions spiraled out of control.

The hell of it was, she was right. But by then, he was tangled in his own legal issues and too busy trying to stay out of prison to spend much time worrying about the woman responsible for tangling him up in the whole mess in the first place.

"We're a family, like it or not," he said now, trying his best to keep his temper contained.

"I don't," she muttered under her breath.

"Look, you've convinced yourself you hate it here but we've only been here a few days. Give it time. I think you'll change your mind. And I promise, first order of business for me is to hire a housekeeper. I'm working through an agency and expect to have someone by the end of the day."

"I don't see why we need a housekeeper."

He couldn't take any more. "Face it, kid. We're slobs. I haven't washed dishes in a long time. We need somebody to clean up after us, cook for us, run you around, be here if you break your thumbs with all that texting."

"I don't have anywhere to go," she muttered.

"You will. Once you've been here awhile and have a chance to make some new friends, you'll probably find all kinds of things to do. Meantime, today I would like

you to come with me and be my moral support. Please.
Just get dressed, Peyton."

He could tell she wanted to offer more arguments but
she finally slid off the bar stool.

He whispered a prayer of gratitude that at least he
didn't get another *whatever* out of her.

"GOOD NEWS. Nothing's broken."

"What did I tell you?"

Charlotte shifted her aching ankle to a little more
comfortable position on the exam table while her pri-
mary care physician, Susannah Harris, examined the
X-ray displayed on the wall-hung light cabinet.

Dr. Harris tucked a strand of steel-gray hair behind her ear. "It's not broken but your ankle is badly
sprained. In my experience, sorry to say, a sprain can
sometimes be more painful than a fracture."

Charlotte closed her eyes, foreseeing a difficult week.
"This is going to be a problem for me, isn't it?"

"It doesn't have to be. But I would recommend you
stay off it for at least a week."

"I can't do that! What about the store? And my running? I have to exercise!"

Susannah had been with her through her whole
weight-loss journey. She knew how deadly a change in
routine could be for someone trying to establish new
habits.

"Calm down, Charlotte. You can do this."

Easy for Susannah to say. She was athletic and tough
and ran marathons for fun.

"Have you done much swimming?" the doctor went
on. "The new pool at the recreation center is wonderful.
James and I went up over the weekend. They reserve

it for lap swimming in the morning and it wasn't very busy when we were there."

When she was young, she used to swim all the time but since she had gained weight, she hated how she looked in a swimsuit too much to subject herself to that humiliation very often.

What other choice did she have? She couldn't run on her ankle. Right now, she couldn't even walk. She had a reclined exercise bike but the thought of pedaling made her ankle give an angry throb.

Yet another reason to be angry with Spence Gregory for coming back to town and ruining *everything.*

She frowned. Okay, in all fairness she couldn't really blame him. How could he have known she would become so off balance to see him there that she would lose track of where she was running?

She could only imagine the trouble she could get into if he happened to walk past while she was swimming at the community center. Susannah would be treating her for a concussion from heedlessly ramming into the side of the pool.

"I'll figure something out. Thanks, Susannah."

"I'm going to write a scrip for some crutches. You can pick them up at our pharmacy here at the clinic. Use them, got it?"

"At least it's my left foot. I can still drive, right?"

"If you're careful." The doctor gave her a sympathetic look. "I'm sorry I can't give you better news. But look at it this way—you don't have to wear a cast."

Small favors. This would definitely complicate her life. In addition to the difficulties at work, she would have to try very hard to make sure she didn't lose hard-fought ground when it came to working out.

Susannah gazed at her computer screen for a moment. "It looks like you've lost another five pounds since I saw you two months ago. That's fantastic, Charlotte. Doesn't that put you right at your goal weight?"

She smiled. "Yes. Three pounds ago."

"You're an inspiration. You've added years to your life, you know. I can tell you that, if you hadn't lost the weight, this injury probably would have been far worse—and I think you'll find your ankle will heal much faster than it would have otherwise, since you're more toned and your diet is more healthy."

Of course, if she hadn't lost the weight, she probably wouldn't have been running in front of Spence Gregory's just after sunrise to go sprawling into the street. But she decided not to mention that little fact to the doctor.

She left Susannah's office with her ankle wrapped and her palm bandaged, wielding a rented pair of crutches.

She drove to work trying to figure out how she was going to handle parking. Most downtown merchants used a lot a block off Main Street in order to leave the prime spots for customers. She certainly had a good excuse to park closer but she couldn't find a more convenient spot. Besides, parking along the street was limited to two hours anyway. She ended up circling around the block and finally pulling back into the off-street parking lot.

Ah, well. It would give her good practice on the crutches and a little of that exercise she and Susannah were just talking about.

By the time she made it half a block, she was reconsidering. Besides the steady throb of her ankle, her hands hurt where she clutched the crutches and her armpits burned.

This would get old fast.

She was walking past String Fever, her favorite place to bead, when Claire McKnight, the owner of the store, and her manager, Evie Thorne, came out the front door.

"Oh, my word," Claire exclaimed, consternation temporarily shunting aside her voluptuous pregnancy glow. She planted her hands on her hips. "Charlotte Caine, what have you done to yourself?"

She was grateful for the chance to take a break and sank onto the conveniently situated bench outside the bead store. "Nothing. It's so embarrassing. I sprained my ankle this morning on my run."

Tripping over my feet, just because Spence Gregory happens to look gorgeous in a pair of jogging shorts.

"Do you have to use the crutches long?" Evie asked. She was a physical therapist by training, though she only maintained a select few clients and preferred to spend most of her time working at the bead store.

Charlotte sighed. "Dr. Harris tells me I'm supposed to keep weight off it for a week. It's really no big deal."

"It is. Believe me, I know how horrible crutches can be," Claire said. "Why don't you come into the store and let me get you a drink and fuss over you for a bit? The fall bead magazines showed up this morning."

Fall, already? She supposed so. It wouldn't be long, anyway. Here in Hope's Crossing, the quaking aspens would start turning gold in another month.

"That sounds tempting, believe me, but I'm afraid I'm already late heading into the store. I missed the whole morning at the doctor's. I hope nobody needs an urgent order of fudge made today because I'm afraid it's not happening."

"You're coming to the book club meeting tomorrow, aren't you?"

She had completely forgotten in the chaos of Spence's return. "I should be there, as long as I can find a convenient spot to prop my ankle."

"We'll make sure you do," Evie promised. "Here. Stand up. Let me help adjust those crutches to a better fit."

Charlotte had learned a long time ago it was best to just obey when her dear friends started trying to order her life. She stood and let Evie fuss over her for a moment.

"There. Try that."

She took a few exploratory steps with the crutches and smiled back over her shoulder. "That's tons better. Wow. Amazing!"

"We all have our little skills. You make the best fudge in the Rocky Mountains. I adjust crutches. Take it easy. Even when your ankle starts to feel better, you can do serious damage if you push yourself."

"So Dr. Harris warned me. Thank you for the double dose of caution. I promise, I'll sit in my office at the store all day long and let my employees wait on me hand and foot."

"Good idea," Claire said. "Or better yet, take the day off. You've got smart people working for you. They can handle things without you during an emergency like this."

Charlotte gave Claire and Evie a warm smile. "I'm a lucky woman to have friends to fret about me."

"Yes, you are," Claire answered.

With a smile and a wave, Charlotte started to hobble toward Sugar Rush when Evie moved up to walk beside her.

"Wait," her friend said. "I'm heading that direction anyway to grab coffee at Maura's place. I'll walk with you."

She had a feeling that wasn't precisely true, and that Evie was manufacturing a reason to accompany her, probably to make sure she didn't take another dive off the sidewalk.

As long as Spence didn't happen to walk by and start some leg stretches, she should be fine.

"So I understand Alex is trying to set you up next weekend with one of Sam's army buddies."

Crap. She had completely forgotten about that. She absolutely didn't want to go out on a blind date while she was on crutches. She would just have to hope she didn't need them by the following weekend.

"I've met Garrett King," Evie said. "He seems very nice. You should have a wonderful time."

Evie was another of her friends who had a great husband. She and Brodie just seemed to fit together, perfectly complementing the other's strengths.

Evie had moved to Hope's Crossing a few years ago from Los Angeles, where she'd had a successful pediatric rehab practice. After Brodie's teenage daughter, Taryn, had been injured in a severe car accident that had killed another teen, Evie had stepped in to help the girl's recovery.

Charlotte started to ask about Taryn, but before she could get the words out, an old blue battered pickup pulled up to the curb beside them and the driver killed the engine.

Tucker's big droopy face hung out the passenger window and a moment later, Dylan climbed out the other side and walked around the front of the truck. He wore his customary scowl but for once, he looked more concerned than angry at the world.

"What the hell happened to you?" he exclaimed. "I just saw you last night!"

She sighed, wondering how many times she was going to have to go over this with people. Probably a couple dozen more that day, at least. "You know me. Clumsy as a deaf bat. I sprained my ankle while I was running this morning."

"That's what happens when you go running. Sorry about that. You need a ride somewhere?"

"I'm heading to the store."

"Let me walk you the rest of the way."

"Okay," she managed to say, so surprised at his gesture, she forgot to point out that she was almost there, that Evie was already babysitting her or that Dylan had parked in a red zone.

When they reached the store, Evie waved and headed back to the bookstore and coffee shop. Dylan lingered in the doorway, his features troubled.

"I was thinking I might have dinner tonight at the café. If you're not hurting too bad, want to come?"

She stared at him, wondering if she had imagined the breathtaking words. Was Dylan actually instigating a social engagement, inviting his sister to have dinner at their father's café? She could hardly believe it. She gave him a careful look but he certainly looked sober to her. He knew better than to get behind the wheel otherwise.

"Yeah. Yes. Of course! I should be done at the store about seven."

"Okay." He shifted. "I'll meet you in front of the store. That way you won't have to walk there on the sticks."

It was only a block away and she could probably walk but she was so thrilled at this new development that she didn't turn him down.

"Yes. Great. I'll see you at seven."

Dylan looked pained for a moment, as if he had half hoped she would refuse, but then he nodded and returned to his pickup. She watched him drive away, effervescent hope bubbling through her.

If twisting her ankle had in any way contributed to her brother agreeing to venture out into public long enough to have dinner at the café, she would trip over her feet in front of Spence Gregory's house every day for a month.

CHAPTER SIX

DUSKY SUNLIGHT FILTERED up the canyon when Spence finally left the recreation center at the end of his first day and headed down the road that paralleled the reservoir toward town.

His day hadn't been *completely* miserable. He had met the new staff at the rec center and spent a little time talking to them, listening to their ideas, trying to assure them he had no plans to come in and radically change what they had already started.

So far, so good. Though he had intercepted a few sideways glances and everyone treated him with wariness, nobody had come right out and called him a drug-dealing murderer. Always a bonus, when he could say that at the end of the day.

The recreation center wasn't finished yet. When it was done, it would have an extensive network of facilities, indoors and outdoors. An equestrian complex, hiking trails, a practice ski jump, even boating docks and a swim beach in the reservoir.

It was an ambitious project for a town the size of Hope's Crossing, created through a complicated mix of taxes and private donations, but he was already excited about the possibilities. For once, he thought he might be able to put to use the college business classes his one-time mentor had encouraged him to take during the off-season.

At the thought of Mike Broderick—once one of his best friends in the world—his hands tightened on the steering wheel and that familiar surge of bitter anger scorched through him. He pushed it away, knowing it was as pointless as ever and somehow didn't belong in the midst of the pure beauty he drove through.

Summer evenings in the Colorado high country were divine, green and lush and full of long, lazy shadows. He had forgotten that in the years he was gone.

He glanced over at his daughter, thumbing her way through what passed for a conversation these days with one of her friends.

"Thanks for coming with me today. I appreciated the moral support."

She made a *hmmph* sort of sound. "Funny. I don't remember you giving me much choice."

"You couldn't have been bored. Every time I saw you, you were doing something. Swimming in the pool, trying the machines in the weight room, hanging out in the lobby with your computer. It looked like you made a few friends."

She shrugged, her eyes still on her phone. "Not really."

"I saw you talking to some girls."

From his perspective, she had looked animated and even happy, but the next time he had walked past, she had been sitting alone with her computer again, with no sign of the other girls.

"I guess."

Little Miss Loquacious, apparently. "Were they nice?"

She hesitated for a moment then shrugged. "Sure.

Until I told them who I was. More important, who *you* were. Then they wanted to ask me all kinds of questions about you and about Mom and everything."

His hands tightened again, this time with anger directed at himself. He hated that his child had been affected by the hot mess created by the adults around her.

And this, kids, is what happens when a stupid nineteen-year-old boy jumps into the deep end before he learns to swim and signs a multimillion-dollar contract, which attracts all the wrong sort of women.

He would give anything to go back and fix his mistakes—except that would mean he wouldn't have this smart, funny, beautiful girl for a daughter.

He just had to hope that things would get better for both of them.

"I don't know what we have to fix in the groceries I had delivered. Feel like going out somewhere tonight?"

"Whatever."

Ah, there it was. He fought down a sigh and turned his SUV toward downtown, knowing just where he wanted to go.

He found a parking place on Main Street, across from the bookstore and coffee bar he'd stopped at his first night in town.

He had heard it belonged to Maura McKnight. Her kid brother Riley had played ball with him, though he'd been a few years older. Maura had once been married to Chris Parker, lead singer of Pendragon—one of Peyton's favorite bands.

He wondered what might be his chances of swinging an autographed poster or something, though he couldn't imagine that would be enough to make Peyton hate him less.

"Where are we going?" she asked as he moved around to open the car door for her.

"Remember how I told you I washed dishes at the café Charlotte's dad runs? I thought you would like to see the place. You might enjoy imagining me elbow deep in dishwater."

She looked intrigued as they crossed the street, with its historic reproduction streetlamps and hanging flower baskets.

"What was her name?" she asked after a minute.

"Who?" he stalled.

"Your mom. You said this morning she had been a waitress there. You never talk about her. She would have been my grandma, right?"

"Yeah." He didn't know what to say about her. He had loved her fiercely and had once beat the crap out of a punk at school, Corey Johnson, for calling her a drunk.

When she was sober, she had been funny and bright, full of stories and jokes. She had played ball with him in the backyard and had taken him cross-country skiing.

Through his teen years, she hadn't been sober very often.

"Her name was Billie," he finally answered. "She grew up here in Hope's Crossing but left to go to college in California, where she met my dad. She was a really talented artist and loved to read."

He could see the wheels turning in Peyton's head. "Really?"

"She used to draw funny cartoons for me on the napkin she packed in my lunch."

Until his dad died, when everything had fallen apart.

"How did she die?"

He didn't want to tell Peyton that the talented, beautiful artist drank herself to death. "She just got sick one day and didn't get better."

It was the truth, anyway. Her liver had finally given up after years of abuse. He had spent New Year's Eve of his senior year in high school not at the big party his friends were having but at the hospital with her while doctors told him she wasn't going to live through the night.

"That's really sad," Peyton said.

"Yeah. It was." Even more tragic because of all that wasted potential.

He didn't want to think about Billie, but it was hard to escape it here in this town. With a weird feeling of déjà vu, he pushed through the door into the Center of Hope Café.

Not much had changed. Oh, it looked like the walls had been painted and Dermot had put a few new paintings on the wall to freshen things up—one that looked like it was done by his favorite artist, Sarah Colville, whom he had heard lived in town. Other than that, he could have been a kid again, running in late after baseball practice for his evening shift.

A tall hearty-looking man with a white apron tied around his waist stopped dead when he and Peyton walked inside. The man gazed at him, an arrested look in eyes the same blue as one of the glacier-fed lakes that dotted the mountains.

"Why, as I live and breathe. Spencer Gregory himself."

At the welcome in those eyes, warmth washed through, sweet and cleansing. To his shock, emotion welled up inside him and he had to clear his throat before he spoke.

"Dermot. It's been too long."

"That is has, son. That it has."

After a moment, Dermot Caine—almost as tall as Spencer—reached out and hugged him hard, not at all afraid to show affection to another man, apparently.

That emotion welled up again and he realized how very much he had been in need of a friendly face in town, someone who didn't seem to paint him with that ugly brush.

Dermot stepped away, wiping at his eyes with the edge of his white apron. "Why ever have you stayed away so long?"

"That's a damn good question," he said, not quite sure how to answer. He could have said that he had lost his way, that he had been too caught up trying to prove himself. Dermot seemed to understand without the words.

"You're here now. That's the important thing. You're here, and it looks like you've brought me someone."

Spence angled his head down to find that Peyton stood a half pace behind him.

"Yes. Dermot, this my daughter, Peyton. Peyton, Dermot Caine is one of the best men I know."

Those blue eyes looked pleased and seemed to water a little more as he reached a hand out and solemnly shook Peyton's hand. "Welcome to our little town, my dear. I hope you'll feel most welcome."

"Mr. Caine, you're related to the lady who owns the candy store, right?"

His features creased into a handsome smile. "Why, yes I am. Charlotte is my only daughter after six big, smelly, farty sons. She's the light of an old man's eye, she is."

"She's nice," Peyton said with a shy smile that warmed

Spencer's heart. "She gave me a big bag of fudge yesterday."

"And doesn't it taste delicious? You need to try her toffee. Better than anything you'll find in a tin, I'll tell you that much."

"Looks crowded tonight," Spence said. "Any chance you've got a free booth for us?"

"For my best dishwasher, always. Let's take a look."

He led them to a booth in the front that overlooked Main Street and the bustle of tourist traffic.

"We've changed a few things over the years but I think you'll still find some of the old favorites. You don't fix what's not broken, right?"

"Thank you, Dermot."

The man paused beside the booth as Spence and Peyton slid in on opposite sides then handed the menus to them and poured water from a pitcher into their glasses.

Before Dermot walked away, he rested a hand for just a moment on Spence's shoulder. How was it possible that one small gesture could convey so much meaning? Sorrow, comfort, concern, happiness at seeing a long-lost friend. It was all there.

Spence sipped at his water glass and opened the menu. Across from him, Peyton frowned.

"Wow. Is there anything *not* fried on the menu?"

He had barely taken a look but he didn't exactly remember Center of Hope being famous for its diet food. "Turkey wraps. Those look good. Or I see a couple salads."

She tucked a strand of dark hair behind her ear, and he thought how thin her wrists were. She did not need to be worrying about her weight at twelve, unless she was trying to figure out how to pack on a few pounds.

Jade had been obsessed with her weight, tracking calories, exercising at least two hours a day. He never could figure out how someone so concerned with being thin, ostensibly taking care of her body, could then abuse it with any little pill that made her feel good.

"I'll just have a hamburger," Peyton finally said. "I guess all that swimming today worked up an appetite."

He couldn't be too worried about Jade's obsession trickling down to Peyton if she could order a hamburger.

"That actually sounds good. I think I'll have one, too."

Dermot sent over a young shaggy blond snowboarder type to take their order. He wondered if Della Pine still worked there. She had been quite a character.

Peyton blushed a little when she ordered and kept her eyes on the menu.

"Good choice," the kid said after he wrote down their order. "The burgers here are killer. Seriously."

Not the most ringing endorsement, but Spence would take it.

They lapsed into silence and Peyton once more pulled out her cell phone, her favorite conversation-butcher of choice, and started sending a text. He looked out the window, wondering how the hell he was going to reach her, when she looked up at a new arrival.

"Hey, isn't that…" Her voice trailed off and she shook her head. "Wow, Dad. Way to go. You broke Charlotte's leg."

He turned around to the door behind him and watched Charlotte, bright and lovely as any Hope's Crossing evening, hobble in on a pair of aluminum crutches.

He muttered an oath. Had she broken her foot this

morning? He really should have taken her to see a doctor instead of just leaving her at her house.

Wasn't it just his luck? He had one real ally in this town, Dermot, and apparently Spence had just broken the leg of the man's beloved only daughter.

Dermot rushed out of the kitchen, his distinguished features a study of paternal concern. "Now what's all this?" he demanded.

"Nothing. I'm fine," Charlotte assured her father, but Spence had an up-close-and-personal acquaintance with injuries of various sorts and knew she was lying. As one who had endured his own aches and pains, including his career-ending shoulder injury, he recognized the pale set features of someone fighting to hide great discomfort.

"You're not fine or you wouldn't be using crutches, now would you?" her father countered. "Tell me what happened to my girl."

Even from here, Spence could hear her sigh. "It's nothing, I promise. I fell while I was out running this morning and sprained my ankle. Dr. Harris assures me I only need to keep weight off it for a week or so, and I'll be good as new."

Her father frowned. "Well, then, why are you standing up? Come on with you. Let's get you to a place where you can sit."

Before he realized what Dermot intended, the man led his daughter to the booth right next to his. So far, she seemed so preoccupied with wending her way on the crutches through chairs and customers to notice him and Peyton until her father helpfully brought their presence to her attention.

"Here you go, my dear. And look who's here, too? Our Spencer has come back at last."

He wasn't sure how it happened but one of the crutches tangled with a chair leg at a nearby table and she started to topple. Dermot, more spry than a sixty-something man ought to be, managed to catch her and right her, then help her into the booth.

Her expression made it quite clear he wasn't *our Spencer* at all. He had a feeling she would like to ignore them—or him, at least—but their proximity made that impossible.

"Hello again, Spence. Hi, Peyton."

"Hi," Peyton answered. "Your fudge was really good. I've already eaten like half of it."

Charlotte looked surprised. "Really? I'm glad you enjoyed it."

A clatter of dishes sounded from around the corner and Dermot cursed in what sounded like Gaelic. "That boy is going to drive this place into the ground with the cost of replacing dishes alone. Excuse me, will you?"

He walked away to deal with the crisis and in the awkward silence he left behind, Spence could tell she would have preferred to just turn back to her booth but politeness deemed that impossible.

"So how was your day?" She addressed the question to Peyton, who shrugged.

"We don't have a housekeeper yet so he made me spend all day at his work. Can you believe it?"

"That must have been truly terrible, being surrounded by all those fun things to do at the recreation center."

Pey didn't look amused at Charlotte's dry tone. "I don't see why I couldn't stay home. I'm almost thirteen. It's not like I'm three or something."

Charlotte met his gaze and he gave her the same argument he'd used on Peyton that morning. "It seemed a long time for her to be alone in a strange town where she doesn't know anyone. Part of my day was spent interviewing housekeepers, though, and we've got somebody starting in a couple days."

"And then I can be bored out of my mind at home instead of at the lame-ass rec center. Excuse me. I need to go wash my hands."

She grabbed her cell phone umbilical cord and trotted toward the restrooms at the rear of the café.

"Sorry about the bad attitude," he said when she disappeared through the ladies' room door. "She's not really thrilled about the move to Hope's Crossing."

"I kind of figured that out." Charlotte's gaze was almost sympathetic. "Give her time. I'm sure she'll adjust to her new situation. Most kids do. When school starts in a month, she'll make dozens of friends and be so busy you'll have to be constantly on her case about doing her homework."

"Great. Something else to look forward to."

She almost smiled but straightened her mouth before one could slip out, tucking a strand of honey-gold hair behind her ear and glancing at the door.

"Things haven't been easy for her. We're both trying to figure things out. With my...legal troubles and then her mother's death, I guess you could say we're in a rebuilding phase here."

Which had been going on for a year, without much forward momentum, but he didn't add that.

Again, that hint of sympathy flickered in her blue eyes. He didn't want her feeling sorry for him but it seemed marginally better than the veiled animosity of the previous day.

"Hope's Crossing is a good place for rebuilding lives and relationships," she said, "surrounded by warm people, beautiful scenery, mountain air."

"I haven't seen that yet on one of the tourist brochures."

"We tend to keep it a secret or the whole world might show up."

"I would like to think you're right. About Hope's Crossing, I mean, being a good place to heal. To be honest, I could use a little hope right now."

She eyed him for a long moment and then turned away, and he wished he knew what she was thinking. When she turned back, her voice was a little softer than it had been.

"I'm sorry about your wife. I don't think I said that yesterday or this morning and...I should have."

He stared, nonplussed at the words. Did she think Jade's death had left him heartbroken? He didn't quite know how to disabuse her of that notion without sounding hard and calloused. He had certainly never wanted his wife dead and had grieved for what their marriage should have been, but that wasn't something he could blurt out to someone he hadn't seen in years.

"Thank you," he finally answered. "It's been hard on Peyton. They were very close."

"I can imagine. It's a tough age for a girl to lose her mother."

Charlotte had lost her mother to cancer at about that age, he recalled. He could remember how helpless he had felt at sixteen to watch people he cared about suffer such a loss.

Even then, in the midst of Dermot's own pain and grief—left a widower with seven children, two still at home—Dermot had been kind to Spence and Billie. He had shared several baskets full of leftovers from all the food people had brought to help the Caines after Margaret's death.

Charlotte had survived something similar to what Pey had been going through this past year. He wondered if she might be willing to help him understand his daughter a little better, offer some perspective that could give him half a clue on how to deal with her.

"Listen, Pey and I seem to get on better with a buffer. I don't suppose there's a chance you'd like to sit with us?"

Her eyes widened at the invitation. She looked disconcerted but at least she didn't appear horror-stricken. "I... Thank you, but I'm actually meeting somebody."

He felt a twinge of something that felt suspiciously like jealousy. Really? Over Charlotte Caine? Where did *that* come from? But for some crazy reason, he found he didn't like the idea of her sharing those sweet, hesitant smiles with anybody else.

"Oh. Sure. No problem."

"It's my... Actually, here he is."

He followed her gaze to the door and saw a rough-looking dude with shaggy longish brown hair and a menacing black eye patch. He could have used a shave a couple days ago and wore a grease-stained pair of jeans and a long-sleeved T-shirt, odd for such a warm evening.

It took Spence only about another five seconds before he recognized her brother Dylan beneath that badass scowl, and he realized what he had taken for a glove on one hand was really a prosthetic arm.

Dylan's scowl lifted and he headed over to his sister, leaning in and kissing her on the cheek. "Anybody ever tell you you're a stubborn thing? I told you I would pick you up. Just because I was ten minutes late, you didn't have to hobble all the way over on your crutches."

"Didn't you get my text? I told you I've been sitting all day and needed to move. Anyway, *all the way over* is only a block and my car was closer to the café than the candy store. So you had a flat tire?"

Dylan took the seat across from her. "Yeah. Must have run over a nail or something or maybe a sharp rock up in the canyon. For all I know, I could have picked up a slow leak a week ago. Ever tried to work a lug wrench one-handed? It's a hell of a lot harder than you might think."

"And you call me stubborn." She made a grumbling noise at her brother. "Why didn't you call somebody to help? Any of the brothers would have come out in a second."

"I managed."

The love between them was obvious. It always had been. When he was a kid, he had been fiercely jealous of the Caines. He could remember seeing them all together sometimes here at the café, squabbling, teasing, laughing. Envy had sometimes threatened to swallow him whole.

Peyton finally returned to the table and picked up her napkin to wipe at her mouth then took a long drink of water.

"You okay?" he asked, suddenly realizing she had been gone awhile.

"I'm fine. I was, uh, just fixing my hair. It's a *mess* after swimming. I hate how frizzy it gets."

It didn't look any different to him, but what did he know? He was just her dad. Their conversation in the next booth must have attracted Dylan Caine's attention. He stood again and approached their table.

"Gregory. I heard you were back in town."

Spence rose and shook hands with him. What had happened to the man? And how the hell had they lost track over the years? His fault, he knew. When he left for Portland, he had basically closed the door on his life here.

Though they were the same age, Dylan had been a grade ahead in school because of what Spence considered his lost year. Dylan had been his catcher all through high school and he had always trusted and respected him.

He had joined the army the year before Spence signed with the Pioneers. Until the scouts started sniffing around his senior year, he had figured he would follow his friend's example and do the same.

"How've you been?" Spence asked, though the answer seemed obvious. The man looked as if he'd been through hell. His clothes hung on his frame and his eyes were shadowed.

"Oh, you know. Can't complain." His light tone contrasted with his bleak expression.

Out of the corner of his gaze, he was aware of Peyton trying hard not to gape at Dylan's prosthetic hand.

"It's good to see you, man," Spence said honestly. "I'd love to buy you a drink sometime and catch up."

The offer seemed to throw Charlotte's brother off guard. "I might take you up on the drink," he answered, his eyes shuttered and dark, "but skipping down memory lane isn't really my thing."

Spence wondered what haunted the man. Suddenly his own demons seemed pretty damn mild in comparison.

"We can start with the drink then."

Dylan nodded. Before he could answer, his father walked over carrying a tray. When he spied his son, Dermot's steps faltered a little but he quickly straightened. "Two of my children here to eat my food. Am I forgetting my birthday or something?"

Charlotte shook her head. "Dylan is taking pity on his clumsy sister and offered to meet me for dinner."

"And you both say I never get out," Dylan said.

"Neither of you should be needing menus then. You can tell me what you want just as soon as I've taken care of Spencer and young Peyton here."

Spence sat down again as Dermot set two plates on the table. "Two house burgers cooked to perfection, if I do say so myself."

His stomach rumbled in anticipation. "Thanks, Dermot. I can't tell you how I've missed your food."

Dermot smiled with a kindness and welcome that overwhelmed Spence. "Then maybe you won't wait more than a decade before coming back again."

"I can promise, I won't."

The café owner gave him a smile and then turned to take the order of his son and daughter, leaving Spence alone with his own daughter, a delicious plate of food and years full of regret.

CHAPTER SEVEN

As AWKWARD MEALS WENT, this one ranked somewhere very close to the top.

Between Dylan's desultory conversation, Pop's frequent stops to check on them, the throbbing from her ankle which should have been elevated about six hours ago and her overriding awareness of the neighboring booth's occupants, she could hardly eat anything, even her favorite Cobb salad.

She wasn't the only one who seemed without an appetite. Dylan picked at his own salad and only took a few bites of his chicken sandwich.

"You're not eating," she pointed out.

"You're one to talk."

"I had a big lunch."

"Liar."

She had packed a turkey sandwich for lunch and some fruit and had eaten on the little picnic table behind the store, enjoying the warmth of the sun.

She sensed Dylan had something on his mind but it seemed every time she tried to encourage him to talk, he backed away. While her impulse was to push and prod, she forced herself to employ one of Pop's better strategies and let her brother work his way around to what he needed.

"So I could use a favor," Dylan finally asked.

Wow, her brother had invited her to dinner *and* wanted to ask a favor, all in one evening. If not for her sprained ankle currently throbbing in time to the country music playing on the jukebox, she might have thought this was her lucky day.

"Of course! Anything."

"I hate when people say that. How do you know that until I ask? What if I want you on my support team while I become the first one-eyed, one-armed asshole to climb Mount Everest?"

"Then I guess I'll have to buy a better parka."

He rolled his eyes. "You're a nut. You know that? It's not quite that extreme. I just need a dog sitter. Can Tuck stay with you for a couple days?"

"Of course!" she said immediately. She loved having that big goofy dog around to fill the empty spaces. He almost made her want to get one of her own, if she didn't hate the idea of leaving the creature alone most of the day.

"I hate to ask when you're on the DL."

"Oh, please. I only have a sprained ankle, I'm not on the disabled list. I might not be able to take him for runs but I can still throw a stick for him in the backyard."

"Thanks. I'll drop him off tomorrow on my way out of town."

"How long will you be gone?" she asked.

"Two nights. Three at the most."

He didn't offer any further explanation about where he was going. She desperately wanted to ask but forced herself to let the silence drag on.

Finally, he sighed. "I've got to run into Denver to the VA for a couple adjustments. Should be easy enough, just a quick surgery, but they might have to keep me overnight. I don't want to leave him at the house on his own or in a hotel room somewhere."

"I'm happy to have him stay. I love the company. I hope you know you can ask anytime. Do you need somebody to come with you to the hospital?"

He shook his head, which she could have predicted. "It's no big deal. I'll be fine."

She wanted to encourage him to ask the doctors to refer him someplace where he might find help through his grim moods. The words clogged her throat and she forced them down. Dylan was reaching out to her—in a small way, yes, but more than he had since he'd come home. She wasn't going to push him and risk losing what little progress they had made.

At the table next door, she heard Peyton make a snide comment to her father but missed Spence's low reply. A moment later, Peyton climbed out of the booth and headed for the ladies' room.

"Do me a favor," Dylan said, his eyes serious. "Don't tell Pop or any of the brothers, would you? It's a minor procedure. I don't want anybody making a fuss."

He couldn't have made that more clear in the past few months if he'd taken out a billboard. She could just picture a big one hanging over the entrance to his driveway in Snowflake Canyon, flashing ten-foot-high letters that blinked Leave Me the Hell Alone.

It went against all her instincts, but she finally nodded. "What if somebody asks me why I'm keeping Tucker?"

"Just tell them I had business out of town."

As far as she could see, the only business Dylan was conducting involved the liquor store and copious purchases of alcoholic substances, but she decided not to comment again. Instead, she pulled her crutches to the side and stood up. "I need to use the ladies' room before I head home."

Her brother nodded and she hobbled through the diner dodging tables. She waved at a few people, hoping the crutches gave her a good excuse not to stop and talk.

When she entered the ladies' room, she was greeted by a retching sound coming from one of the stalls.

"Peyton? Are you okay?"

It had to be her, since Charlotte hadn't seen her come out yet, but a long moment stretched out before she answered. "Yeah. Fine."

"That doesn't sound very fine to me. Do you need some help?"

"No. No, I'm okay."

She waited before going into the other stall, concerned for the girl. A moment later, the toilet flushed and Peyton came out wiping her mouth with tissue.

Charlotte thought she looked pale, but that might have been the lighting.

"I hate that feeling of throwing up. I'm so sorry."

Peyton rinsed her mouth with a little water she cupped from the sink. "I'm okay now, really. I don't know what happened. I guess maybe I ate too much, too quickly. I was starving after I spent all afternoon at the pool."

"Why don't we get you back outside with your dad and I can have Pop bring you some crackers or toast? That always helps me feel better."

"No. You don't have to do that. I just probably need to go to bed early." She fumbled in her messenger bag for a moment before pulling out a stick of gum, unwrapping it and sliding it into her mouth.

"Hey, can I ask you a question?" Peyton asked after a few chews.

"Sure." Still concerned that she might be ill, Charlotte studied her carefully. Peyton didn't seem at all fazed to be in here tossing her dinner.

"What happened to your brother?"

Okay, she hadn't seen that one coming. She pursed her lips, trying to figure out how to answer in a way a young girl could understand.

"Sorry. Was that a rude question?" Peyton asked.

"Not rude at all. It's just a little hard to talk about. He used to be an Army Ranger. He was wounded in an ambush in Afghanistan. He was…the only survivor. He shouldn't have made it out at all."

"No shit." Chewing gum forgotten, Peyton stared at her.

"It was kind of a miracle, really," she answered. She thought so, at least. Dylan didn't seem as convinced. He seemed haunted by his survival, as if he believed he had done something wrong to walk away when the rest of his team didn't.

"Coming back from something like that can be hard," she went on. "Dylan is having a pretty rough recovery, if you want the truth. He nearly died from a couple nasty infections and he's struggling to learn how to do things that used to be easy for him."

"That's way sad," Peyton said.

For all her bristly anger around her father, the girl seemed genuinely concerned.

"Since he's been back in Hope's Crossing, he's become something of a hermit, hiding out alone at this cabin he has in the mountains. It's kind of a big deal that he invited me to have dinner with him tonight here.

I'm hoping this means he's ready to begin venturing out and about more."

Peyton appeared thoughtful as she touched up her lip gloss in the mirror then slipped it back into her bag. "Makes me feel stupid for bitching so much about having to leave my friends, you know? At least I can still text my friends and Skype them and stuff. They didn't die in a bomb or something."

"Your friends are lucky to have you. Before you know it, you'll make plenty more here in Hope's Crossing, trust me."

On impulse, Charlotte hugged the girl. Peyton froze as if not quite sure how to respond. After a pause, she relaxed a little and Charlotte thought she almost hugged her back, but that might have been the crutches moving with the weight shift.

"Feeling better?" Charlotte asked.

The girl's gaze slid away. "Yeah. Guess I'll go back out. Thanks for telling me about your brother and stuff."

"You're welcome."

When Charlotte walked out of the restroom a few minutes later, she was dismayed to see Spence and Peyton sitting in their booth, carrying on what appeared to be mostly a one-sided conversation with Dylan while Peyton's thumbs once more danced over her cell phone screen.

"Don't get me wrong," Spence was saying as she approached. "I still think the recreation center is a great idea. A place for the community to gather and have fun together. Hiking trails, horseback riding, ski runs. It's going to be fantastic when everything is finished. Just can't help wondering if we could make it, I don't know, something *more*."

"Like what?" Dylan had a faraway, unreadable look in his eyes, as if he was there in body but not really present. She was the recipient of that look quite often but Spence didn't seem fazed by it.

"I don't know. Unite for some kind of common purpose, maybe. Hope's Crossing has a lot to offer. Stunning scenery, a quiet kind of charm. Generally nice people. Maybe there's some population out there we could help through the center. Inner-city kids, single mothers, visually impaired children."

Dylan didn't answer, shifting his attention to Charlotte when she approached with half a mind to end the evening and head out while she was already on her feet.

"What about wounded veterans?" Peyton asked suddenly.

All three of them gazed at her with various expressions. Charlotte was stunned, touched again at her compassion, and sat down next to Dylan now to hear out this discussion. Dylan just raised an eyebrow and sipped at his drink, while Spence looked at his daughter as if he had never seen her before.

"That's an idea," Spence said slowly. "Actually, it's a really fantastic idea, Peyton. Wow. Wounded veterans. I'll definitely have to think about that one."

"Waste of time," Dylan said tersely. "Stick with your inner-city kids."

Peyton's face fell and she shifted her attention back to her phone. "It was just an idea."

Charlotte wanted to smack her brother for hurting the girl's feelings when she had only been trying to help, especially since it was just about the first positive thing she had heard Peyton say.

"Why do you think it's a waste of time?" Spence

asked. "I can't think of a population that would benefit more. Water sports in the summer, skiing in the winter, hiking and horseback riding. It seems like a perfect fit."

Dylan tossed his napkin onto his plate, apparently done moving his food around. "On the surface, maybe. But you don't know Jack about what some of these guys have been through. Hate to break it to you, but a horsey ride won't fix the damage an IED can do."

"I don't know Jack. You're right," Spence acknowledged. "But I'm willing to learn. Maybe you and I could talk about this over that beer sometime."

Instead of answering, her brother reached into his pocket and pulled out a couple bills. He tossed them on the table and stood up to go, long and lanky in the narrow space between the table and the banquette, leaving Charlotte no choice but to hobble to her feet to let him out.

"Not interested. Point your little charity wand in another direction, why don't you?"

"Dylan," Charlotte said.

In one of his rapid-fire moods, tension rippled off him and she wanted desperately to make things better. This rude, irritable stranger wasn't the brother she knew.

"I should go. Tucker is home on his own."

His hound was perfectly fine by himself for a few hours and both of them knew it. Dylan obviously wanted to escape, and she didn't know how to prevent it. She supposed she should be grateful she had enjoyed a relatively peaceful hour with him.

"Thanks for dinner, Charley. I'll drop Tuck off in the morning before I head out of town."

"All right."

A muscle worked along his jaw beneath the shadow of growth. "Good to see you again, Gregory. And to meet you. Peyton, wasn't it?"

She nodded, though she didn't look at him. After that brief moment of clarity and kindness, she had apparently subsided back into her truculence.

Charlotte watched her brother walk out of the restaurant without even stopping to say goodbye to Pop and she again wanted to smack him. People cared about Dylan. Their overflowing family wanted to help and support him through his transition back to civilian life.

Yes, it would be a very different one than he had known before but that didn't mean it had to be worthless.

"Sorry," Spencer said quietly. "Looks like we drove away your dinner companion. Why don't you join us?"

"I was finished anyway," she answered. Even if she had only just received her order, she probably would have had Pop toss it into a take-out box rather than try to make conversation with Spence.

"I'm done, too. I'm totally stuffed," Peyton said.

Spence smiled. "I knew you'd like this place."

Charlotte frowned. This was the girl who had just thrown up in the ladies' room? Had she told her father about her upset stomach at all?

Before she could ask whether Peyton was feeling better, Dermot approached their table. His eyes darted around the restaurant. "Where did that brother of yours get off to?"

"He left to take care of Tucker."

"What's the matter with that boy?" Dermot glowered. "I swear, he would rather spend time with that dog than with his own flesh and blood."

"Tuck is a pretty great dog," she answered, though both of them knew Dylan would probably rather spend time with a tree than his family right now.

"Everything was delicious, Dermot. Better than I remembered," Spence said. "I haven't had a burger that good in years."

"I expect you to come back soon for another one, now that you're in town."

"You can bet on it."

"Can we go?" Peyton muttered under her breath.

"Sorry, can we get our bill?" Spence asked.

"No charge this evening. It's on the house."

"What is it with you Caines? How do you expect to make a living if you won't let anybody pay you? Just give me a lousy bill."

"Nothing doing. Consider it your welcome-home gift."

Did Spence consider Hope's Crossing his home? She didn't think so.

"Don't argue," Charlotte said quietly. "You'll only waste your breath. He never backs down."

Spencer's gaze shifted from her to her father. "I'm not a freeloader. Want me to wash a dish or two? See if I've still got it?"

Dermot chuckled softly. "Not necessary. I've no doubt that you do."

His blue eyes suddenly took on a crafty sort of light that made nerves flutter in her stomach.

"You're not paying for dinner, lad. But happens you could do a little favor for me, though."

"What?" Spence asked.

"I don't want my girl walking on those crutches by herself to her car. I would accompany her myself if we weren't so busy, of course. It would surely put my heart at ease some if you would consider helping her to her car, just to make sure she arrives safely. I can't believe that scamp brother of hers would leave her to fend for herself."

She did *not* want his help. She wanted to hobble to her car, drive home and put her foot up somewhere quiet, peaceful and Spencer-free.

"It's only a short way. I'll be fine. I think I've done my share of tripping today."

"Never hurts to have someone along to make sure," Dermot said. "You don't mind, do you, son?"

"Not at all. We'll be glad to see Charlotte safely to her car, won't we, Peyton? It's our neighborly duty."

"Sure," his daughter answered. "Especially since she's only using those crutches because you scared her half to death and made her fall."

Dermot raised an eyebrow at that and Charlotte winced. She did *not* need Pop getting any ideas in his head about her and Spence. Just the thought of it made her hands start sweating on the crutches.

She hadn't exactly been great at hiding her crush on Spence when she was a girl. Seriously, how many times could a girl doodle *Mrs. Spencer Gregory* on her home-work folder without somebody spying it?

She had a feeling her father knew. Probably every-body in town had known. Every time she thought of how transparent she must have been—going to all his games, blushing whenever he talked to her—she wanted to die.

She didn't need Dermot remembering her stupidity.

"Nobody made me fall," she said quickly. "It was my own two clumsy feet."

"Which would probably have stayed on the sidewalk if I hadn't suddenly yelled out and startled you."

"Who knows?" she argued. "A dog could have barked and I still might have fallen."

"Well, either way, we would be happy to walk you to your car. I could even go drive it up front for you so you don't have to walk at all."

"Going into the valet business now?" she asked, her tone more waspish than she intended.

He didn't snap back. "It's an idea. If the rec center thing doesn't work out, I might need a fallback."

She turned away, embarrassed that she could sound so bitchy when he was only trying to help. "Seriously, my car is just around the corner. I don't mind walking and I don't need a babysitter."

"Not babysitters. Just a little added peace of mind for your pop."

She sighed, knowing she had no choice. She led the way out of the café, to be met by a lovely cool night. July evenings in the mountains seemed to last forever, one of her favorite things about Hope's Crossing in the summer.

She headed in the direction of her car, moving as swiftly as she dared on the crutches. Forget her sprained ankle. Her arms were what ached most after all day of trying to maneuver on the stupid things.

Spence looked up Main Street, where downtown marched up a pretty substantial grade. "That's quite a sight," he murmured.

The sun wouldn't set for another hour or so and the light was soft, sweet. The streetlights hadn't come on yet but all up and down Main Street, tourists were eating at restaurants that spilled tables out onto the sidewalks.

"Have you missed Hope's Crossing?" she asked him, noting that Peyton had fallen back a few paces and shoved in earbuds.

He glanced down at her then back at Main Street. She wondered if she had imagined that glint of *something* in his eyes, something warm and sultry that sent heat pooling low in her abdomen.

"You know, if you had asked me a few days ago, I would have said I hadn't missed my hometown one bit over the years. Funny how the mind sometimes chooses to dwell only on the bad, isn't it?"

"In some cases. Sometimes you see only the good and ignore all the things that made you miserable about a situation."

"In this case, I think I'd forgotten all the nice memories I had of Hope's Crossing. The moment we drove back into town, it seems like this flood of good moments surged back. Things I had completely forgotten. Swimming with Dylan and our buddies at the reservoir on lazy Saturday afternoons. Fishing that creek your dad took me to once in Snowflake Canyon. Parking up at the Sweet Laurel Falls overlook with a pretty girl."

"You had plenty of those kinds of memories, I'm sure," she said tartly.

A corner of his mouth danced up. "I've suddenly recalled this town seemed to have more than its fair share of pretty girls. That certainly hasn't changed."

She didn't quite know how to respond—was he making fun of her somehow?—so she quickly changed the subject.

"All that talk in there with Dylan—were you serious about coming up with a program for injured vets?"

Somehow the idea of him as a caring philanthropist

didn't quite gibe with the media's image of him as a heartless, hard-living partier.

"It has definite possibilities. Ideas have been spinning in the back of my head since Peyton mentioned it. Tomorrow, I'll start looking more seriously into what similar programs might be doing and how we can complement their efforts. I can't imagine it would be too hard to add a recreational therapy kind of effort to the other offerings at the center. From everything I've seen today and what I learned before I took on the job, the facility is already state-of-the-art."

"Harry Lange likes the best of everything."

"It shows. The center is in a perfect setting. I just keep thinking how serene it could seem to somebody who's been battered by the hell of war and just needs a little help finding his way."

Naturally, she couldn't help thinking of Dylan. If she thought he was finding peace in Snowflake Canyon, she would be happy to leave him to it. On the other hand, maybe it wasn't her place or Pop's or the brothers' to try dragging him down the mountain when he was working things out on his own.

"They would need somewhere to stay," Spence said, obviously thinking aloud.

"There are quite a few condo developments in the canyon, not to mention the ski resort."

"Yeah. That would do for a start. But you know, come to think of it, when I was touring the facilities today, I saw this beautiful stretch of unused land right along the creek. I don't see why we couldn't work toward some on-site lodging. We could build five or six small accessible cabins for them to stay with their families, maybe for a week or two at a time. This could be really life changing for people."

His enthusiasm was infectious, she had to admit. His hazel eyes glittered with an excitement she very much wanted to share.

This *was* a wonderful idea. She could see vast potential for the good in it, both in the population he wanted to serve and in the town. The citizens of Hope's Crossing could really mobilize around this sort of thing.

The town had its own Angel of Hope, someone—or a group of people—who went around performing secret acts of kindness. An envelope full of rent money on one doorstep, a new bicycle for a child diagnosed with cancer on another. The Angel had inspired copycats, she knew. She had even dropped a few care packages filled with books and CDs and chocolates on the front porches for people she knew were struggling.

Helping others whenever possible had become kind of the town's unofficial motto and she was sure people would be eager to reach out to honorable men and women who had been wounded in service to their country.

She wanted to sign right up to volunteer. On the other hand, this was Spencer Gregory, who had broken her heart more times than she could count—and, worse, broken the collective heart of this town that had placed him on a pedestal.

He would have many obstacles to overcome, not least of which would be public perception of him as a scandal-ridden drug peddler.

"I can see the possibilities," she said warily, when they were almost to her SUV. "I can also tell you straight up that if you want to have any chance in hell of doing this, you're going to need Harry Lange on board."

"I figured as much."

"Harry has the deciding vote on just about anything that goes on in this town, like it or not. If he backs you, you'll be golden. If not, you're going to have to, like Dylan said, point your little charity wand somewhere else."

"How do I get Harry Lange on board?"

They had reached her SUV as he asked the question and she was grateful to ease her weight against the metal while she considered how to respond. The answer came to her as suddenly as an August thundershower.

"Harry is engaged to Mary Ella McKnight."

"I remember Mrs. McKnight. She taught me eleventh grade English. I seem to recall I wouldn't have passed her class if someone hadn't helped rewrite my essays."

She was once more fourteen and painfully in love, sitting with a much older Spence, eighteen and brawny, gorgeous as anybody in her favorite boy band. Though he had been very smart in some areas—math, for instance—putting his thoughts down on paper had been a fierce struggle for him. She had spent many winter nights sitting at the café while snow fluttered outside the window, helping him organize his thoughts into coherent order.

"Somebody had to," she said.

"Did I ever thank you properly for helping me survive high school?"

She thought of the one thing she had asked him, of all those foolish hopes and dreams that had died an ugly, painful death.

Heat burned her cheeks and she looked away. "Yes, well, if you want to bring Harry on board, go through Mary Ella," she said stiffly. "If you have her support,

Harry will follow. He generally supports anything she wants."

"Why not go straight to Harry? He hired me. Seems to me I could just call him up and tell him I think it's a good idea and we should consider it."

"That could work. The thing is, Harry can be… stubborn. He obviously has his own ideas for the recreation center and they might not necessarily include opening it up to people from outside the community. He might need a little creative persuading. Mary Ella would know the best way to do that."

"You would know all these intricacies better than I do. I trust you."

She should just bid him good-night, hop in her car and go home to that quiet moment on the sofa with her foot up. Anything that thrust her into closer proximity to Spence probably wasn't wise. But she really *did* think this could be good for the town.

"Mary Ella is a good friend of mine. If you want, I can talk to her. Lay the groundwork for you."

He looked startled. "Really? You would do that?"

"I can't promise anything but I don't mind talking to her."

"That would be fantastic. Thank you, Charlotte!" His eyes glittered in the fading light. "Give me a couple days to do some preliminary research, maybe come up with a prospectus, and I'll get back with you."

"Sure." She knew she shouldn't have that little tingle of anticipation. This was Spence, she reminded herself firmly. The last man on the planet she should be excited about seeing again.

She reached into her bag for her keys then unlocked the car door. Spence opened the door and waited while she did a ridiculous little hopping dance with the crutches, trying to keep weight off her foot while climbing into the high seat of the SUV with any semblance of grace.

"Thank you for walking me. I hope you don't have far to go to your car."

"No, actually. We're just on the other side of this lot."

Parking was a major pain in Hope's Crossing. The town streets were narrow, the infrastructure never designed for the tourist traffic that had sprung up in the past fifteen years.

Peyton pulled one dangly white earbud out. She didn't look any the worse for wear after heaving up her stomach contents. She seemed a little more pale than usual, but that could have been a trick of the twilight.

"Can I have the keys?" she demanded. "Victoria wants to call me and my phone is about to die. I need to plug it into the charger."

Spence pulled them out of his pocket and handed them over. When Peyton disappeared, he turned back to Charlotte.

"Are you sure you're okay to drive? We can follow you home since we're heading in the same direction."

"That's not necessary. Driving is fine. It's my left ankle that's sprained."

"Okay." He seemed distracted and she could almost see his thoughts racing. Against her better judgment, she found it rather endearing that he was becoming so enthusiastic about helping wounded veterans like Dylan.

"Good night," she said. "Thank you for walking me."

He stopped her when she would have closed the door. Though her SUV had a higher suspension than a sedan, he was still taller than the roof and had to lean down to be on level with her in the driver's seat.

"Thank you," he murmured.

She couldn't seem to breathe as the scent of him, masculine and sexy, seeped into her senses. "Why are you thanking me?"

"This idea."

"It was Peyton's," she reminded him. "Thank her."

"I know, but she never would have come up with it if we hadn't seen you and Dylan at dinner." He paused. "I've been wondering what I have to offer. If I'm crazy to take this job, to come back here."

"Why did you?" she couldn't help asking. He could have gone anywhere. He had to know people here in Hope's Crossing would have taken the scandal, the criminal charges, harder than someone in some small nameless town back East. He had been a hometown hero here. Children had Smoke Gregory's poster on their bedroom walls, housewives kept scrapbooks full of his newspaper clippings.

He was quiet for a long moment, his features still, and she thought he wasn't going to answer.

"You can probably imagine how things have been for me the past year," he finally said. "Needless to say, I haven't had a lot of offers."

He shrugged. "I don't need to work. Not really. I made good investments during my career and I've still got a few things cooking. I could spend my time golfing and working on my portfolio."

"Why didn't you?"

"That's what I've done the past year and it's driving me crazy. Anyway, what kind of example is that for Peyton, to see her father sitting around on his ass?"

His words didn't make sense. If he cared that much about the example he was setting for his daughter, why would he make all these stupid choices? What kind of example was it when he was supplying steroids and prescription drugs to his teammates?

For the first time, she wondered if perhaps there might be more to the story than she had heard in the media.

"Anyway, Harry Lange called me and asked if I would be interested in helping with the recreation center. Most people don't even want to take my calls anymore but Harry was willing to give me a break. I haven't had many of those lately."

She gazed at him, at the way his cheeks creased a little when he smiled, at that full, sensuous mouth. Something inside her did a long, slow shiver. She wanted to touch his hand, press her mouth to that hidden dimple, dip her fingers in his hair....

Oh, good grief. What was *wrong* with her? Five minutes of cordial conversation and she was ready to fall headlong back into her infatuation with him, despite everything.

"Good for Harry," she said curtly. "I'll warn you that you're still going to be fighting an uphill battle. Not everybody else is as willing to overlook the past as Harry."

He blinked at her cold tone and straightened. "You don't have to tell me that," he answered, his voice curiously calm and without expression.

One part of her wanted to apologize, to go back to that moment of quiet accord between them. She knew she couldn't. She had developed willpower in all other aspects of her life. She just had to be tough about resisting him, too.

"Good night. Let me know when you've come up with enough solid details about the wounded vets program and are ready for me to talk to Mary Ella."

"I will. Good night."

He stepped back and closed the door with a hard thud. She sat for just a few seconds, surprised to realize her hands were trembling a little, but she quickly turned the key, reversed out of the parking stall and headed for home without looking back.

CHAPTER EIGHT

Four days after that dinner at the café, Spence rang Charlotte's doorbell, a restless energy seething through him.

Maybe he should have waited until the next morning, when he could have tried to catch her at the candy store.

The papers in his hand rustled in the slight evening breeze. No. She told him to let her know when he was ready to talk to Mary Ella. He had been on the phone, online videoconferencing, tossing emails back and forth nonstop since early Thursday and after an exhaustive amount of research, he was ready to start the ball rolling.

He was always this way with a project. Once he was ready to go, even another day's delay seemed too long.

Besides that, he wanted to see her. He hadn't been able to stop thinking about her all weekend. By yesterday morning, he had even considered taking Peyton out for breakfast and then casually peeking into Sugar Rush. He might have, except she said she had a stomachache and wasn't hungry so he'd made waffles and bacon at home—of which she'd eaten a half-dozen pieces.

He rang the doorbell again, that energy bubbling along his skin. Under other circumstances, he would have thought nine o'clock on a Sunday night a rude time to be making social calls. She would understand—if she was home, anyway.

He was pretty certain she was, considering the light spilling out from a couple different windows and some kind of mellow jazz that eased through the summer night, sultry and warm.

Of course, she could always have left the lights and the music going while she left the house. Or she could be occupied with a date and not at all inclined to answer the door to a neighbor she quite obviously disdained.

The thought of her sharing her time with someone else left an uncomfortable ball of discomfort lodged under his ribs—and the renewed realization that he would even entertain such an emotion left him even *more* uncomfortable.

Jade had cheated on him regularly. Toward the end of his marriage, he hadn't given a rat's behind about his wife's other men—until the final betrayal that had sent his world tumbling.

With some vague idea now that maybe the doorbell was broken—even though he was quite sure he had heard it chiming through the house—he reached a hand out to knock. Before his hand could connect with the blue-painted wood, the door swung open and she stood there, haloed by the light seeping out from inside.

She was barefoot, wearing a gauzy white summer dress with a thin ribbon of lace around the hem, propped up on her crutches, and beside her stood a big black and tan hound dog, who watched him out of doleful droopy eyes.

"Spencer! Oh. I... Hello."

"I forgot you had to hobble to the door on the crutches. I'm sorry."

"It wouldn't have been a big deal but the dog sort of got in my way."

"I didn't know you had a dog."

"I don't. This is Tucker. He's my brother's. I'm dog sitting for a couple days." Worry, cloudy and dark, crossed her expression. "Dylan had to go into the VA for a procedure."

He wanted to say something to comfort her but was pretty sure anything he tried would fall flat.

"What a great dog," he said instead, crouching a little to scratch the hound's jowly chin.

He loved dogs and had wanted a dozen when he was a kid. He'd even brought home a stray one day, a shy little mutt he found crouching beside the road on his way home from school. He had kept her secret in his room, feeding her whatever scraps he could sneak from the kitchen, until Billie found out. The next day, he came home from school and the dog was gone. Billie said she must have run away but even at eleven, he was pretty sure his mom had probably dumped her somewhere.

One of the first things he had done after signing with the Pioneers was buy a couple big gorgeous purebred German shepherds.

If the dogs were his first big indulgence, tangling up with the wrong woman was his second. Jade had hated the dogs, said they scared her to death. After Peyton was born, Jade claimed one of them growled at the baby, and she wouldn't have them in the house. After he stopped caring about his wife's opinion, it had seemed too much trouble while he was traveling with the team to change the status quo.

He supposed there was nothing to stop him from getting a dog or two now. It might even be good for

Peyton to have the responsibility of caring for an animal. He would have to check his lease to see if it was allowed at the rental.

He wasn't here to pet her brother's dog, he reminded himself, and he straightened up.

"Sorry to drop in so late like this. I wanted to be sure to catch you tonight. May I come in?"

She glanced behind her at the warm welcome of her cozy house and then back to him, and he saw a tumult of wariness in her expressive blue eyes.

"Sure." She turned on the crutches with adroit skill and gestured inside to her living room, bright and cheerful.

"Can I get you something to drink? I could probably find a beer in the refrigerator. With six brothers, I try to keep some around."

"No, thanks. I'm good."

He didn't take chances with any kind of potentially addictive substance since he'd completed rehab. Though his issue had been the mix of prescription painkillers that had kept him playing long after he should have walked away, he knew his genetic soup as the child of an alcoholic predisposed him for addiction.

"Water? Ginger ale?"

"I'm good. Please. Sit down."

She finally took a seat in a wingback armchair patterned with bold flowers and he sat adjacent to her on a sage-green sofa he noticed matched the stem color of the flowers.

The dog settled at her feet in what looked like a customary arrangement between the two of them.

"I won't keep you long. I wanted to catch you up on the status of what we talked about the other day, the idea of using the recreation center to help wounded veterans. It's got a tentative name now. A Warrior's Hope."

"Oh. Oh, that's perfect!" Her smile was warm, approving, and he wanted to sit right there in her cozy living room for a couple hours, letting her approbation wash over him.

"I can't take credit for it, to be honest. When I was talking with the director of a similar program in Idaho, she suggested the name and it seemed to fit."

"Definitely."

"I've actually spent several days talking to other people situated in these groups across the West. Sun Valley, Park City. California. They gave me some fantastic ideas. I really think we could make this work."

He waved the documentation he had collected and printed out over the past few days. He held it out so she could see better, and as he moved closer to her, a soft, seductive mix of citrus and vanilla whispered to him.

"If the population is already being served by these other programs, wouldn't A Warrior's Hope be redundant?" she asked.

He forced his attention back to the documentation. "From what I understand, the need far outstrips available resources. We could definitely fill a much-needed niche. I'm thinking we should start small. Ideally, I would like to see a series of intensive recreational therapy sessions, maybe eight or nine a year. We can augment that if we see more demand and can find the resources."

He shifted through the papers until he found the sample brochure he had worked with his assistant to design. "In the summers, we can focus on hiking and water sports at the reservoir, climbing, maybe some fly-fishing and horseback riding. In the winter, we've got sledding, adaptive skiing, snowshoeing. There are boundless natural recreational possibilities here, not to mention the pool and exercise equipment at the recreation center."

He hadn't been this excited about anything in a long time. Before, his charitable giving had always involved writing a check but this was hands-on, boots-on-the-ground kind of service and he relished the possibilities. Hearing stories from other groups that had started similar programs only fueled the fire of his enthusiasm.

"Initially, I'm thinking we could arrange transportation and lodging for five or six soldiers at a time and their families for weeklong sessions," he went on. "In addition to the physical therapy possibilities, I want to help them reconnect, since it's not only the soldiers whose lives are changed forever by an injury. It's spouses, girlfriends, children. What better place to do that than Hope's Crossing?"

He wanted her to jump with enthusiasm, to exclaim over the research and the ideas. When she only gazed down at his information, a distant, unreadable expression on her lovely features, air began to seep from his passion like a pinpricked balloon.

Did she hate the idea? She had liked the name. What about the concept didn't work for her?

"You've really done your homework," she said.

"This is a major undertaking. I wanted to be sure it was really viable before pursuing it further. From my interactions with other programs, I think we can pull this off, especially with the infrastructure we already have in place. We can make a real difference here."

"What about the cost? How do you imagine funding

this? Bringing in veterans and all? I can't imagine the city council will let you use taxes."

This, at least, was one concern he could address. "Here's the thing. I've already got a charitable foundation, and we've been looking for a new direction lately, for various reasons. I know others who might be in similar situations. I want to do this, to help people like Dylan who might be struggling to come to terms with changes in their lives after war injuries. This is a worthy cause, helping a population that tends to be forgotten."

She leafed through the papers for a moment and, while he sensed her interest in what she was reading, he also guessed she was trying to collect her thoughts.

"I need you to answer a question for me," she finally said.

"Of course. What is it?"

The dog snuffled near her feet and she looked down at him before lifting her gaze to meet Spence's.

"Why are you doing this?"

He gestured to the pile of research in her lap. "It's obvious, isn't it? There's a great need. More than forty thousand soldiers have been injured overseas, with three-quarters of those having life-threatening or life-changing injuries. And here's something staggering. Nearly 20 percent of soldiers who've seen combat in the Middle East have sustained what could be classified a traumatic brain injury. An estimated 30 percent of returning soldiers have psychological or post-traumatic stress issues."

"I know that's all true. We've seen it firsthand with Dylan. You haven't. Your life has been baseball for the past fifteen years, about as far removed as a person can be from the horror of war."

The words stung. "That doesn't mean I can't care about people who need help."

"This goes beyond simple concern. This is going to take millions of dollars and a huge commitment in time and energy."

He had no answer to that. He only knew that he had spent four days pouring exhaustive effort into developing a preliminary plan for A Warrior's Hope. He wanted her to be excited about it, too.

"I've got millions of dollars. And nothing *but* time."

"And don't forget, you also have an image to repair."

Fury, hot and sharp, burst inside him. "What the hell is that supposed to mean?"

"I'm sure you can figure it out." She pressed her lips together, eyes flashing.

Had he ever seen her angry before? He couldn't remember it. She had always been sweet Charlotte, quiet and kind.

"You think this is a publicity stunt. You think I want to use the plight of injured soldiers and their families to throw some kind of sparkle-clean over my mistakes?"

"You wouldn't be the first celebrity who seemed to think giving mouth service to a few good works will make everybody willing to forgive and forget, just gloss over an ugly past."

He stared at her. "Wow. You don't think very highly of me, do you?"

"No," she said bluntly.

The single word hit him like a line drive to the gut and he couldn't breathe for a moment.

"Fine." He gathered the papers, wanting to shove his fist through her pretty sage walls. "Screw you. I'm doing this, with or without your help."

The droopy-eyed dog lifted his head and watched as Spence stalked to the door but she didn't get up from the chair.

"Never mind. I'll talk to Harry myself. It's better that way. I thought so all along. I don't need you or Mary Ella McKnight to run interference for me."

He opened the door to storm out, then something—anger, pride, hurt, he couldn't have said—sent him back into her living room.

"This is a good proposal and you know it. I just hope to hell there are enough people in Hope's Crossing who aren't as judgmental and myopic—who are open-minded enough to look at the merits of the idea, not focus only on the past sins of the person presenting it. Somehow I expected more from you."

He couldn't believe he had ever been so excited to talk to her about this. He had thought the other night that maybe, just maybe, she might be one of his few allies in town but apparently she couldn't see beyond his reputation.

"Why would you?" she demanded. "You don't know anything about me."

"I know you used to be a kind person. You were one of the least judgmental people I knew, with a nice word for everyone. You and Dermot were the only ones who bothered to come to my mother's funeral. It meant something to me, that you cared. I've never forgotten that."

"Bull," she whispered. "You haven't given me a thought since you left town."

That was probably true, he had to admit. When he walked away from Hope's Crossing, his good sense had been clouded by unimagined wealth and sudden fame.

He had never expected to come back at all, much less under these far-from-stellar circumstances.

She *had* been his friend. He shouldn't have relegated that to some dusty corner of his memory. He frowned. At least, she had been his friend until near the end of his senior year, a few months before he signed with the Pioneers and left town. After that, she had stopped talking to him, he remembered, and completely ignored him at the café, though he couldn't for the life of him think what he might have done. Something immeasurably stupid, probably.

"I was an asshole. I think that's been well established by now."

Amazing how simple arrogance could ruin a person's life. He had worked damn hard to be a good baseball player, staying later than anybody else, honing his technique, working out for hours each day to stay in top shape.

A healthy ego and a fierce competitive streak had been requirements at the level at which he had competed, but that same ego had forced him to ignore a body that was wearing down from years of throwing ninety-five-mile-an-hour fastballs.

And it had been colossal, unmitigated gall to believe he could cover up somebody else's mess without it slopping back on him.

He sighed, the sharp edge of his temper dulling. He was responsible for his own mistakes. None of it was Charlotte Caine's fault and he couldn't blame her for thinking the worst about his motives.

"The truth is, I want to do this. I'm ready to throw my own charitable organization behind it. Whatever you think about my past, I also still have plenty of connections among professional athletes who have their own charitable organizations and might be looking for a cause."

He could call at least a dozen guys right now, in both the American and National leagues, who had stood by him when it mattered. Any one of them would be willing to donate at least high five figures, enough to seed the project.

"I think we could make A Warrior's Hope a force to be reckoned with. You can think what you want about my motives. I can't deny there might be some element of truth to what you say. Would I like to walk down the street without people spitting on me? Okay. Sure. But I want to do this because it's a damn good idea and because it could help people who deserve a break."

Gazing at him, brow furrowed, she reached down and scratched the dog behind his ears. What was she thinking? Did she believe him? And what would he do if she didn't want to help?

He could certainly make this happen without her but it wouldn't be nearly as much fun.

After a breathless moment, she held her fingers out. "Give me that."

He offered her the research, and she snatched it away and reviewed it once more.

He sank down on the sofa and the clever dog, apparently sensing her attention was elsewhere, shifted his haunches on the carpet so his head was just at Spence's hand level.

He sat in her cozy living room while the mountain-sweet evening breeze danced in through the open windows and fluttered the curtains. Her whole house smelled like her—vanilla and citrus, completely delectable—and he decided this wasn't at all a bad way to spend a Sunday evening, with a lovely woman reading next to him and his fingers petting a dog's warm fur.

She nibbled on her bottom lip as she read, and he found himself utterly fascinated by the sight. She used to do that, he remembered, when she would read over his piss-poor English papers.

He still couldn't believe she was the same person he had known before. He wanted to think he hadn't been so shallow that he couldn't see the loveliness inside her but he had been a stupid teenage boy whose idea of the perfect female body was the one on the current *Sports Illustrated* swimsuit issue. Hell, he'd married a supermodel, hadn't he? And look how delightfully that had turned out.

As he watched her read, her features becoming more animated with every page, a fine tension tightened his insides. He wanted to kiss her, just reach across the space between them, slide his fingers into silky honey-gold hair and capture that lip she was tugging between her teeth with his own....

"This could work!"

Her excited voice jolted him out of a very pleasant fantasy involving the two of them, this comfortable sofa and a great deal less of that gauzy white dress.

He cleared his throat. "Yeah. I know."

"I really like this idea about adding wheelchair-accessible cabins behind the recreation center."

"I think that has to be an urgent priority. We can use condos or hotel rooms at the resort at first but it would be better having more of a village feeling with our own small cabins."

"You might want to talk to Sam Delgado about that.

He runs a construction company in town and has a reputation for fast, excellent work."

She blushed a little when she said the name, and he had to wonder why. He jotted the name down, curious to meet the man.

"Katherine Thorne is on the city council. She might be able to help you fast-track the construction through the permit process."

Charlotte must know everybody in town. She would be an invaluable asset.

"This is fabulous information," he said. "Thank you."

"I can talk to Mary Ella tomorrow, if you'd like. We're having a birthday lunch for a friend of ours."

"You know, now that I think about it, I prefer going straight to Harry. It seems devious to go around him and manipulate him that way, and I don't want to start out on the wrong foot. Still, it can't hurt to have the support of his future wife, too. We can take a double-team approach. Thank you."

"You're right. It's a good cause."

She organized the papers, then faced him with a half curious, half wary expression. "Do people really spit on you in the streets?"

The question came out of nowhere and it took him a moment to remember he had hurled those words at her in the heat of their argument.

He didn't really want to talk about this but didn't see how he could avoid it, since he had been the one who brought it up.

"Not literally. More than a few have probably wanted to. I did have somebody break through my security system and spray paint PUSHER on the side of my house. We never caught the guy."

His tone, casual and light, didn't deceive her. What had it been like to tumble so quickly from hero to goat? He had been vilified in the national media, had been made an example of all that was wrong in professional sports. How it must have hurt when his team members, his fans, jumped on board to denigrate and condemn.

She caught herself. Spencer Gregory did *not* need her sympathy. He was rich, he was gorgeous, he had a sweet daughter—and he obviously had insane luck and darn good attorneys if he could escape prison time when it seemed all the evidence against him had been overwhelming.

Still, it had probably been a heavy blow to lose his career and his reputation so abruptly.

She looked down at the papers on her lap. He had accumulated an amazing amount of research in only a few days, had taken what had only been a vague concept and turned it into something concrete and eminently viable.

She didn't know what to think. Which was the real Spence? The hardworking teenage boy she remembered, who had juggled two or three jobs at a time to support his drunk of a mother, while going to school and trying to play sports? The nightclubbing, irresponsible partier the media had made him out to be after the accusations emerged?

Or this earnest, caring man who appeared to be trying to do something worthwhile with his life, to become something more than he had been?

She couldn't discount the last, especially when she—of all people—knew it was certainly possible for a person to make radical changes and to reshape his or her direction.

Yes, she had very personal reasons to be angry with

him. It didn't seem right to let those stand in the way of something that could be of benefit to many people.

"I don't see anything in here about creating a network of community volunteers to help out," she said.

He frowned. "I hadn't thought that far ahead."

"You need to. That should be part of the whole concept for A Warrior's Hope from the beginning."

"You think so?"

"The recreation center was intended for use by the community. If you want to repurpose a portion of that mission and open the facilities to a wider population, it seems only right that you give the people of Hope's Crossing a chance to be part of the effort."

"How?"

"I can think of dozens of ways. Fund-raising, organizing welcome parties for the veterans. Restaurants could join in to help feed them. I'm sure Pop would love to cater some meals and so would my friend Alex McKnight, who is the chef at Brazen. My friend Evie Thorne is a rehab therapist and she might have insight on what kind of activities would be most helpful for certain injuries. Oh, and I happen to know somebody who's really good at making fudge and would be happy to donate a steady supply."

Skepticism flickered in his eyes. "That all sounds wonderful but do you really think people would be so willing to step up to help perfect strangers?"

She gave him a long look, then shook her head. "You obviously haven't spent enough time in Hope's Crossing lately. The town has changed since you were here."

"Yeah. That's fairly obvious. Every time I turn around, I see a new business or condo development."

"The growth is only part of the difference. Tourism

has taken over as the leading industry since you left. It was already headed that direction fifteen years ago, I guess. As more and more people have moved in to buy vacation homes and condos, the year-round residents have had to make a conscious effort to stay united."

"Seems like that wouldn't be an easy task."

"It hasn't been. I think Harry's idea behind the recreation center was to help foster the sense of community. We also have our own annual day of service. We call it the Giving Hope Day and it was started to honor my friend Maura Lange's daughter Layla, who was killed in a car accident a few years ago."

"Giving Hope. Catchy."

She narrowed her gaze, trying to detect sarcasm in his tone or expression, but he appeared genuinely interested.

"It's really wonderful. You just missed this year's event. It's held in early June and it's a time when everybody comes together to make the community better. Painting the bleachers at the football stadium, cleaning up yards, preparing meals for senior citizens. The day ends with a big benefit gala and auction up at the ski resort. All proceeds go to a scholarship fund."

"You really think a one-day event is enough to bring a town together?"

"No. We have other things. There are weekly summer concerts in the park—in fact, that's where I was earlier tonight—a townie ski day every month when the resort gives reduced lift tickets to residents, a couple different parades throughout the year. Oh, and I can't forget the Angel of Hope."

"Somebody mentioned that to me the other day. Who is the Angel of Hope?"

"Wouldn't we all like to know? Actually, I have suspicions but I'm happy to leave them unanswered. I can tell you the Angel is someone who goes around helping people in need. Bags of groceries left on the doorstep of a struggling family, rent or utilities mysteriously paid, a sudden delivery of needed medical equipment. The Angel has attained folk hero status around here."

"All in secrecy? I find that hard to believe. Really, nobody knows who it is?"

She couldn't say that with certainty. Maura and Mary Ella had once said something that made her think they knew who might have started the whole thing but she hadn't pressed them.

"I suspect some people do know, but they're keeping it zipped," she answered. "After more than two years, the Angel has become a symbol of the need for increased kindness than an actual person. People do nice things anonymously and are happy to give the Angel credit."

She herself regularly figured out who to help each week, which had become one of her favorite pastimes. When she ran out of ideas, she often took a different route for her workout, thinking about the people whose houses she passed as she ran and what their needs might be.

Since the whole point was anonymity, she didn't mention that to Spence.

He remained skeptical. "You're right. The town must have changed, then. This all sounds rosy and sweet but I have to tell you, my memories of Hope's Crossing tend to be a bit more…gritty."

Yes, he would have seen the uglier side of the town, the part where a mother stayed out all night at The Speckled Lizard. Again, that sympathy fluttered through her.

"It's still not a perfect town," she said. "We have our problems. Pain, loss, financial troubles. Overall, it's a pretty nice place full of caring people. I'm sure more than a few of them would be eager to jump on board a project like this as one more way to give back."

"Okay. We will definitely incorporate a community volunteer effort in the planning. Thank you for looking through everything and for offering a different perspective."

"You're welcome."

He stood to go, all big rangy muscles, and she suddenly wanted him to stay, for reasons she wasn't quite ready to examine.

Deep down, apparently she was still that giddy teenage girl when it came to Spence Gregory.

He moved in the direction of the door, and she got up and followed him. As it was only a short distance, she didn't bother with the crutches. "I think A Warrior's Hope could really be amazing, Spence."

"Thank you for seeing that this isn't about me and whatever you might think of…my past."

He gazed down at her and the moment seemed charged, somehow, glittery and sweet. She couldn't seem to catch her breath. Her lungs felt tight, achy, as if she had just run hard up the Woodrose Mountain trail.

"You're welcome," she whispered, then felt stupid. Why had she whispered?

She opened her mouth to repeat the words louder but before she could, he was leaning down, all those big hard muscles coming closer, and then he pressed his mouth to the corner of hers.

CHAPTER NINE

SHE FROZE, her heart pounding so loudly she was certain he could hear. His mouth was warm and he tasted of mint underlined with a hint of something sweeter.

He wasn't moving, either, just standing so close to her she couldn't think, couldn't breathe, and then the soft whisper of a kiss shifted to something else. Something more. His mouth slanted over hers and he was kissing her, really kissing her.

Spencer Gregory was kissing *her,* as if he couldn't get enough.

This was crazy. She should say something. Shove him away, wipe her mouth, tell him to go to hell. But, oh, my. All her girlie parts were doing handsprings of joy.

She raised her arms and wrapped them around his neck, telling whatever small rational part of her brain that was still working that she only needed the support to keep from standing on her ankle. He helpfully complied, leaning back and absorbing her weight.

At the same instant, he intensified the kiss, his mouth searching, exploring, *devouring.*

She had never really been kissed before. Not this sort of kiss, with passion and fire and urgency.

How ridiculous. She was nearly thirty years old and had no idea how to handle a man like Spence, completely unprepared for the onslaught of sensation. It felt as if a whole factory's worth of fireworks was exploding inside at the same time, bursting with bright color and heat, sound and wonder.

In a weird way, she felt as if her body had been sleeping for all these years, just waiting for this moment. Every part of her wanted to sink into him, to drag him back into her house and spend all night just like this.

She didn't want it to stop. She wanted to stay right here forever, until their lips fused together and they starved to death. She couldn't imagine another experience on earth that could possibly be as wonderful as right now, his mouth on hers, his arms holding her against those hard muscles, the scent of him, masculine and sexy, filling her senses.

Life sometimes took strange twisting journeys. In the tiny corner of her brain capable of stringing two thoughts together, she remembered being fifteen years old and painfully in love, watching him on the baseball diamond or the football field or joking with customers at her father's café and wanting nothing in her entire life as much as she wanted him to see her, really see her.

Okay, and maybe to love her back a little.

How very odd that all these years had passed with her minding her own business, living her life—establishing a successful store, loving her family, changing old habits—and here she was at last in the arms of the man…the same man she had convinced herself she now detested.

"You taste like strawberries and something else. I can't tell what, but it's delicious."

Every single nerve ending seemed to shiver at his hoarse voice against her skin.

"Prosecco," she murmured, the single word sounding ragged. "I…had a glass at the concert."

"Nice. Very nice."

He kissed her again, his tongue sliding along hers in ways that made those girlie parts start leaping around again, doing corkscrews and triple spirals.

She wanted more. She had a nice convenient sofa just steps away. How could she maneuver him inside so she could explore all these gorgeous hard muscles?

A low sound suddenly pierced the glittery haze of hunger. A long musical *wooo-wooo.*

Tucker.

She had completely forgotten about the dog but his bark was enough to bring her back to her senses, to realize she was standing in her entryway, tangled up with Spence Gregory like peppervine around a cottonwood.

She slid her mouth away, mortified. Was she that desperate that she completely lost her mind the moment a gorgeous man kissed her?

Spence gazed down at her, those changeable hazel eyes looking murky and dark.

She didn't know what to say or do, especially not when he was looking at her in a way that seemed to send her thoughts ricocheting around her head like a six-year-old set loose in her store.

She desperately wished she could be like her friend Alex, someone breezy and confident—the kind of woman who thought nothing of kissing a gorgeous, athletic, complicated man like Spence Gregory.

But she had had no idea what to even do with her tongue, for heaven's sake. He must have realized how inexperienced she was.

When he looked at her, how could he not see the dumpy, awkward girl she had been?

Somehow—drawing on reserves she had no idea

existed—she managed to produce a casual smile. "You know, you didn't have to kiss me to seal the deal. I was going to help you with A Warrior's Hope anyway."

He eased farther away, those eyes going murkier still. "You can't honestly think I kissed you only to make sure you were committed."

She shrugged. "You probably figured it wouldn't hurt."

"That's ridiculous. I kissed you because I *wanted* to kiss you—because I've wanted to kiss you since I came back to Hope's Crossing."

She couldn't honestly believe that, but the words still sizzled through her. She fiercely tamped down her reaction.

"I guess it's good we got it out of the way, then, isn't it?"

His mouth tightened and she realized he was seriously growing annoyed with her. She was feeling so flustered, so discombobulated, she couldn't figure out how to respond.

This was stupid. It was only a kiss, certainly nothing to send her spiraling into a panic attack.

Her ankle throbbed as if someone had kicked it. She firmly ignored the pain. "I'll be sure to let you know what happens after I talk to Mary Ella and the others tomorrow."

He ran a hand through his hair, his narrowed gaze studying her intently. His mouth opened for an instant.

"Good night," Charlotte said quickly, before he could spill out the argument she could see forming in his expression. Her lips still throbbed and tingled and it was all she could do not to touch her finger there, to feel the heat that still lingered.

"Yeah. Okay. Good night." He headed out but paused in the doorway, his gaze on hers. "For the record, that was one hell of a kiss, Charlotte. You know I'm not going to be content with just a little taste, don't you?"

Before she could come up with any sort of answer to that, he walked out and closed the door behind him.

She waited on the other side of the door until she heard footsteps going down her porch and along the sidewalk before she moved. Only when she was convinced he had truly left did she hobble back to the sofa and lift her aching leg up.

She again wanted to touch a finger to her lips but she curled her hand into a fist instead.

Why had he kissed her? It made no sense. She couldn't believe he had suddenly discovered some consuming passion for her.

Why, oh, why hadn't she worked a little harder to lose this stupid virginity when she was in college? Yes, she had been overweight but she knew plenty of other big girls who were popular and well-liked and had dates all the time.

In Charlotte's case, she had been burdened with a deadly combination when it came to having an active social life. She had been shy *and* fat—not to mention studious and far too serious. She had driven home from the university most weekends to help Pop at the café, even though he had discouraged it. Now she wished she had spent more time putting herself out there. Maybe then she would have a little experience under her belt and know better how to deal with a man like Spence.

If not for this pesky virginity, maybe she might be tempted to indulge in a fling.

She frowned and scrubbed at her face. So he was attracted to her. Yes, she found that insanely flattering. She would be lying if she said otherwise. He had been married to a *supermodel,* for heaven's sake.

But for crying out loud. The man had hurt her enough for one lifetime, hadn't he?

Tucker nosed her hands, probably still trying to figure out what the weird humans he'd been saddled with were up to. She braced herself with one hand on the door while giving the dog a dutiful scratch.

The things he had said once about her had been burned like acid in her heart. If she were truthful with herself, that one horrible moment, more than anything else in her life—a few words said casually by the boy who held her heart and didn't even know it—had led her to this moment. They were a big part of the reason she sometimes felt like a dry, frigid wasteland.

She had given him and those words—and the vast betrayal from someone she thought was at least a friend—far too much power over her.

All through the rest of her teens and into her early twenties she had let them shape who she was, what she did. Right after, in that hot miserable time, she had thought she could lose the weight. She had tried starving herself, even forced herself to throw up a few times. But after two months—once he left Hope's Crossing for the Pioneers—she had only lost ten pounds and felt worse than ever, so she had given in to the inevitable.

She ate Pop's food all she wanted, she added ice cream to her giant slice of pie, she stashed junk food under her bed for a late-night snack, all while she watched Spence's career in the major leagues explode.

She let out a painful breath she hadn't realized had been clogging her chest.

There were plenty of decent guys in Hope's Crossing. Okay, maybe they weren't exactly popping up like wildflowers in August, but she could find a few if she looked hard enough—or widened her search to other surrounding towns.

She had a date with one this coming weekend, actually. She had been thinking about calling the whole thing off when she saw Alex the next day at the birthday lunch but she abruptly changed her mind.

A big tough army buddy of Sam Delgado's was exactly what she needed to take her mind off the one man in the world she shouldn't want.

"Good friends, good food and birthday cake. What more does a woman need in a day? I mean, seriously?" The very pregnant Claire McKnight beamed at her group of friends while a soft breeze rustled the leaves of the trees in her small patio garden behind the bead store.

Sweet scents floated around them from the flowers growing in bright clumps around the edges of the little fenced garden and sunlight filtered through the trees.

Nearly all the members of the book club, Books and Bites, had gathered during the lunch hour to celebrate the birthday of one of their newer members, Janie Hamilton, a widowed mother of four who had moved to Hope's Crossing a few years earlier.

"Thank you all for coming," Janie said. "I know how busy everyone is. It means a lot that you would arrange your schedules to be here."

"Are you kidding?" Maura McKnight smiled at her. "This is the perfect way to start out the week."

"Why can't everybody's birthday fall on a Monday this year?" Charlotte asked with a smile.

"This cake is fantastic," Katherine Thorne said. "Lemon angel food cake with strawberries. Delicious."

"Of course it is," Alex McKnight said smugly. Alex had no problem taking praise for her cooking, which was always divine. Charlotte also appreciated the low-fat choice in a cake.

"Everything has been perfect," Janie assured them.

"I'm only sorry I didn't think to invite some sexy guys along for you single girls," Alex said.

Janie rolled her eyes. "Who has time for sexy guys?"

Katherine raised her hand, earning laughs all around.

Charlotte didn't have time to spare, either. That didn't keep her from replaying in her head, again and again, that kiss with Spence the night before.

"I know people are busy and some of you have to get back to work," Claire said, "but I can't host a birthday party without throwing in some beading. I was in a mood, so this morning I put together some bracelet kits for a party favor. They're memory wire with beads in pretty summer colors. Nothing too time-consuming. Of course you could always stay out here and chat, if you'd rather take the kits home for later."

"I could use a new bracelet," Mary Ella said. "I haven't done nearly enough beading lately."

She, Katherine, Claire and Claire's mother, Ruth, headed inside. Charlotte went, too, watchful for an opportunity to talk to Mary Ella.

"This is what I was thinking," Claire said. "If you don't like the colors, you're welcome to pick out some that work better for you."

The bracelet was simple, seed beads and glittery crystals strung on a quadruple coil of memory wire.

Claire had picked turquoise, a pale rose and a soft, warm brown.

For some reason, the colors made Charlotte think of Peyton and the cute shirt she had been wearing the night Charlotte had seen the girl and her father at Pop's café.

She didn't have anything that color but she could make it for the girl, she thought. Maybe it would help cheer her up about the prospect of living in Hope's Crossing and possibly spark an interest in beading.

She sat down and started organizing the beads for the project into one of the trays Claire provided.

Mary Ella sat beside her and, as their hands worked the beads onto the wire, the conversation between the women drifted around Claire's upcoming birth, Alex's restaurant and a new boutique coming to town. Finally, during a lapse in the conversation, Charlotte made her move.

"Mary Ella, I need your help."

Her former high school English teacher raised an eyebrow above the rim of her little glasses. "Of course, my dear. Are you having trouble with the pattern?"

"Not the bracelet. I need to ask a favor. It's kind of a big one."

She was aware that everyone at the worktable was now listening in, curiosity on their features. Maybe she should have taken Mary Ella aside separately. If she didn't think A Warrior's Hope was a good idea, the others might be slow to throw their support behind it.

"Actually, I could use help from everybody. I know you're probably thinking we have enough going on and don't need to take on more projects. I agree, I really do. But I think this could make a difference."

"You haven't said what it is," Mary Ella pointed out. "What do you need?"

Charlotte's fingers fumbled with the crystal she was trying to pick up. She was nervous, she realized, afraid they would think the idea was stupid. She hated these moments when her confidence seemed as tiny and hard to manage as the blasted seed beads.

"It's Spencer Gregory's idea, actually. He enlisted my help, for obvious reasons."

Alex looked intrigued. "Obvious reasons? What obvious reason would Smokin' Hot Spence Gregory have for asking your help?"

Charlotte could feel herself blush, which only made Alex look at her more curiously. "Why, Dylan, of course," she answered.

She was screwing this up. These were her friends, women she loved and admired, and she had no reason to be nervous to talk about anything with them.

She drew in a breath and tried again. "He had this idea. Spencer, I mean. I think it's a wonderful one but it's something that will take a great deal of effort to organize, and we'll need community support. That's where you all come in, if you're willing to get behind it."

"Why would we want to get behind a drug dealer?" Ruth Tatum, Claire's mother, spoke with her usual blunt negativity.

Charlotte usually tolerated the older woman and sometimes even found her amusing, rather like a crusty old man constantly yelling at all the kids in town to stay off his lawn, but in this case she wanted to accidentally stick a headpin in the cranky old biddy.

"Ruthie, let's hear the idea before we jump in and say we oppose it." Mary Ella's voice was calm, serene, as if she were addressing a seventh-hour class full of bored and restless teenagers.

Charlotte deeply admired the woman's class and style. She didn't wonder that Harry Lange had fallen hard for her. The only mystery was why Mary Ella returned his affection.

"As you all know very well, the recreation center is open now and people seem to be enjoying it. Harry did a good thing for Hope's Crossing."

"He has been known to do a good thing here and there," Mary Ella murmured.

Looking amused, Maura cleared her throat in a meaningful way that Charlotte didn't quite understand.

"Anyway, Spencer had the idea of taking these great resources, both the recreation facilities at the center and the natural resources around Hope's Crossing, and opening them up to a wider population. He would like to start an adaptive recreation therapy program for injured veterans."

Nobody said anything, they only watched her, and she felt itchy and uncomfortable, wishing she knew what they were thinking.

"I know it's ambitious. Spence has done a great deal of research over the weekend and he believes it's feasible. The first major task would be constructing some lodging near the recreation center. He's thinking several small wheelchair-accessible cabins on that strip of land near the river."

"That won't be cheap," Katherine pointed out.

"No, but I was thinking we can use volunteer labor for some of the work. Like we do with Habitat for Humanity. You and Jack help out with that, don't you, Maura?"

"When we can," Maura answered. Charlotte knew now that Maura and Jack had a small active one-year-old as well as her bookstore and his architectural firm, their schedules were hectic.

"I realize we just finished our Giving Hope Day, which is a really wonderful way to help each other. I love that about our community, and I think it's safe to say everyone else who lives here loves it, too. Hope's Crossing is such a warm, friendly place. Don't you think we could reach out now and take that same spirit of caring to others? Offer a little lift to many who have sacrificed a great deal for our sakes?" she finished in a rush, then held her breath, waiting for their reaction.

Katherine Thorne was the first to speak. "Recreation therapy for wounded veterans. How could that help?"

Charlotte thought of the information she had scrutinized the night before and her own research online, long into the night when she should have been sleeping.

"Similar programs have been amazingly effective, providing safe, comfortable, fun opportunities for them to heal and to push the limits of their capabilities. Spence is suggesting adaptive skiing and snowboarding in the winter and the rest of the year focusing on water sports like boating, fishing, waterskiing. Hope's Crossing is beautifully situated to take great advantage of our natural resources as well as the innate welcoming kindness that resides here."

Katherine pursed her lips. "Spencer Gregory came up with this?"

"It was his daughter's idea at first. Dylan and I were having dinner at the café the other night while Spence and Peyton were there. She asked me what happened to him. I gave him the short version, then when Spence was talking about how he would like to expand the recreation center's mission, she suggested something to help wounded veterans like Dylan."

"What a thoughtful girl," Mary Ella said.

"She is," Charlotte answered.

Katherine gazed at Charlotte, forehead furrowed a little. "I'll admit, I wasn't thrilled when Harry threw his weight around, as he tends to do—I'm sorry, Mary Ella, you know he does—about bringing Spencer Gregory back to town. After everything he's done, I didn't see why we had to entrust him with that kind of responsibility. But if these are the kinds of ideas he has, I'm a big enough woman to admit I might have been wrong."

Some of the tension in Charlotte's shoulders eased at what amounted to a bold declaration of support. Katherine was on the Hope's Crossing city council and gracefully wielded plenty of influence of her own.

"Thank you, Katherine. I'm sure he'll appreciate that. As Spence rightfully pointed out to me last night, we should look at the merits of the idea itself, not the personal history of the man who wants to make it a reality."

As she spoke, she felt that stab of sympathy for him again. How difficult it must be to have no choice but to face his mistakes everywhere he turned.

"I mentioned to him that you might be in a position to help fast-track any necessary building permits."

"I don't know about that but I can probably bring Mayor Beaumont around."

"Thank you. I'll let him know."

She turned. "Mary Ella?"

The other woman gave her a long considering look that would have made her nervous if she didn't catch a hint of amusement in the depths of her green eyes. "Let me guess. You want me to convince Harry this is a good idea."

"Yes," she said shamelessly. "Spence planned to talk to him this morning but I didn't think it would hurt to appeal to the real power brokers in Hope's Crossing."

Mary Ella and Katherine both laughed roughly. "Is that what we are?" Mary Ella asked.

"Why not? The women at this table take care of business. You don't wait around for somebody to tell you what to do. You dig in and do it yourself."

It was true and she loved them all for it.

"Well, I think it *is* a good idea. I love this community but I'm not sure we always have our arms as open wide to outsiders as we ought. We can sometimes be too insular, I think. I've heard that from new people moving into town," Mary Ella said.

"I didn't see that at all," Janie said. "You all welcomed me from the very beginning."

Mary Ella smiled at her and touched her hand softly with one of hers. "I'm glad. But there's always room to improve. This could be an excellent way to take that spirit of hope and caring we've had the past few years and help people outside of Hope's Crossing."

Charlotte nodded, more of that fine tension seeping away. Why was she ever worried? Even if her friends had hated the idea, they would have been kind in their rejection of it. "Yes. That's exactly what I was thinking."

"What do you need from us?" Claire asked, always ready to step up, even though she was in the last weeks of her pregnancy.

"Spencer is still in the very early planning stages. He came over last night with pages of research he's done on similar organizations. He's talking about committing funds from his own charity and talking to friends in professional sports who might be looking for a cause."

She tried to push away the memory of everything else that had happened the night before but it seeped in anyway. *That* was the real reason she had spent the night awake, trying to distract herself from the warmth and wonder of his kiss.

"Do you think Harry might be on board?" she asked quickly. "Without his support, we all know this idea won't go anywhere, no matter how worthwhile the cause."

Mary Ella looked pensive. "I can't answer that with certainty but I could easily see Harry supporting something like this. I won't mention that I have ways of bringing him around to my way of thinking."

"Please don't," Alex urged.

Mary Ella laughed. "I don't think I need to resort to them. Harry and I have talked before about starting some sort of organization to help people outside of Hope's Crossing. And unfortunately, when it comes to wounded soldiers, the need just seems endless, doesn't it?"

"I think it's a great idea, too," Katherine said. "I'm ready to help in whatever ways you need."

"Same here," her daughter-in-law, Evie, said. "I'm sure I could convince Brodie to host a fund-raiser at one of his restaurants or cater something at the ski resort."

"I mentioned to Spence we might be able to turn to you for advice in a professional capacity."

"I don't know about that." Evie shifted in her chair. "I'm a pediatric therapist, remember. I have no experience with wounded veterans."

"True, but you have far more knowledge about rehabilitating people with injuries, especially brain injuries, than anyone I know. I think your help would be invaluable in coming up with the kinds of activities that would be both effective and fun."

"I would have to talk to some of my connections in therapy circles. I can make some calls and see if I can find someone a little more qualified who might be willing to consult on a pro bono basis."

Ruth remained silent, which Charlotte considered another victory.

"Thank you. Thank you, all." Charlotte felt a little teary as she looked around the beading table full of women she admired and loved who were immediately ready to jump in and help, simply because she asked it of them.

She thought of Dylan, lost and isolated up in his mountain retreat. Why couldn't he see the healing peace that opening his life and his heart to others could bring?

The other night at the café, he had implied that no one could help a wounded soldier except somebody who had gone through the same thing. Now that the project was moving from a vague idea to something more concrete, would he be willing to see the benefits? Or would he continue to tell her she was wasting her time?

Maybe, just maybe, this might be a way for her brother to move outside of his own pain to help ease someone else's.

CHAPTER TEN

BY THE TIME she finished working at the shop that day, her ankle throbbed and she desperately wanted nothing more than to throw on her most comfortable nightgown, incline her foot on some plump pillows and find something brainless to watch on television for the rest of the evening.

As she turned onto Willowleaf Lane, the small gift basket full of fudge and a certain turquoise and rose memory wire bracelet seemed to flash a big blinking neon sign pointing at her.

Me. Me. Me.

She frowned at the thing. Later. She could drop it off another night. She was tired and achy and was quite certain she didn't have the emotional strength to handle another encounter with Spence tonight.

She drove past the house he and Peyton were renting but the neon seemed to become more garish, to blink more insistently.

She hated leaving things like this undone. She had gone to all the trouble to make the bracelet and package it with a few pieces of a new flavor of fudge, white chocolate and lemon, which she thought Peyton might like. Now she needed to follow through and actually *give* it to the girl.

It would only take a moment to stop at the house, hand

the basket to Peyton, then be on her way. With luck, she wouldn't even see Spence. And if she did, she could update him on the enthusiastic response from her friends to A Warrior's Hope. It was the neighborly thing to do, she told herself. No ulterior motives, she was simply being kind, trying to help Peyton feel better about the move.

As part of her efforts at rebuilding herself, she was trying hard to force herself to face all the things that made her nervous. This past winter, she had gone skiing, even though it had been many years since she had braved the slopes. She had bought a punch pass for ten all-day lift passes and had used all but two of them, which she had given to one of her brothers.

She had taken a karate class and quite enjoyed it.

She had even agreed to chair a committee on the library board to help finance new computers.

She had been brave enough to do those things. How hard was it to find the courage to face Spence again, for the sake of a girl who could use a friend or two?

With a heavy sigh, she turned around in her driveway, gave a hasty wave to Tucker, who was peeking at her over her backyard fence, then drove the short distance back to Spence's house.

She grabbed the crutches—only a couple more days on those, yea—and climbed out of her car, then hooked the basket over her hand and walked up the sidewalk.

She could do this. So they had kissed. So her world had been slightly rocked on its axis. So she had spent all night and most of the day remembering it.

That didn't mean things had to be awkward.

Ha.

She rang the doorbell and waited, trying to do the circle breathing she had learned in her yoga class. In through her nose for five counts, hold for five counts, out through her mouth for five counts.

She was on her third round of exhales when the door swung open and Peyton answered, her cell phone in her hand.

Her eyes widened when she saw Charlotte, and she actually stopped texting and shoved her phone in the pocket of her jean shorts.

"Hi there," Charlotte said with casual cheer. "May I come in?"

Peyton shrugged. "I guess. My dad's not home, though, if you came to see him."

She told herself she completely imagined that stab of disappointment. "Oh. That's okay. I'm here to see you anyway."

Peyton looked surprised and a little suspicious, which was probably a healthy trait in a young girl. "Me? Why?"

"You're probably going to think this is weird but I made you something." She held out the basket. "I went to the bead store for a birthday party today and this was the project my friend Claire had for us. As soon as I saw the colors, I thought of that shirt you were wearing the other night, with the flowers around the neckline. I don't have anything that matches those colors nearly as well. I thought you might like it."

Peyton continued to look suspicious but also a little flattered. Maybe she should have talked to Spencer first to make sure he didn't mind her giving his child something small.

"You really made this?"

"These are super easy. It's just a matter of stringing the beads onto the wire and closing the ends. The wire is cool because it stays into the shape you bend it. It's called memory wire and it works really well for bracelets *or* necklaces. My friend Claire's daughter, Macy, makes these very cute rings, too, out of seed beads and a couple charm dangles. I'm sure she could show you sometime."

"Why do you want to give it to me?"

She again felt stupid. She doubted Peyton would understand if Charlotte told her she saw a great deal of herself in Peyton. She sensed Peyton was reacting to the turmoil of her life the past few years by drawing inside herself, just as Charlotte had done.

She shrugged. "I've made so many bracelets for myself over the past few years, I wouldn't be able to wear them all if I put a new one on every day for a month. And to tell you the truth, as much as I like them, bracelets aren't very practical when I spend most of my days elbow-deep in chocolate."

Peyton looked down at the basket and then back at Charlotte, and her wariness seemed to ease. "Wow. It's really cool. Thanks."

She pulled it out and put it on her left wrist, where it dangled loosely. Charlotte had tried to make the bracelet small but maybe she should have tightened it more.

Charlotte frowned, struck again at how slight the girl was—thin, angular, with those narrow shoulders and thin birdbones for wrists. She definitely needed a little fudge.

"You're welcome."

"How do you hang the little dragonflies on there?"

"That part's easy. It's the same as making earrings. You make a dangle by stringing beads on a headpin and then creating a loop at the top with your round-nose pliers, then you just put on a jump ring and hang it on your bracelets."

"Okay, you lost me at headpin. I don't know what that is but it doesn't sound very easy."

"I'm not really the expert but my friends Evie and Claire can do just about anything with beads. You ought to stop into String Fever one of these days. They love to help people make things. Earrings, necklaces. Whatever you like."

"I'm not very artistic." Peyton looked down at the bracelet on her wrist with a glum expression.

"Who says you're not artistic?"

"Me. I can't play any instruments or anything, and I almost failed art class last year. I never could draw very well. Even with crayons, my mom could never tell what I was trying to make. But I'm good at math and stuff, so it's okay."

Charlotte was only too well acquainted with the habit of accepting what others said about her as truth.

"I don't believe it," she said promptly. "We all have some spark of creativity inside us. You just haven't found what lights yours yet."

"I guess not."

"Give it time. I didn't think I was very artistic until I started dipping chocolates and making fudge and discovered I had a real talent for it. And I was a college graduate by then."

"Really?"

"Honest. I certainly never believed I could make jewelry until I took a couple classes at String Fever. In fact," she added, "I happened to notice Claire's daughter is teaching a teen class in a couple weeks on making back-to-school earrings. You would love Macy. She's about your age and is really fun."

"Do you think I could do it?"

"Yes! I know it. You could learn the basics of beading from Macy and create something pretty in the process. Wouldn't it be fun to make a bunch of new earrings to wear when school starts again?"

Peyton made a face. "Don't remind me about school. It's going to seriously suck being the new girl."

"You'll be fine, especially if you use opportunities like this bead class to make new friends before the year starts."

"If I do it, will you come with me?"

The request caught her off guard. "You want me to come with you?"

"I don't know. Forget it. I just thought, you know, so I would have at least one friend there."

Peyton considered her a friend. Charlotte wanted to cry, like the big baby she was. "I love any excuse to spend time beading. I'd love to come. I'll try to arrange my schedule at the store so I can take the time, as long as it's okay with your dad. Would that work?"

"Great," Peyton said, and she smiled. She actually *smiled*. When she did, her face lit up with a sweet, rare beauty.

"Great. I'll plan on it."

"Thanks again for the bracelet. It's totally cool."

"You're welcome. I'll see you later."

She thought about asking Peyton to tell her father Charlotte needed to talk to him about A Warrior's Hope but decided against it. Exhaustion pulled at her after the long day, and she wasn't sure she had the energy.

As she hobbled on the blasted crutches back to her

SUV, though, the garage door started ascending and a sleek, sexy Range Rover pulled up next to her vehicle.

Drat. She hadn't moved fast enough.

Spence climbed out wearing khakis and a black polo shirt, looking dark and dangerous.

"Charlotte! Hi."

He smiled widely and she had the clear impression he was happy to see her. If she weren't so darn tired, she probably wouldn't have been weak enough to let slip the sweet burst of warmth surging through her at his smile.

"Hi," she murmured.

The memory of their kiss the night before seemed like a living creature suddenly, silky and sinuous, entwining around and through them, tugging her toward him. She could feel herself flush and tried to block the remembrance of the taste of him, the heat of his hands on her skin.

He cleared his throat and she had to wonder if some of those images haunted him.

"We needed milk." He held a gallon up by the handle.

"You might not know this but Hope's Crossing has a very good delivery service. Clover Hill Dairy will bring you eggs, milk, butter, cheese. It's quite convenient." The dairy supplied many ingredients to Sugar Rush, though she still purchased some things through a wholesaler.

"I'll have to look into it. Thanks."

Her ankle throbbed and she opened her car door. "I was just leaving. I only stopped to drop something off for Peyton. A bracelet I made today at the bead store."

He looked startled. "That was nice of you."

She really hoped he didn't think she was some psycho stalker, trying to get to him through his daughter.

"It's a long story but my friend Claire made up these kits and the colors reminded me of something Peyton was wearing the other night." She wasn't making this better. She ought to just shut up now and leave but she couldn't seem to stop. "I don't know what it's like to move into a new town where you don't know anybody. But I do know what it feels like to lose a mother when I was around her age."

"Thank you, Charlotte. You've been more than kind. If she warms up to Hope's Crossing, it will be in large part because you've made her feel welcome."

He smiled again and she completely lost her thread of thought.

She had to stop this. She couldn't afford to be sucked in again. She forced herself to focus. A Warrior's Hope. Mary Ella. Katherine.

"I'm glad I caught you, actually. What happened with Harry this morning? Did you talk to him?"

"Yes. We had lunch today at the resort. I presented everything to him."

"And?" she prompted.

"So far, so good. He wants to do some research of his own about the practicalities and the finances. I expected nothing less, but he's offering tentative support and made a verbal commitment for a hefty amount to start building the cabins."

"Oh, Spence. That's wonderful." With any of her other friends—and under any other circumstances—she would have rushed him for a hug. She couldn't quite bring herself to be that forward with Spence. Plus the crutches...

"He seems to think we could have the funding in place to start one session by the fall and have the cabins finished by Christmas. I'm not as optimistic, but we'll see."

"If Harry wants something, he tends to find a way to make it happen."

"After I spoke with him, I spent the day on the phone with some former teammates and guys I know I can count on. We're planning a media event fund-raiser in about three weeks."

"Wow. You and Harry have a lot in common in the getting-things-done department."

"No reason to wait, is there? With the seed money in place, we could have at least a couple sessions before Christmas."

"Adding to your win column here, I spoke to Mary Ella and the others today."

"You did?"

"Everyone's very excited about the possibilities. Several people volunteered for the organizing committee. Evie said she and Brodie would host a fund-raiser at one of his restaurants and she also agreed to reach out to some of her contacts in the rehab profession for tips on the therapy side of things."

He looked stunned. "Seriously? I don't know what to say."

"I told you the people of Hope's Crossing come together for a good cause. You would be astonished at what we can accomplish."

"I'm already amazed. I can't believe things are moving so fast. We've gone from idea to concept to reality in only a handful of days."

"I'm glad. A Warrior's Hope is going to be *amazing*."

He gazed at her, his hazel eyes a glittery green right now, and she wanted to bask in the warmth of his expression like Dylan's lazy hound dog in a pool of sunlight.

"Because of you. *You're* the amazing one. The project never would have made it this far without you."

Before she realized what he intended, he leaned down and wrapped his arms around her. The crutches clattered to the ground with a hollow clang.

She returned the embrace briefly, convincing herself it was only because she was glad A Warrior's Hope was coming together. It had nothing to do with how delicious he smelled—clean, masculine, sexy.

The memory of that kiss whispered into her mind again and before she could control the impulse, her gaze flicked to his mouth. In an instant, the moment changed from casual and friendly to something else, something bright and heated.

Awareness bloomed between them. His muscles tightened with sudden tension and her breasts felt achy, heavy where they pressed against him.

When she lifted her gaze to those hazel-green eyes, her breath tangled in her chest at the heat and hunger there.

No. She had spent all day telling herself she couldn't kiss him again. She wasn't a silly girl anymore, desperate for the object of her crush to notice her. She was a grown woman, smart and resilient. She wasn't going to let him twist her around like this again.

With great effort, she managed to block every impulse that urged her to lift her mouth for his kiss, and managed to slip out of his arms to put a few inches of distance between them.

"I need to go," she said in a voice that only shook a little. She gripped her door handle and tugged it open.

"Dylan's coming back from Denver tonight and I need to…to make sure Tucker's ready."

It was a flimsy excuse and both of them knew it but Spence didn't call her on it. He only nodded and held open the door for her, then gripped her elbow to help her inside and tucked the crutches in after her.

"Thank you," she murmured, then closed the door firmly between them, backed out of the driveway and drove the short distance to her own home, telling herself the entire way that she had had a lucky escape.

A few more kisses, and she might find herself exactly where she was at fifteen—hopelessly in love with a man who didn't deserve it.

Spence watched her drive down the street to her house. He waited until she pulled into her garage and he saw the lights come on inside the house a moment later.

He didn't know what the hell was happening to him.

Every time he was around her, he wanted to yank her against him and kiss her until neither of them could think straight.

He had dreamed about her the night before, slick, heated, erotic dreams that left him aching and frustrated.

Her soft, sweet, almost hesitant response the night before—that hint of innocent desire—had worked on him like nothing else. He couldn't remember ever being so affected by a simple kiss—or so determined that he couldn't repeat the experience, as much as he might hunger to do just that.

This was completely crazy. Even if he wasn't neck-deep trying to rebuild the shattered pieces of his life, he couldn't start a fling with Charlotte Caine.

She was gentle and kind, the sort of woman insightful and compassionate enough to make a spontaneous gift for a lonely young girl.

She deserved far better than a washed-up baseball player with an ugly past and a disaster of a failed marriage, a man who couldn't walk down the street without people pointing and whispering.

He hoped that his time here in Hope's Crossing would help rehabilitate that image a little. If nothing else, he wanted to prove to himself he could do something good and worthwhile that didn't involve a split-finger curve.

He certainly didn't plan on sticking around longer than the six months he had been given at the recreation center. He wanted this to be a springboard to other things, maybe help him go into coaching on a university level.

Charlotte was well-liked and popular in town. He had seen the way people talked to her the other night at the café and had a feeling her friends agreed to help with A Warrior's Hope in no small part because of their friendship with her.

He didn't think Dermot or any of her brothers—or Harry Lange, for that matter, who had spoken of her highly at lunch earlier—would think kindly of Spence blowing into town and starting something with her, then kissing her off on his way out again.

CHAPTER ELEVEN

By THE END of the week, as July eased into August, Charlotte convinced herself her life was slowing returning to pre–Hurricane Gregory normalcy.

In the short time Spencer and Peyton had been in Hope's Crossing, it seemed as if everything had been in constant tumult. Sprained ankles, new exciting projects, intense kisses that left her aching for something she couldn't have.

The throbbing in her ankle had subsided to a manageable level and by Saturday morning, she was more than ready to return to some aerobic exercise. Dr. Harris gave her the go-ahead three days earlier to put weight on it again. The pain had subsided considerably. She had even tolerated standing up for a couple hours at a time yesterday at work.

Before that, she had been forced to be creative with her workout, focusing on upper body weights and exercises that strengthened her noninjured leg. It gave her a great deal of appreciation for adaptive sports programs.

Twice that week, she had gone swimming at the recreation center early in the morning and had been grateful each time that she didn't run into Spence.

She could continue that for a few more days before returning to more aggressive weight-bearing activities, but she thought maybe biking would be a way to ease into her regular routine. She figured she would start out with one of the more level trails that didn't require a great deal of uphill pedaling but could still get her heart rate going.

Cautiously, she rode down her driveway. Her ankle twinged a little with each rotation of the pedal but seemed to be firmly supported. So far so good. She increased her speed a bit, wishing for a little company. Tucker had gone home several days earlier when Dylan had returned from Denver, and Charlotte didn't want to admit how lonely her house had seemed without the big dog.

"Hey! Charlotte. Hi!"

She was so busy concentrating on keeping her balance and protecting her ankle from too much exertion that she didn't notice Peyton standing out on her driveway.

Charlotte hit the hand brake just as she would have passed the house and put her feet to the ground for balance as Peyton walked down to greet her.

"How was your week?" she asked the girl.

"Okay, I guess. The new housekeeper started. Gretel. Like *Hansel and Gretel*. She's pretty nice."

"Great."

"And some of our stuff came from Portland." She gestured to the garage behind her and Charlotte saw a stack of boxes. "We're still leaving a lot up there for when we go back but my dad had his assistant send down more clothes and some other things he thought we would need. We're going on a bike ride, too."

"Are you?"

At that moment, Spence emerged from around the corner of the boxes rolling one gleaming mountain bike beside him, a smaller one hefted over one shoulder by the frame.

"Finally found them, Pey. No flat tires. That's a minor miracle. Are you ready to go?"

In that moment, he caught sight of Charlotte and his stride faltered a little. "Charlotte! Hi!"

She instantly wished she had picked something a little cuter to wear for her ride than lycra shorts and an old Sugar Rush T-shirt.

She forced a smile, thinking it was completely unfair how good he could look first thing on a Saturday morning, probably with no effort whatsoever. "Good morning."

"Our stuff finally showed up yesterday, including the bikes."

"That's what Peyton was just telling me."

"It seemed like a good morning to head out, explore a few of the trails I remember."

"I'm sure more have been added since you were here. Hope's Crossing is renowned for its biking trails. We're no Moab but we have some good terrain for it."

"Looking forward to seeing what we find out there." He paused and gave her a considering look. "Are you supposed to be on a bike again, so soon after hurting your ankle?"

Yes. She was supposed to be on it right this moment, riding hard and fast away from him. "The doctor gave me the okay to resume weight-bearing activities earlier in the week. I'm trying not to push it. I thought biking would be a good middle ground."

"Don't force it."

"I plan to be careful." About bike riding and particularly gorgeous former baseball players, she thought. "You two have fun."

She lifted her foot back to the pedal, intending to take off. Peyton's words stopped her.

"Why don't we just ride with Charlotte?" she suggested to her father. "She probably knows all the good trails, then we won't waste time trying to figure out where to go."

Her stomach dropped. Hurricane Gregory had apparently decided to make landfall again.

Spence must have seen some of the dismay in her expression. "Charlotte doesn't need to play tour guide. I'm sure I can figure out where to go. We could just ride through town, for that matter."

"My ankle still isn't very strong," Charlotte said. "I can't go very fast, and I probably won't make it far before I have to turn back."

"Sounds perfect to me," Peyton said. "I didn't even want to go for a bike ride but my dad made me. I can't have my phone back until I exercise for thirty minutes. How dumb is that?"

She gave her father a look of such dramatic disgust that Charlotte had to fight down a laugh. "Terrible."

"Yeah, yeah. I'm a complete tyrant. How brutal, to want my kid to move a little once in a while."

"Bring on the slow, easy bike ride," Peyton said. "That still counts, right?" she appealed to her father, who gave a rueful laugh.

"We don't need to drag Charlotte into this. You and I can find a slow, easy bike path."

"But I would rather go with her," Peyton countered and Charlotte thought she saw a spasm of pain flit across Spence's features.

Charlotte felt torn—she didn't want to spend more time in Spence's company than she had to, given how weak she apparently was around him. On the other hand, she sensed the fragile, tense relationship between father and daughter might benefit from a third-party buffer. He had said as much at the café the other night.

"How about this? I'll help you find a good trailhead and ride as far as I can handle, and then the two of you can go on without me?"

"Sounds great to me," Peyton said.

"Sure. Okay," Spence said.

"There's a new trail that runs along where the railroad tracks used to come out of Silver Strike Canyon. It goes through town and then out into the fields. It's really pretty and quite level. You could actually ride all the way to the next town over, if you wanted. Does that work?"

"Which direction to the trail?" Spence said.

"Left at the corner. You can take whatever way you want to get there through town. Just head over toward the mouth of the canyon."

Peyton rode beside her and Spence took off ahead of them, which had the added benefits that he didn't see her struggling along on her bum ankle—and also that it afforded her a lovely rear view of a well-built male.

She was so busy trying not to gawk at him like some sex-starved housewife at a male stripper revue that she didn't pay attention to the route they took. He braked abruptly a few blocks from their destination— so abruptly, she almost ran into him.

"It's gone," he exclaimed.

She and Peyton stopped their bikes and looked in the direction he was gazing.

"What's gone?" Peyton asked.

"The house I grew up in was right here."

He pointed at a new six-unit luxury development that had been built a few years ago.

"William Beaumont bought a bunch of houses in this neighborhood and tore them all down to rebuild condominiums." And made a fortune, she remembered. One of the units had been on the market the summer before, and Charlotte remembered seeing that the asking price was more than twice the cost of her entire house.

"I forgot you grew up in this neighborhood," she said.

She *should* have remembered. Why hadn't she? Really, how many times had she ridden her old ten-speed past his house in the hopes of seeing him outside mowing the scraggly lawn or something?

She could only hope he had never seen her pathetic attempts to look casually unobtrusive.

"Everything is different," he said, a funny expression on his face.

When he had lived here, the neighborhood had been filled with small clapboard houses, built cheaply and quickly to house workers at the silver and copper mines that dotted the area. She remembered it being a pretty low-income subdivision—small grim houses with shutters hanging off, peeling paint and mostly unkempt lawns.

A few of the original miners' houses remained around town but they had all been renovated and added to—or, as in the case of Spence's old house, completely torn down to make way for new developments.

"A million memories have just come flooding back," he said, gazing at the spot where the house would have been. "I used to climb that tree back there. I guess they chose to keep that. Deer would come down in the winter and browse on those bushes there. I can remember watching them out of my bedroom window."

He paused, looking at some distant past neither Charlotte nor his daughter could see. "In the summer, my mom used to sit me on the top rung of a step stool while she cut my hair, there on the lawn."

In Charlotte's memory, Billie Gregory was a larger-than-life character. When she was sober at work, she was a pretty good waitress who knew just how to make the customers feel comfortable. She was funny and nice and obviously adored her son.

On her bad days, she forgot orders, dropped plates, even fell asleep on the floor of the office once.

"It wasn't all terrible," Charlotte said quietly.

He flashed a quick look at her, something dark and disguised in his eyes. "No. Not all of it."

"What was terrible?" Peyton asked from beside Charlotte. "You were king of the world when you lived here. Star of the baseball team, quarterback of the football team, blah, blah, blah."

"I did have sports, yeah." He looked at the space where his house would have been, and Charlotte wondered what else he was seeing. "But life at home wasn't that great."

"Why not?" Peyton looked genuinely interested, almost thirsty for knowledge, but Charlotte could tell this particular line of inquiry left Spence uncomfortable.

Had he really never told Peyton about the chaos of his childhood? Why not? Their relationship baffled her. It was almost as if Peyton didn't really know her father at all. Maybe he had been too busy building his career to spend much time with his daughter.

"It doesn't really matter," he said now, every line of his body taut as if he wanted to ride away from this spot.

Charlotte wanted to shake him. Couldn't he see his daughter wanted to hear about his past? If Peyton knew a little more about Spence and his life in Hope's Crossing, it might help bridge the distance Charlotte sensed between them.

After her own mother died, at least she had had six older brothers and a loving father to help her through. Peyton had nobody except a distant man she seemed to barely know.

Charlotte wanted to tell him so but knew it wasn't her place—still, something of her thoughts must have showed in her features. Spence gave her a quick look and after a long pause, turned back to his daughter.

"It was pretty chaotic," he finally said. "You know my dad died when I was young. My mom took it… hard. Eventually we came to Hope's Crossing from California to live with my grandmother in the house that used to be right there. My mom, your grandma, started drinking and basically didn't stop. She drank a lot. She barely held a job through the kindness of Mr. Caine, Charlotte's father."

By the time he finished, Peyton looked stunned, her eyes huge and dark amid those slender features. "That's why you washed dishes at the café? And had a newspaper route? And swept the hardware store?"

He shrugged. "We had to eat, didn't we?"

She glanced at Charlotte as if for confirmation. Charlotte gave her a half nod.

"Why didn't you ever say anything?" Peyton demanded. "I always thought you had it so great when you were a kid. All I ever heard about was the sports and stuff."

"I figured there wasn't much sense looking back."

"Your house was right there?"

"Yeah. But it was pretty different. Not much of a house, really—a couple bedrooms, a living room, bathroom and kitchen. My grandparents left the house to my mom so we didn't have to pay rent but it was falling apart and we—she—never did much to fix it up. The windows were so thin, I could put a glass of water beside my bed in the winter and wake up with a crackle of ice on the top."

Charlotte had known enough about his situation to guess that life wouldn't have been easy for him when he was young but her heart turned over at the picture he painted, especially when she contrasted that with the big house she had grown up in on Winterberry Road, full of noise, chaos, food and especially love.

"I think that makes it even more remarkable that you found something you were good at and worked so hard to change your future," Charlotte said promptly, then immediately wished she hadn't, especially when he shifted that veiled expression in her direction.

"I guess," he murmured. She had a feeling he was thinking about everything that came after, the turmoil and scandal of the past two years. "Come on. No sense looking back. Let's go find the trailhead."

He took off, leaving her and Peyton no choice but to follow after him.

He maintained a steady pace, turning where she indicated until they ended up on the trail that ran along the old railroad tracks that used to carry ore from the mines. Her ankle throbbed a bit but the rest of her muscles felt loose and relaxed.

"Hey, can we stop for a second?" Peyton called when they reached the trailhead.

Spence complied. "What's the matter?"

"I really need to use the bathroom. I thought there might be one here before we took off on the trail."

"No. Sorry. The closest public bathroom is down at Miners' Park," Charlotte said. "It's about a half mile away. We can head there instead."

Peyton shrugged. "No. That's okay. I don't really feel like a bike ride anymore. I think I'll just go back home."

"Peyton." Spence said her name in a chiding tone.

"What? We've been riding at least fifteen minutes, haven't we? By the time I ride back home again, that will be a half hour and you said I could have my phone back if I went for a half-hour bike ride with you. I did it. You can't say I didn't."

He sighed. "No. I just thought once you were out and moving, you might like to go a little farther."

"I have to go to the bathroom, and I don't want to use some gross public stall at some park. I just want to go home and call Victoria. Before you took my phone away, I told her I would call her today."

"Can you find your way back to the house?"

She gave him a disgusted look. "I'm almost thirteen. It's not like I'm some three-year-old loose in the neighborhood on a Big Wheel."

"Be careful. Call my cell if you run into trouble."

"How can I? You haven't given me back my phone."

He sighed again but reached into the cargo pocket of his shorts and pulled out her device. Peyton rode up and snatched it from his hand with a gleeful look.

"See you later," she said, and rode off in the direction they had come.

Spence's worried gaze followed her. He swore under his breath.

"You can probably catch up with her in about thirty seconds if you think she's going to get lost. Don't worry about me. I'm fine."

"She doesn't *want* me to go with her. She would prefer if I dropped off the face of the earth."

"I'm sure that's not true."

"Oh, I'm sure it's fairly accurate." He said the words evenly but his expression was bleak. "She thinks I killed her mother."

She sensed he hadn't meant to say the words. They hovered between them, ugly and dark. She didn't know what to say. Before she could come up with anything, he rode forward onto the trail, leaving her to either ride after him or go home. After a moment's hesitation, she pushed down the pedal and followed.

"Aren't you going to ask me if she's right?" he asked when she joined him. The trail was wide enough here for two or more cyclists to ride abreast in either direction.

"No," she answered.

He glanced over at her. "Because you don't want to know or because you don't care?"

She considered her answer as they rode through trees on either side of the trail that created a tunnel of sorts, blocking the pretty view of downtown and creating an intimacy she knew was an illusion.

"Stow this in the confession drawer," she finally said. "I occasionally read *People* magazine when I'm in line at the grocery store. I've even been known to pick up *Us Weekly*."

"Shocking," he murmured.

"I know. I know. Because I…knew you a long time ago, I—and most of the rest of Hope's Crossing—followed the news reports about your wife's death. You were at a court hearing when she drowned in your swimming pool. The autopsy showed she had enough antidepressants and painkillers in her system to knock out the entire Pioneers outfield."

He sighed. "I might not have been present at the moment, but I knew she was spiraling down. She had been for weeks. Months, even, and I…didn't stop it. She needed help and I refused to admit it."

"Do you think she killed herself?" She couldn't believe she dared ask the question everybody wanted to know. She waited for him to lash out but Spence only shook his head.

"I don't. Not that anybody cares what I think. Jade was…troubled but she loved Peyton. I don't believe she would leave her like that. She wasn't herself, though, toward the end, so I can't be certain."

"Why would Peyton blame you? She had to realize you weren't there."

"You want the whole ugly story?"

She didn't but she sensed he needed to share it. All her intentions to maintain a healthy distance between them seemed to float away on the soft breeze.

"Peyton might not hold me directly responsible for her mother's death but I believe she thinks the…allegations against me, the scandal, was too much for Jade. Suddenly her so-called friends weren't calling her back, she wasn't being invited to the A-list parties anymore, she lost… well, a few people she cared about, people who couldn't afford to be mixed up in my mess. They dropped her, and Jade couldn't handle it. She retreated into alcohol and drugs, both legal and not."

Like his mother, she thought. Oh, poor Spencer. He must have felt as if history were repeating itself. A troubled mother and a troubled wife and he couldn't save either of them....

"I didn't want to see how bad things had become. I told myself I was dealing with my own stuff. I figured once I didn't have the threat of prison hanging over me, I could make her go into rehab. Things didn't quite work out that way. Obviously. I came home from court that day and found police swarming the house and Peyton traumatized. At least she didn't find her mother. The groundskeeper did, and he and our housekeeper had the wisdom to keep her inside."

Charlotte remembered media reports she had seen, the pictures of a pale, gaunt Peyton at her mother's funeral, and her heart ached for the young girl. No wonder she seemed very angry and troubled.

"I'm so sorry," she murmured. "For both of you."

SPENCER HEARD THE sympathy in her voice and couldn't believe it. He was telling her his darkest failure, the knowledge that haunted him, and Charlotte only gazed at him out of steady blue eyes that were drenched with compassion.

He felt something hard and ugly shake loose inside him and slink a little further into a corner. He wanted to tell her the rest. Everything.

"You should probably know, my marriage was over by the time Peyton was about three. We all lived in the same house but Jade and I were virtual strangers. Generally polite to each other, but that was about it. Toward the end, even that broke down."

It had been a little tough to be cordial after he found his wife in bed with the man he considered his mentor and best friend.

"We stayed together for Peyton but...the two of them were very close. Jade made sure there wasn't a lot of room left over for me to have much of a relationship with her. I can't blame her. I know I should have tried harder."

He didn't know why he was telling her all this. Charlotte Caine had a way of looking at him that made him want to unload his burdens, to ease into the quiet peace she offered.

"Is that why you didn't tell her about how things were for you here?"

"I've spent most of the past dozen years trying to convince myself my life started when I signed that contract with the Pioneers. The rest was just the prequel and who cares about backstory?"

"Everything that happens to us becomes part of the whole. Your past here in Hope's Crossing helped shape your drive and your character."

They rode in silence for a few moments while he mulled that.

"On those rare times when Pey would ask about my childhood," he finally said, "I just told her memories from before my dad died, glossing over our life here. I think she probably figured, since I didn't want to talk about it, I was still grieving for my parents or something."

He did grieve for his father, who had loved baseball and had taken him to a major league game when he was barely a toddler.

He also grieved for his mother and tried to focus on those happier times. He had loved Billie, even when he had despised her weakness.

"Well, this is a pleasant discussion to have on such a lovely day. Sorry to ruin your workout."

"It's not much of a workout for either one of us," Charlotte said.

He managed a smile. "I ran five miles before Peyton woke up. This was just supposed to be a recreational ride with her. I guess that didn't turn out so well."

They rode for a few more moments, until he realized she was falling farther behind him.

"Sorry. Can we stop for a second?" she asked when he looked back.

He braked and returned to her, then waited while she pulled out a water bottle and took a long drink. A monarch butterfly flitted around her and she watched it with a soft smile but when she lowered her water bottle, he noticed for the first time the lines of pain bracketing her mouth.

"You pushed too far, didn't you?"

"A bad habit of mine."

They had ridden maybe only a mile from the trailhead—not far, but it would be painful for her to return.

"As I see it, we've got a couple options," he said. "You can wait and I'll go see if I can find somebody with an ATV to ride up here and get you. Or I can leave my bike and walk you on yours back to the trailhead."

She gave a surprised-sounding laugh, as if she couldn't quite believe he would do that for her. "I only needed a little rest. Now I'm perfectly fine to turn back."

"Liar."

"Am I?" With a laughing, defiant look over her shoulder, she set her feet on the pedals. In the dappled late-morning sunlight, she made his mouth water.

What the hell was he going to do with her? He had told himself he needed to stay away from her, that he couldn't afford to alienate everyone in town willing to help him with A Warrior's Hope. But he was rapidly finding he needed Charlotte Caine far more than he needed the approval of everyone else in town.

"You're not even going to pretend to let me save the day?"

"I'm fine," she repeated. "Yes, it aches but nothing unmanageable. It's mostly downhill anyway, at least to the trailhead. I can coast most of the way. Go ahead and keep going if you want. There's a turn that will take you back to the Woodrose Mountain trail, though that would probably take you a couple hours. Well, it would take *me* a couple hours. You could probably finish it off in half that."

"You really think I would just leave you here, Charley? What kind of jackass do you think I am?"

She gave him a rather pensive look in return but took off the way they had come.

He could tell her ankle hurt by the tentative way she used her left pedal compared to the right but she didn't complain. She didn't even wince, as far as he could tell. Several times, he urged her to wait where she was while he rode home for his Range Rover. He wasn't surprised when she refused. While he wanted to insist, he sensed this was a point of pride for her so he subsided into frustrated worry.

By the time they reached her house, she was pale and a fine sheen of perspiration covered her skin. He quickly climbed off his bike, letting it fall to the grass, and barely managed to catch her when she wobbled as she tried to dismount.

In one movement, she was in his arms. "Come on, you stubborn thing. Let's get you inside. You're done."

"Put me down, Spence. Right now," she exclaimed as he headed up her steps then wrestled open her door. "I'm way too heavy."

"You're exactly right," he replied. He hadn't meant the words to sound sensuous, but somehow his voice came out husky.

The mood instantly shifted between them. She gazed up at him, and he saw her gaze flit to his mouth and then quickly away.

"You've really got to stop carrying me."

"What if I like having you in my arms?" he murmured.

And then—because she was gazing at him out of those big eyes, because she made him feel things he hadn't in a long time, because he *wanted* to, damn it— he kissed her.

CHAPTER TWELVE

SHE FROZE FOR just an instant and then she returned the kiss, tentatively at first and then with growing enthusiasm. Her tongue slid against his and her arms wrapped around his neck and his body went instantly hard.

She made a low, sexy sound, her breathing ragged, and pressed all those luscious curves against him. Heat exploded in his gut and he couldn't think of anything but how very much he wanted to touch her, taste her everywhere.

With their mouths fused, he carried her into her living room and lowered her to the sage sofa he had sat on the other night. She made a sound of protest, her arms tight around his neck, and he followed her down, their mouths still together.

She squirmed beneath him, her full sexy breasts brushing his chest, and he felt like a kid, desperate to get to second base. He had to touch her. It was a primal need he couldn't seem to control and, while exploring the wonders of her mouth, he eased a hand to her waist, slipping under the edge of her T-shirt. Her skin was warm and deliciously soft, and she made little needy noises with each inch he moved his fingers.

Finally, he feathered a touch just on the underside of her breast. She gasped and jerked her mouth away.

"What's wrong?"

"You…surprised me, that's all," she said after a moment. "You, um, don't have to stop."

Her voice sounded breathy, hollow. He eased away from her and saw her eyes were dilated, her cheeks flushed. She looked wanton and innocent at the same time, a heady combination.

Some of her hair drifted from her ponytail, and he wanted to pull it all free and run it through his fingers, savoring each silky strand. He was so aroused, he ached with the need to lose himself inside her.

"Really. Don't stop," she said, her voice a little shy, color high on her cheekbones. She shifted restlessly on the sofa then winced a little when she moved her foot. Suddenly, he remembered her ankle. She was still on the DL, had just survived the ordeal of riding her bike much farther than she should have, and here he was mauling her on her own sofa.

"You're in pain."

"Only my ankle, which I'm fairly sure doesn't have to be heavily involved in this."

Damn it. He couldn't do this, as much as every particle of his body was crying out for him to carry her somewhere with a little more room, strip them both to bare skin and spend hours exploring those curves.

He would hurt her. It was what he did, even when he started out with the best intentions. She trusted him, had become the closest thing he had to a friend in Hope's Crossing, and he couldn't betray that trust by complicating everything with sex.

"I find you incredibly desirable, Charlotte."

A startled sort of heat flared in her eyes and she gazed at him, her lips parted and her heartbeat pulsing rapidly beneath her skin at her neck.

"You...do?"

"Isn't it obvious?"

She blushed again. For some reason, he had a flash of memory. Charlotte's round cheeks used to flare with color whenever he would smile at her in the halls or slap his books down at the booth where she was studying at the café.

He had some vague recollection that she once had asked him out on a date. A girl's choice, if he remembered correctly. For the life of him, he couldn't think why they hadn't gone.

Even more reason why he should stop things before they flared out of control. Charlotte was sweet and kind. Decent. She cared about her family, her town, even a troubled young girl who needed a friend.

He didn't want her developing feelings for him. He would break her heart, smash it into pieces. She would end up despising him, and he would hate that. "You're a beautiful woman. I would love nothing more than to follow up on this...heat between us. But I think we both know this would be a terrible idea."

She stared at him silently for a long moment, her blue eyes hiding her emotions.

"Horrible," she finally agreed, tugging down her T-shirt.

"Unwise, anyway," he amended. He suddenly didn't necessarily want her associating the word *horrible* in any degree to the idea of making love with him.

"No. You're right. It would be disastrous." Her hands trembled a little as she tucked her loose hair behind her ears.

He sighed. "Charlotte. You know I'm not...in any kind of position for a relationship."

She sniffed. "Who said anything about a relationship? Maybe I just wanted wild, crazy sex with a hot celebrity athlete. Sure, you've got a reputation now, but maybe that's part of the appeal. Maybe I like bad boys."

He had certainly been with other women who only wanted to say they'd been with Smoke Gregory. Not many, but enough to add another check in his personal self-disgust column. Hearing sweet, kind Charlotte say something like that seemed terribly wrong.

He remembered the compassion in her eyes when they had talked about his time here as a kid, the concern when she had asked him about Jade. He couldn't hurt her.

"I don't have many friends right now, Charlotte. I hope…that is, I would very much like for you to be counted among those few. I don't want to ruin it. I hope I haven't."

For some reason, she blushed an even rosier shade. "It was just a kiss, Spence. Relax."

It wasn't *just* a kiss. The two times he had kissed her had been explosive. He didn't like thinking maybe they hadn't been the same for her.

She rose, once more composed and in control, while he stood there fiercely aroused and sorry as hell he had put on the brakes.

"Thanks for helping me home," she said. "I'll see you later."

It was a clear dismissal and they both knew it. He gave her another searching look, wishing he knew what she was thinking. With nothing left to say, he kissed her on the forehead and walked out of her house, feeling the strangest sense of loss.

LONG AFTER HE LEFT, she sat on the sofa staring into space, trying to figure out what had just happened.

He had told her he liked having her in his arms, had kissed her until she couldn't think straight, had obviously been aroused—she wasn't *that* naive—and then had come up with an excuse not to take things further.

He only wanted to be friends. Right. That was just a handy excuse guys used on women they didn't want to sleep with.

On the other hand, Spence really *did* need people on his side. She guessed he didn't have very many. Maybe he really *did not* want to ruin their friendship with sex.

Not that his reasons mattered. The truth was, she was glad things hadn't progressed further. She had come too far, had worked too hard to let him tangle her up again.

The ring of her cell phone interrupted that pleasant thought. She considered ignoring it, not really in the mood to talk to Pop or any of her brothers. It could be one of her employees from Sugar Rush, though. Out of habit, she picked it up and checked the caller ID and decided to answer when she saw it was Alex McKnight.

"We're still on tonight, right?" Alex said after a preliminary greeting.

It took her several beats to process what Alex meant.

"You forgot. Tell me you didn't forget."

"I didn't," she lied. "I've just had a…bit of a crazy morning, and it slipped my mind for a second. But I remember now. Tonight. You and Sam, me and one of Sam's friends whose name I just forgot."

How could she be expected to remember her *own* name when her tongue had just been tangled around Spencer Gregory's?

"Garrett. Garrett King. I really think you'll like him,

Char. He's great looking, he's super funny, he's smart and hardworking."

She gave a small laugh. "Wow. I'm not sure I'm ready for all that perfection."

"He's not *completely* perfect. He's not Sam, after all. But he's a close second. I can't wait for you to meet him. We're coming to pick you up about seven. I think I told you we're going to Le Passe."

"You did. Yum," she said. She would have to stick to a plain salad for lunch to save calories for the sauce-heavy deliciousness that was Le Passe Montagne, one of Brodie Thorne's restaurants.

"I know. Wear something sexy, okay? And promise me you'll give Garrett a chance."

"I swear to you. I'm completely open to any possibilities."

"Good. I'll see you tonight, then."

She would love nothing more than to fall hard for Sam Delgado's friend, she thought as she severed the connection. Or even to seriously lust after the man. Any distraction would be a welcome relief from the inevitable heartache she knew would follow if she were foolish enough to let herself care about Spence again.

Usually, she loved Le Passe Montagne.

The decor was French elegant—tasteful chandeliers, discreet tables, sophisticated paintings on the walls— and the food was fantastic.

When she came here, she had to choose her meal carefully. Tonight she had chosen grilled salmon and steamed haricot verts. It might lack the typical rich sauce the restaurant was famed for but she still found it delicious.

"I'm so glad we were finally able to make our schedules mesh so we could do this," Alex said.

Charlotte smiled at her friend and the man beside her. Sam Delgado looked gruff and rather scary on the outside, with his close-cut hair and tattoos, but he was really a sweetheart beneath the layers.

"I am, too. This has been great."

Her date—who was indeed quite gorgeous, in a California surfer-dude sort of way, with sun-streaked hair and a killer tan—lifted his glass of wine and they all clinked glasses.

"To new friendships," he said.

I don't have many friends right now, Charlotte. I hope…that is, I would very much like for you to be counted among those few.

She shoved the thought of Spence out of her head, once again.

"Where's Ethan?" she asked Sam. She should have thought to ask him about his son an hour earlier when they picked her up but she had been too busy fighting a killer case of first-date jitters.

"He's gone camping with Riley and Owen and some of Owen's friends," Alex said, referring to her brother and his stepson.

"He's not all that excited about the fishing but he can't wait for the roasted marshmallows," Sam said. "No messy chocolatey s'mores for my son. He's all about the marshmallows."

Charlotte smiled, a little envious at Alex's good fortune to find a great guy like Sam who obviously adored his child. Envy aside, Sam and Alex were so crazy about each other, it was hard not to be happy for both of them.

"Me, I'd take the fishing and leave the marshmallows," Garrett said.

She really, really wanted to like him. He seemed nice enough, though a little distant, as if he wasn't quite sure he wanted to be here, either.

The only sparks between them had come from static electricity when he had helped her into the car.

"Do you fly-fish or bait fish?" Alex asked.

"Fly," Garrett answered. "That's one of the reasons I agreed to help Sam out for a few months after he called. The trout fishing nearby is supposed to be fantastic."

"I have brothers who fish," Charlotte said. "There are supposed to be some good streams up around Snowflake Canyon."

"I might need to talk to them. Do you know where they go?"

She mentioned a few places she remembered and was racking her brain to come up with more when her attention was diverted by the hostess leading another group in her direction.

Some sixth sense had her lifting her gaze away from Garrett for just an instant, long enough to spot the identity of the new guests.

Harry Lange walked in with Alex's mother, Mary Ella. They made a very handsome couple—Harry, distinguished and well-dressed, and Mary Ella, still lovely in her sixties.

It was the man following them, obviously with Harry and Mary Ella, who drew her gaze.

Charlotte wanted to cry. Okay, this was bordering on the ridiculous. Couldn't she go anywhere in town without Spence showing up?

She was trying so *hard* to keep from returning to

the old days when she had seriously crushed on Spence. The man had broken her heart too darn many times. She had so many patches over it, it was a wonder the thing still worked. She refused to give him another go.

Just her luck, the hostess showed Harry's party to the best table at the restaurant, with a lovely view out the windows to Harry's own resort—and, of course, the table happened to be right across from theirs.

How was she supposed to fall for Sam's Army buddy with Spence right here in her face? There were dozens of other restaurants in Hope's Crossing. Seriously, why did he have to come to *this* one, on the night she was here with the man she really had hoped would become the love of her life?

She knew exactly when he spotted her. His steps faltered a little and he almost ran into a chair. Their gazes met and, for a split second, she was back on her sofa, his body hard and urgent as he pressed her into the cushions, his hungry mouth slanting over hers while his clever hands found all her most sensitive spots.

He blinked first, his gaze shifting to the man who sat beside her and then back to her with a glittery expression she couldn't read before he sat down in a chair that, unfortunately, offered him a clear view of their group.

After all of them had taken their seats, Mary Ella spotted her daughter. She waved and rose again, gracefully heading to their table.

"I didn't know you were off tonight or we would have had you join us," she said to her daughter. "I suppose if you're here, instead of in your kitchen, it's a good thing we chose to eat at Le Passe instead of Brazen for dinner."

"I hope you know by now that my well-trained staff can deliver the goods even when I'm not there."

Her mother laughed. "What? Are you actually telling me you're not completely indispensable, my dear?"

"I don't believe I said anything of the sort." Alex sniffed. "Not completely, anyway. Sam, darling, do you need a drink of water? I swear, if you clear your throat any louder, they'll throw us out."

"I'm fine. Thanks." He stood and kissed Mary Ella on the cheek. "You look stunning, as always."

She smiled at him and then at Charlotte. "I don't believe I've met your friend."

Alex stepped in to make the introduction. "Oh, sorry. Mom, this is Garrett King. Garrett, this is my beautiful mother, Mary Ella McKnight. Garrett and Sam were in the same unit together. He's going to be in town for a few months to help Sam catch up on all the work that's been coming his way."

"Lovely to meet you." Mary Ella gave Garrett a welcoming smile. Charlotte so envied her the class and dignity that seemed as innate to her as her green eyes and dimples. "I hope you enjoy your stay in Hope's Crossing. If you'll all excuse me, I should probably return before Harry orders something completely outside his dietary restrictions."

"Go. Save the man from himself," Alex said.

After Mary Ella returned to her group, Sam and Alex started a rather intense conversation about escargots, which she adored and he apparently hated. While they were debating the wisdom of eating anything that left a trail of slime, Garrett leaned closer to Charlotte and spoke in a low voice.

"Okay, am I crazy or is that Smoke Gregory over there?"

The very last thing she wanted to do was talk about the man she had been making out with a few hours ago on her sofa but she couldn't find a way to directly avoid the question.

"Yes. He's a Hope's Crossing native," she said carefully.

Her date studied the other table out of the corner of his gaze, and she *really* hoped Spence didn't notice and wonder if they were talking about him. "I saw him pitch a no-hitter against the Giants. Man, he had a hell of an arm. Shame about everything else."

Why did everybody say it like that? "Yes," she murmured. "Yes, it was."

"I mean, think about it. How weird would it be to be on top of the world one minute and in prison the next?"

"He never went to prison. The charges against him were dismissed."

"But everybody knows that's only because he had a team of high-priced attorneys. If there had been no evidence against him, he never would have been charged in the first place."

She opened her mouth to argue that sometimes not every story was as clear-cut, good versus evil, black-and-white, as it appeared and that sometimes the reality was much more complicated. The words clogged in her throat, and she practically had to bite her tongue to keep them from bursting out.

What was wrong with her? She was on a date with a great-looking guy, the most interesting man she'd met in ages, and here she was wanting to hotly defend someone she still wasn't entirely sure deserved it.

She really didn't know anything about Spence's case, other than her own gut instinct that he was hiding something. And just look how spot-on her gut had always been about him.

"What's he doing in Hope's Crossing? Does he have a house here or something?" Garrett asked, oblivious to her internal struggle.

"Who?" Alex asked. Apparently she and Sam had settled the great escargot conflict.

Garrett gave a slight head jerk toward the other group. "We were just talking about Spence Gregory, over there with your mother. I'm from Portland and have been a big Pioneers fan since the franchise started. Gregory won't win any popularity contests around the City of Roses, I'll tell you that. Plenty of people think he had something to do with his wife's death. I was just wondering how a person comes back when his life turns into that kind of hot mess?"

Charlotte thought of his efforts to make a better life for him and his daughter, of the guilt he carried for not helping his troubled wife, of the hardworking boy he had been who had tried to take care of his mother despite her abysmal neglect of him.

"Inch by excruciating inch," she answered softly. "You asked what he's doing here. He's the director of the community's new recreation center. You might be interested to know, he's working with veterans' organizations to set up a recreational therapy program here for wounded soldiers."

She wasn't really surprised when Garrett's hard features tightened. Like Dylan, he apparently had a cynical streak.

"So he's just another do-gooder hoping for some positive press on the backs of the hardworking men and women of the military."

"I don't think so, actually," Sam corrected mildly. "He came to talk to me about the project the other day, asking if I could help build some cabins up there. He seemed quite sincere when he talked about what he hopes to achieve and the financial commitments he's already made. I think it sounds like a great idea. Hope's Crossing has a lot to offer these guys who need a safe, warm place to heal. I say, if he can make it happen, more power to him."

Charlotte wished Spence could have heard Sam defending him. He probably wouldn't have believed it.

"I hope he's successful," she said. "My brother was severely wounded in an ambush in Afghanistan. He lost some good friends and came back without an arm and an eye. He's had a tough road back. I guess the way I see it, it's the outcome that matters in this case, not necessarily the motive."

Their server approached their table to see if anyone wanted dessert. After she left, the conversation turned to lighter topics, a movie Sam and Alex wanted to see, Charlotte's taste in music, Alex's long, vastly entertaining treatise on how to make a perfect crème brûlée.

At one point, Garrett put his arm across the back of her seat while he emphasized something. She didn't flinch away, but she did make the mistake of looking up at Spence's table.

He was watching her, she saw with a little thrill of dismay, and the big tough ex-soldier she sat beside. She quickly jerked her gaze away but not before seeing a hot glittery light in his eyes.

He couldn't be jealous. She would never believe it. It was probably only her fickle heart.

Though she was tempted to lean forward, away from even that slight physical contact, she forced herself to sit casually, to smile with bright enthusiasm at Garrett, to try her very best to fall for him—as hopeless as it might seem right now, when all she could think about was Spence's arms around her that morning and the wild heat of his kiss.

CHAPTER THIRTEEN

"THAT'S WHAT I SAID. A million and some change, along with that strip of land you want along the river, as long as you agree to put your money where your mouth is and match it."

With far more effort than it should take, Spence managed to wrench his attention away from a glowing pretty Charlotte and the hard guy she sat beside. He forced himself to focus on Harry Lange and the unbelievable donation he had just offered to A Warrior's Hope.

"I don't know what to say."

"Here's where you say yes or no. Fish or cut bait, boy. Trust me, I've got plenty of other places to put my money if you're not committed to your wounded warrior project."

"No. I am. You just took me by surprise."

"I read through everything you gave me. You've done your homework. I like that. The way I see it, this is just what I want for this town. Something that takes us out of ourselves to reach out to those who might not have it as well."

"I agree."

"That should give you enough to build the cabins you're talking about. You can have Sam Delgado over there get started as soon as possible. Be up and running by Christmas."

He blinked, not quite sure what just happened. Harry Lange had committed a substantial sum to make A Warrior's Hope happen much faster than he expected.

"Thanks. This is…thank you."

"You can thank my Mary Ella here. She's the one who convinced me."

He had a hard time calling his former English teacher by her first name. "Mrs. McKnight. Thank you."

"I love the idea. From the moment Charlotte mentioned it to us the other day, my mind has been racing with possibilities. I'll help you in any way I can."

"Fantastic. I'll definitely take you up on that."

He wanted to celebrate. He wanted to order champagne for everybody in the place. He wanted to yank Charlotte away from the big granite-jawed asshole pawing her and kiss her until neither of them could think straight.

Instead, he sipped at his ginger ale. "Where do we go from here?"

"As soon as all the paperwork is in order for the charitable trust, my attorneys will make everything tight and legal with the land transfer. You do remember this is a matching grant, right? You're good with that?"

"Absolutely," he said promptly. "I was already planning on at least that, whether you matched or not."

"Good man." Harry gave him an approving smile. "Hard to believe you're the same kid who used to deliver my newspaper."

"I was probably the best carrier you ever had," he countered.

Harry gave a raspy chuckle. "True enough. You never missed my front mat, not once in five years. Never met such a stubborn little punk. Why do you think I reached out to you to run my recreation center? I figure a kid who takes that much pride in doing the small jobs the right way won't fail when it comes to the big ones."

The man's trust in him was humbling. All of them at the table knew he had failed quite spectacularly when it came to his baseball career. The injury hadn't been under his control, no, but everything that came after was.

He refused to fail with A Warrior's Hope.

AS HE DROVE through the streets of town after several hours at Harry Lange's house working out details, he was aware of a strange unsettled restlessness simmering through him.

This late on an early August weekend evening, only the bars were still open and active. He wondered idly if going into one of those might ease this restlessness but the craving didn't last long. He had never enjoyed alcohol much, not after seeing how the abuse of it could be so devastating. Having gone through rehab for his painkiller addiction, he was rarely even tempted to drink.

It wasn't the alcohol that drew him to the bar, anyway, but the company. That was the one thing he missed about the Pioneers. His team had been his family. At times like this, when he truly had something to celebrate, he missed not having somebody he could call to share good news.

There were still players he considered brothers, guys who had stuck with him through the worst of everything, despite the evidence. He would never forget their loyalty, though something subtle yet powerful had changed between them. They were still in the game, their lives revolving around their statistics, their swing, their ERAs or RBIs.

As he turned onto Willowleaf Lane and drove past Charlotte's little cottage, he was vaguely aware of slowing down. Her lights were on and, when he glanced up at her house, he saw the shadow of a figure move past the window.

He slowed down further, looking more closely to see if another shadow—maybe a tall muscled dude with a tattoo on his forearm—might join her. He couldn't see anything but her. And, he noted quickly, her driveway was completely empty, the garage door closed tightly.

Apparently, her date had ended early.

The surge of relief was inappropriate and unwarranted but he couldn't seem to tamp it back down. Some of his excitement from earlier in the evening returned.

Charlotte. Charlotte would understand, would be just as excited as he was that A Warrior's Hope was actually coming together.

He suddenly wanted to share the news with her. Without thinking about how foolhardy it would be to stop at her house so late, he pulled into her driveway, shut off the engine and headed for her door. He didn't give himself time to reconsider, he just rang the doorbell and stood inside the square of light spilling from her front window onto the porch.

Only after, while he waited for her to answer, did he start to second-guess the wisdom of coming here, especially given the awkward way they had left things that morning.

The moment she answered the door, looking graceful and lovely in the tailored white blouse and slim pencil skirt she had worn to dinner but with a red frilly apron over both, his doubts subsided. Just the sight of her seemed to ease his restlessness, though it was replaced by an entirely different kind of tension.

"Spence! Is something wrong?"

"Nothing's wrong. Nothing at all. I just saw your light and figured you were still up. May I come in?"

She glanced behind her and he saw indecision flicker across her expressive features but she finally stepped aside. "You had to have seen at the restaurant that I was on a date. What if I were…entertaining?"

He pointed to the empty driveway. "No other car. The guy could have walked, I guess, or parachuted in, but I took a chance."

"Is there something you needed at—" she glanced at a clock above her small white mantel "—ten after eleven?"

With the low heat thrumming through him as he was surrounded by the enticing citrus and vanilla scent of her, he could think of plenty of things he needed but this didn't seem the appropriate time to mention them.

"I had news. I thought you might want to hear it."

"You could have waited until tomorrow."

"Yeah. You're right. But what's the fun in that? By then it will be old news."

"Not to me," she pointed out.

"True. But I was excited and I didn't really have anybody else to tell. Peyton is probably in bed and the housekeeper barely knows me."

She studied him for a long moment and he wondered what she was thinking.

"I'm assuming this has to do with Harry and your dinner."

"Yes. And A Warrior's Hope. Since you've been in

on the planning from the beginning, you deserve to be the first to hear."

Finally she held the door open. "Come on in to the kitchen. I was just cutting up some fruit."

This struck him as odd but he wasn't about to question fate when she led the way through her house. He could smell the sweet-tart scent of pineapple when he walked into the cozy little kitchen.

He eased onto one of the high chairs around her breakfast bar. "If you're making piña coladas, I'll have a virgin."

She looked down at the cutting board and he had to wonder what had turned her cheeks pink. "No piña coladas here, I'm afraid, but I can maybe find you a beer or something."

"Water is fine. So what's with the pineapple?"

"I like fresh fruit in the morning for breakfast, either alone or in a quick yogurt smoothie. If I don't prep as much as I can the night before, I'm usually too rushed on my way to the candy store and end up grabbing something full of carbs and sugar deliciousness."

"Makes sense. Need a hand?"

"No. I've got it." She went back to wielding a knife expertly. In a few slices, she finished with the pineapple and pulled out a cantaloupe from the refrigerator.

He enjoyed watching her and felt more of his tension seep away. Who would have guessed he could find fruit slicing so relaxing?

It wasn't the fruit, he knew. It was Charlotte. She just had this calming way about her, and he discovered he was beginning to crave it worse than any little pill.

"How did your date go?"

Her hands paused their slicing briefly and she raised

an eyebrow. "Do you want a play-by-play? I'm afraid I didn't do a very good job of keeping track."

He waved a hand. "Just the highlights are fine."

"He was…nice. He served in the Army Rangers with Sam Delgado, who is dating Alex McKnight."

"I've met Sam. He seems like a good guy."

"I think so."

Again her color seemed rosy and he wondered why.

"Anyway, Garrett is in town for a few months, helping Sam with his construction company. Alex has been trying to set us up for a couple weeks. Our schedules finally meshed tonight."

He didn't want to think of any *meshing* going on. Could he take a trained Army Ranger? He figured he could, if he had to.

"So what happened with Harry?" she asked.

Oh, right. The reason he had stopped at her house after eleven. "Good news. Great news, actually. He's agreed to donate a cool million to A Warrior's Hope, for starters."

She stared at him. "Dollars?"

He laughed. "No. Toothpicks. What did you think?"

She set down her knife. "Let me get this straight. Over dinner, Harry Lange—the most notorious tightwad in the county—agreed to give that kind of gift to an organization that hasn't even really taken off yet?"

"Yes. In addition to the land we wanted for the cabins. I'm thinking we can break ground within the month."

"That's fantastic!"

"It's a good cause. He had to see that. I told him I feel like we can really make a difference here. There's something almost *healing* about Hope's Crossing. Harry agreed with me that it's past time to bring that healing to others."

"You said all that?"

He shifted his weight on the chair, uncomfortable with the soft note in her voice, for reasons he couldn't have explained. "I don't know what I said, if you want the truth. I had a nice spiel prepared but ended up just talking about your brother and how much he had sacrificed. We owe Dylan and others like him more than just empty platitudes and Veterans Day programs at the elementary school."

She resumed slicing the cantaloupe, but he was almost certain she looked at him with a different light in her eyes, something almost like…approval.

"It sounds stupid, I know."

She shook her head. "Not stupid." Her smile was sweet, and her watery eyes glistened. "Perfect."

"Well, whatever I said must have worked. Harry pulled out his checkbook on the spot."

He didn't mention Harry's condition was a matching grant from his own foundation. She didn't need to know that part.

"You know," she said, "I may just have to reconsider my general philosophy that Mary Ella has gone a little crazy this past year while she's been dating Harry Lange."

Spence had to smile. He had wanted to share his news with someone and now he realized Charlotte was exactly the person he had needed to tell. Her reaction was just as he hoped. He wanted to bask in it, just sit here in her kitchen amid the glow of knowing he had finally done something right.

Now that he had told her the news, however, he realized he had no real excuse for sticking around, other than the simple fact that he couldn't imagine another place he would rather find himself right at this moment.

"Are you sure there's not something I can do to help you here?" he asked, before she thought to throw him out.

Her mouth twisted into a little smile. "You mean you don't have some philanthropist to meet for drinks somewhere? Surely you could use another million in seed money."

"No. And besides, I don't drink anymore."

Curiosity danced across her features but she said nothing, only reached into a drawer and emerged with a melon baller she held out to him.

He washed his hands and then joined her at the work island. She pulled out a watermelon and handed it to him, and for a few moments they worked in silence, shoulder to shoulder. Her sweet scent teased his senses along with the intoxicating scents of the fruit and every once in a while her shoulder brushed his.

This was nice. Soothing.

He hadn't spent much time in a kitchen as an adult. He always figured he had done his time washing dishes and busing tables at the café but maybe he had missed out on something peaceful.

"You really don't drink at all?" she asked after a moment, the question not unexpected.

"I quit everything. Rehab, remember?"

She sent him a glance under her eyelids then turned back to the fruit. "I thought celebrities generally only went through the motions to keep the tabloids off their backs."

"Not this one. I've been clean since I walked through the doors of the rehab facility."

"But you still had no problem supplying the little happy pills to others."

The enjoyment of the moment dissipated on a breath and something hard and cold lodged under his breastbone. He didn't want to talk about this. What he really wanted to do was kiss her, distract her from this topic he abhorred, but he had told her that morning it was a mistake. Nothing had changed.

He remained silent and didn't look at her, though he could feel the weight of her stare for several long moments. Finally, he heard the clatter of a metal knife on the wooden cutting board.

"You didn't do it."

He jerked his gaze to hers. "Didn't do what?"

"Didn't supply drugs or steroids to your teammates."

Something surged inside him, something bright and heady, but he couldn't take time to examine it right now.

"The charges *were* dropped," he pointed out, feeling oddly breathless.

She made a dismissive gesture. "Yes, after six months and a grand jury indictment. But the grand jury was wrong, weren't they? You were innocent."

A tangle of emotions threatened to choke him. She believed him. Sweet Charlotte, who had been his friend long ago, whose father had been so very kind to him.

He wanted to grab her right there in her kitchen and kiss her fiercely for looking at him out of those shining eyes, for daring to believe he wasn't everything awful and ugly the world had said he was for nearly two years.

"Why would you say that?" he asked hoarsely, a bid for time as he honestly didn't know what to say.

"Gut instinct," she answered, her voice pitched low. "I've known you for a long time. That was the part that always bothered me about the case against you. You saw firsthand how substance abuse destroyed your mother. I always had a tough time understanding how you could supply illegal drugs to others, after surviving your childhood and seeing the devastation personally."

"I was addicted to painkillers, Charlotte. I never denied that. After my shoulder injury, I tried to play through the pain but discovered it was so much easier to throw a ball ninety-five miles an hour again and again with a little Percocet on board. And then a little more and a little more—and before I knew it, I was taking five or six at a time and couldn't play without them. Yeah, I went through rehab but since I was an addict myself, why is it such a leap to think I would have a problem supplying steroids and painkillers to others?"

"I don't believe it. Pop never believed it either, for what it's worth."

It was worth more than he could ever tell her, but he couldn't seem to get the words out past the sudden lump in his throat.

"So the question of the hour. How did that very large supply of drugs end up in the trunk of your car in the Pioneers parking lot? And why didn't you defend yourself to the grand jury? Your pleading the fifth was as good as a confession in the minds of many people."

He wanted to confide in her, to spill every ugly detail he had pieced together in the year since Jade's death but long habit held his tongue.

"You're not going to tell me, are you?" she finally said when he remained silent.

"Nothing I could say, then or now, would have made

a difference. I had no proof of anything and...several innocent people would have suffered if I had voiced my suspicions."

She leaned against her kitchen counter, and he again felt breathless at the warmth in her eyes, a look he never dreamed of seeing there. He felt as if he had been walking alone in the high desert for months, thirsty, starving, slowly freezing to death, and she had just held her arms wide to welcome him to wander inside by her fire.

"You were protecting someone else. Of *course*. I should have known. Oh, Spencer. Has anybody ever mentioned you have a very bad white knight complex?"

"You're crazy," he murmured, but somehow the husky words came out more like an endearment.

"I'm beginning to agree," she said, her voice thready.

He had no choice in the matter. Not really. He had to kiss her. In the space of a breath, he moved to her and lowered his head. With a sigh, she kissed him and her arms around his neck felt like a benediction.

CHAPTER FOURTEEN

A BREEZE SCENTED with pines and some kind of night-blooming flower fluttered the curtains at her window but he was barely aware of it, lost only in the wonder of her kiss.

Was it only that morning that he had kissed her last? It felt like eons ago, another lifetime. How had he forgotten the taste of her, honeyed and luscious, how perfectly she fit against him, the funny little way she had of splaying her hands across his back as if she didn't quite know what to do with them?

He wanted to shove aside the rinds and bowls, knives and cutting boards, to lift her up onto the work island and bury himself inside the succulent wonder that was Charlotte Caine.

"You are just about the sweetest thing I've ever tasted," he growled.

"It's the fruit," she murmured, her voice low and her skin a luminous, delectable pink. "I like to, um, sneak a taste here and there while I'm prepping."

"It's not the fruit. It's all you."

He kissed her again and she tightened her arms around him, kissing him back with an enthusiasm that humbled him. What had he possibly done in his life that made him worthy of being the recipient of this kind of heated response?

He kissed her until both of them were trembling, until his body was a hard, heavy ache, desperate for completion.

With an oath, he wrenched his mouth away from her and rested his forehead on hers. "I need to go, before I won't have the strength to leave."

She stared into his eyes, and he saw a tangled jumble of emotions there. Foremost among them was a fierce, naked yearning. He wasn't sure anybody had ever looked at him that way. He already wanted her frantically. Seeing that answering hunger just about sent him tumbling over the edge.

"You don't have to. Go, I mean," she whispered.

The implication of her words rocketed straight to his gut, and his mind went blank for just a moment. When she kissed him, her mouth soft and sweet and warm, he gave in to what felt like perfect, beautiful inevitability.

He still meant everything he had said that morning, every reason not to do this. But she trusted him. She believed in him. He couldn't hold back the tide of emotion and need pouring through him because of it.

He deepened the kiss, pressing her back against the counter, devouring her.

"Bedroom?" he growled, long moments later.

She pointed vaguely through a doorway, and he refused to think about the wisdom in what he was doing, he let all the hunger inside him take control. Mouth locked with hers, he swept her up in his arms. He opened the first door he came to and luck smiled on him when he found an airy, feminine room dominated by a queen canopy bed.

He was vaguely aware of lowering her to the bed and following behind, and then all he could think was the sweetness of her mouth, the sexy little noises she made, the heat of her arms around him and her curvy, mouth-watering body beneath him.

This couldn't be happening.

Was she really here, in her frilly, flowery little bedroom, with Spence Gregory? The moment seemed hazy, unreal. Yes. It was him. That was definitely his tongue tangling with hers, his hard thigh nudging between hers, his hand...oh.

They shouldn't be doing this. Some tiny corner of her mind kept whispering that, telling her that this was a huge mistake, but she ignored it. She was on fire. Every touch, every caress, sent sensuous flames licking through her, and all she could think about was *more*.

She arched against his thigh through the layers of skirt and slacks and sparks exploded, a shiver coursing through her as he began to work free the buttons of her blouse. Oh, mercy. Why hadn't anybody told her how very incredible it felt to have his hand against the bare skin of her abdomen? The caress that morning had been so fleeting she hadn't really had time to appreciate it but now his fingers trailed slowly across her body and she wanted him *everywhere*.

She didn't want to think, to analyze why he was here, after he had pushed her away that morning. For now, she only wanted to feel.

Her bra unclasped in the front, and he seemed to have the necessary skill to work it free. And then she lay exposed to him and she shivered, suddenly fearful. Though she had dropped five bra sizes and two cup sizes, she was still big. A memory pushed into her subconscious that had to do with him and her breasts, something ugly and dark.

He didn't seem to mind. He made a low growl in his throat she took for approval, and she shoved the half-formed memory aside. And then he moved his thigh between her legs and more of those delicious sparks shot out. She pushed against the delicious pressure a little and then a little more. Okay, now she was beginning to see what all the fuss was about.

It was all too much suddenly. His mouth on hers, his tongue stroking her, the hard muscles surrounding her. She was close to something she couldn't have explained, pressure building and building, and then his thumb brushed her nipple, his tongue slid along hers, and she exploded, wave after wave of delicious pressure carrying her under....

When she finally caught her breath, she found Spence staring at her, his eyes glittery and dark.

"That was...wow," she managed to say, her voice ragged.

"Funny. That's exactly the word that came to my mind."

"Um, what is a girl supposed to say after that? *Thanks* hardly seems...adequate."

He continued staring at her, his hand sliding away from her. What had she done wrong?

"Doesn't that...usually happen?" she asked, feeling extremely stupid.

He cleared his throat. "A guy certainly hopes so. Any decent guy will make sure of it. Several times, if he can." He edged back a little, hazel eyes locked on hers. "You've done this before though, right?"

She couldn't answer. The words just wouldn't come. So to speak.

At her silence, he continued to stare at her. She might as well have told him she liked to drop-kick puppies in her spare time. The abject shock in his expression made her want to yank the quilt over her head.

"I'm a freak. I know."

"I didn't say that."

"You don't have to say it. I can guess what you're thinking."

She sat up, hooked her bra closed and began working the buttons of her blouse.

He seemed almost openmouthed with surprise. "How can you be—"

"The opportunity never came up, okay?"

She didn't know when she had ever felt this humiliated—and that was saying something, all things considered.

He looked rumpled and gorgeous, and she couldn't believe five minutes earlier her hands had been under his shirt, splayed on the warm bare skin of his back. She remembered that incredible moment of flying and she wanted more.

"Why not?"

She sighed. She really, really didn't want to talk about this, not when she was all loose and relaxed and feeling wonderful.

"I was fat, Spence. You have to remember. So fat you couldn't even bear to go to a girl's choice dance with me."

"Whoa. What?" He raked a hand through his hair, and she saw genuine confusion in his expression. "I remember something about a dance, and you backed out at the last minute. You were sick or something, right?"

Okay, happy feeling gone. "Right. I backed out."

He frowned at her tight tone. "Isn't that what happened?"

"Technically, yes. I canceled."

"What else happened?" he demanded. "If I did something, I'd sure as hell like to know."

Okay, apparently she could slip a notch further down on the humiliation scale. She was going to have to talk about the darkest moment of her adolescence—with the architect of her shame.

All the remembered pain and hurt washed back, inky, bitter.

She couldn't have this conversation with him here in her bedroom, where a few moments ago they had been tangled together so deliciously on her bed.

Without another word, she slipped from the bed and walked back to her living room. After a pause, he followed her.

Oh, how she suddenly longed for the days when men still wore hats. It must have been so easy to just hand a man his hat when a woman was done with him and send him on his way.

"I really don't want to talk about this right now. It happened years ago."

"Why didn't we go to that dance together, Charlotte? Tell me."

He wasn't going to stop. Having grown up with six older brothers, she knew that implacable tone of voice and knew he wouldn't rest until he had wormed the information he wanted out of her. She might as well just tell him, get it over with.

"Fine," she finally said. "We didn't go to the dance because I...I heard you."

He gave her a blank stare. "Heard me what? Can you be a little more specific?"

Amazing how one moment in time could have such a lasting impact on a person's life. She had the entire conversation memorized, burned into her brain as if etched there by a soldering iron.

"It was after school, two days before the dance. Thursday afternoon. You were working at your other job at the hardware store."

It had been a gorgeous April day, she remembered, one of those rare spring afternoons when it seemed the long mountain winter was finally done.

She knew he had a baseball game at another school the next day so she wanted to talk to him Thursday to work out all the details of their date. Though she had looked for him all that day at school, their schedules hadn't coincided.

She had been so excited, she remembered now, beyond thrilled. Dreams sometimes did come true! Spence Gregory had actually said yes when she had summoned every nerve she possessed (and several she didn't) and asked him to the final girl's choice dance of his high school career.

He was graduating in a month and was already close to signing to play major league baseball. This was her very last chance.

She had built up so many plans for that one dance, had invested way too many unrealistic expectations, including the secret, most cherished dream, that he would see her in the awesome new formal dress she'd bought in Denver and declare undying love for her.

She had decided at fifteen that loving somebody who only wanted you for a friend was just about the most painful thing in the world, and she had been desperate to come up with a way for him to see the real her.

"And?" Spence asked now, and she jerked her mind back to the present, to find him watching her with an impatient sort of curiosity.

"I needed to talk to you about what time I was picking you up for the dance. Well, what time my friend Patty was picking you up. We were doubling with her and Matt Barnes, and since she had a driver's license, she was driving."

He doesn't care about that, she told herself. *Get to the miserable part.*

She let out a breath, amazed at how this memory still burned, years later. "When I showed up, Mr. Litchfield told me you were in the stockroom unloading a new delivery."

She could almost feel that moment, the metallic and rubber scent of the hardware store, the squeak of her shoes on the old wood floor, the cramped, tight aisles.

"You were talking with Ronnie McCombs."

He blinked. "Wow. There's someone I haven't thought about in years. Wonder what he's doing now."

"He joined some kind of survivalist cult a few years ago and moved to Montana, last I heard."

"The guy always was a bit of a whack job, as I remember. He was a good team manager but used to drive me crazy, always wanting to know every detail about my life. Parties I went to, classes I was in. He called me a couple years after high school to see if I could get him a job with the Pioneers but I had to tell him I didn't have that kind of pull."

She wondered if Spence had any idea of all the people who had wanted to be like him. Even in high school, he had an air of command that drew people to him, made them instinctively want to be around him. She wouldn't have been surprised if Ronnie McCombs had only taken a job at the hardware store in order to hang out with Spence.

"So what did Ronnie McCombs have to do with us not going on a date?" he asked.

She sighed. So much for hoping he would be sidetracked enough to forget what had originally started the whole conversation.

"When I walked to the stockroom, neither of you noticed me. I overheard him asking who was taking you to the girl's choice dance."

Even after all these years, the pain could still slice sharply.

He frowned. "I told him, didn't I?"

She wanted to make something up, something benign and relatively harmless but couldn't think quickly enough—and besides, he sounded as if he genuinely wanted to know what happened. Maybe it would be cathartic to tell him, sort of like a stomach being pumped after taking poison.

"Oh, yes. You told him you were going with me. You were quite nice about it but Ronnie laughed and said, *'Big fat Candy Caine? Why are you going out with that cow? Man, she's so big her feet don't get wet when she showers. Be careful, man. A guy could suffocate in that rack.'*"

Yes, she had the whole conversation memorized. He could make of that what he wanted.

"He said that? What an ass. I hope I decked him."

She couldn't say anything. Everything would have been different if Spence *had* punched Ronnie—or at least stood up for her. They were friends, after all. She had helped him get a passing grade in English class for four years running. She would have thought that meant something.

"Okay, I didn't deck him." His expression shifted from annoyed to embarrassed as he correctly interpreted her silence. "That doesn't explain why you had to back out of our date, just because some weird little prick made a rude comment."

She picked up a pillow and hugged it to herself, unable to speak. Good grief. Why had she ever started on this excruciatingly uncomfortable conversation? She should have enjoyed her first real orgasm and just kept her mouth shut about her inexperience. If she had, by now said inexperience wouldn't have been an issue.

"That's not everything, is it?" he asked, wariness in his voice, as if he wasn't sure he wanted to hear the rest.

She shook her head, remembering the pain cutting through layers and layers of flesh to the bone, of hearing someone she had loved with all the passion of her silly fifteen-year-old heart say things that devastated so deeply.

"No. That's not everything." She took a deep breath and faced him. "You didn't deck him. You didn't even disagree with him. In fact, you told him it was a pity date. You didn't know how to say no when I asked you out because you owed my father. You and your mother worked for my pop and he had paid for your sports fees all through high school."

"Charlotte."

She went on as if she didn't hear him. "You also added that no way in hell would you be going anywhere near my giant rack. You didn't even plan to dance, if you could avoid it. You were going to wrap things up with me as early as you possibly could, and then you had a date to meet Becky Brinkerhoff at her house by ten. Her parents were out of town, and you planned to spend all weekend getting laid."

He growled a quite appropriate oath but she went on as if she didn't hear him.

"I didn't want my fat butt to be the one thing standing in the way of your fun or be a pity date only because of my father, so I told you I was sick. So did you?"

He blinked. "Did I...?"

"Spend the weekend with Becky Brinkerhoff?"

He didn't answer but she saw the truth in his eyes. How ridiculous, that she could still be hurt by that, all these years later.

She gave a ragged little laugh. "In the interest of fairness to you, I should add that I do remember that most of the time you were nice to me. That was the only time in all the years we knew each other that I ever heard you say anything...hurtful."

"Damn. I'm sorry, Charlotte. I was a bigger ass than Ronnie McCombs."

"It doesn't matter."

"Yes. It does. We were friends. Friends don't treat each other that way."

"I had a stupid crush on you. You had to know."

He raked a hand through his hair but didn't deny he'd known. Mortified heat burned in her stomach and the fat girl who still lived inside her skin wondered if that was the only reason he was here kissing her, touching her, making her feel so many wonderful things—because he had some vague idea that she was one of the few in town he might be able to bring around again. She had worshipped him once. How tough would it be to convince her to idolize him again?

The worst realization of all was that he might not be completely wrong.

She pushed that thought away as unworthy of both of them.

"It doesn't matter. It was years ago," she repeated. The words hid so much misery, she ached for the remembered pain of being fifteen and in love with someone completely unreachable. "I'm not that fat shy girl anymore standing in the doorway at Litchfield's Hardware with my heart in little pieces at my feet. We're both different people."

"I was a prick in high school, cocky as hell—especially toward the end of my senior year when the scouts were already filling my head with all these dreams of how drastically my life would change after I signed that first big contract. That's still no excuse."

He had been nineteen, with the world at his feet. Why would he have wanted to waste even a minute with a homely awkward fat young girl? She still wondered that.

"So back to the point at hand," she went on, before she lost her nerve, "as you can probably imagine, after my one disastrous foray into the dating scene, I wasn't particularly motivated to ask anybody else out after that, and there weren't that many guys around here willing to look past my weight or my shyness."

"What about college?"

"I dated a few times, but there was never any kind of spark. After I came back to Hope's Crossing, I told myself I was too busy building up Sugar Rush to have much of a social life. I was still heavy but by then I had a little more confidence in myself to know that wasn't the sum total of my parts. I'm funny, I'm kind, I'm compassionate."

"I agree," he said softly.

"I knew all that but I still wasn't taking care of myself. When Dylan nearly died in Afghanistan, it was a wake-up call that life was…passing me by, because of my own choices. I knew I needed to make some changes."

"You do look fantastic."

"I still have a ways to go, mainly toning and strengthening, but I finally feel as good about the outside as I should have all along about everything I had to offer on the inside. Things I can't really blame a teenage boy for not seeing."

He reached a hand out and gripped her fingers. "I wish I could put things right somehow. Make up for what I don't even remember saying."

She really should have slept with him when she had the chance, she thought ruefully. They certainly couldn't go there now because she would forever be wondering if he was only trying to *make it up* to her.

"Please. Not necessary. Yes, you broke my heart, but what girl survives being a teenager without having a little piece of her dreams smashed to bits? It's a rite of passage, isn't it? I can tell you that after that, I became far more selective in the caliber of person I trusted with my heart."

"Um, ouch."

Despite the tumult of emotions that lingered from dredging up this painful episode in her life, a little bubble of laughter emerged at his pained expression.

"Sorry. I didn't mean it that way." It wasn't true anyway. She hadn't trusted *anyone* with her heart after

Spence. "Really, I still find it quite amazing you agreed to go with me in the first place, even if it was only out of a sense of obligation to Pop. Plenty of teenage guys in your situation would have been far more concerned about maintaining their Stud of the Year position in the eyes of their friends. They wouldn't have cared about repaying a debt of honor to someone who had helped them and certainly wouldn't have taken it to the extreme of agreeing to go out with any fat daughters."

"Whatever I said to Ronnie, my obligation to your dad wasn't the only reason I said yes, Charlotte. We were friends," he repeated. "You were always good to me, even when I was a jerk. If I hadn't been such a self-absorbed ass, I would have been smart enough to see all those wonderful qualities beneath the surface and asked you out myself."

A tiny corner of her heart wanted to ask if he would have been here with her right now if she hadn't lost eighty pounds but that was one of those impossible questions. They both probably knew the answer, and it didn't matter anyway. She *had* lost the weight. He obviously found her attractive now—and more important, she had the confidence in herself to know she was much more than that.

"Now that we've skipped hand-in-hand down that particularly cheerful memory lane, you should probably go. I imagine Peyton is wondering what's happened to her father."

He made a face. "I doubt that. She's probably hoping I don't come back so she can take my credit card and buy a one-way plane ticket back to Portland."

"She'll come around," she said, grateful the conversation had turned to his daughter instead of her. "She asked me to go with her to a bead class next week. Did she tell you that?"

"She didn't mention it. A bead class. That's a good sign, isn't it?"

"I think so. It's taught by Claire's daughter, Macy, who is around Peyton's age. Maybe this will be the start of a solid friendship that will help her feel more settled here."

"I hope so."

She rose pointedly, wishing again for those darn hats. A nifty fedora would come in really handy right now to get him to take the hint that she wanted him to go.

He did rise but gave her a searching look. "I don't feel like we can leave things like this between us."

"Like what? We cleared the air, we reminisced about old times, we hashed out in great lengths why I'm still a virgin and likely to remain one for some time. I'd say we've covered everything."

He shook his head. "You make me smile, Charlotte. It's been a long time since anyone or anything has."

Before she knew what he intended, he pulled her to him and wrapped her in his arms. After a startled moment, she hugged him back, aware that this soft, sweet tenderness was more seductive than any heated kiss.

"You should know," he murmured against her hair, "I'm not a stupid kid anymore, too self-absorbed to see what's in front of me."

She closed her eyes, already aching at the pain she had a feeling was in store for her, then found just a particle more grit, enough to step away and hold open the door. "Good night, Spence."

He studied her for a long moment then kissed her softly one last time and walked out into the night.

Though she wanted to call him back, drag him to her bedroom to finish what they had started, she firmly closed the door behind him.

She was in serious trouble here. She had mostly mended from that cruel betrayal. It hadn't been easy, and after a brief bout with unhealthy habits that hadn't worked out, she had once more turned to muting the pain with more unhealthy habits, including copious amounts of ice cream and macaroni and cheese.

She was halfway in love with Spence all over again. Maybe even a smidgen more than that, but who was keeping score?

Somehow she suspected he had far more ability now to leave her devastated.

CHAPTER FIFTEEN

THE LIGHTS WERE off at his house. So much for Charlotte's theory that Peyton was pacing the floors, wondering where her father was. She was probably sound asleep in bed, exactly where she was supposed to be.

He sat in the driveway for a moment before going inside, still reeling from the combined force of all the evening's events. How was a guy supposed to process so many shocks in one night?

He didn't know which he found more astonishing. That moment when—without knowing any of the facts—she had expressed complete faith in his innocence would probably hit close to the top. He could have told her the complete story, all the ugly details, but she hadn't needed them. She had quietly told him she believed in him, and the sweetness of it still overwhelmed him.

Then had come that heated embrace that had led to her bedroom and that sudden, unexpectedly erotic climax that had shocked both of them…and her confession that she was a virgin—and all the reasons why, which could squarely be shoved onto his shoulders.

He couldn't believe she would even be willing to *talk* to him after how despicably he had treated her all those years ago. She had carried around that betrayal ever since. He still couldn't fathom how he could have been so cruel. And for what? To look better in the eyes of a little pissant nuisance like Ronnie McCombs?

It made him feel sick and ashamed. He sighed. What the hell could a guy do to make up for something like that? He didn't have any idea; he only knew he wanted to try.

What was it about her? She was undeniably lovely. The prettiness had always been there. He could see that now. That smile had always captivated him. He remembered now how much he used to love teasing it out of her at the café, and she had those blue, blue eyes that made a guy want to do anything for her.

It was more than that. Charlotte Caine was just a good person. Kind, loving, sweet. If he ever doubted it, he only had to look at what had happened a few minutes ago—in the middle of a conversation about how he had been a jerk and broken her heart, she focused her attention outward and wanted to help his daughter.

He felt small in comparison.

He had spent most of his life being a selfish bastard. On some level, all professional athletes had to carry around a fairly healthy ego. Because of his screwed-up childhood, he had learned early to take care of himself by necessity. A mistake of a marriage had done nothing to change that.

Charlotte made him want to be something else. Something better.

He was going to have to figure out a way to make amends for the hurt he had caused her. How the hell was he going to do that? He was pretty certain relieving her of her virginity wouldn't qualify. More's the pity.

He was too tired to figure it out tonight, he decided, and climbed out of his Range Rover. Inside the house, he was surprised to hear a faint murmur of voices and then canned laughter coming from the media room.

Maybe the housekeeper had stayed up late to wait for him, though that would be a first.

When he followed the sound, he found not the starchy Gretel but Peyton, sound asleep on the sofa. MTV played in the background, some kind of lame reality show, by the look of it. In the blue glow, his daughter looked small and delicate, almost frail, with her mother's high cheekbones and slender features.

A few years ago, he might have scooped her up into his arms and carried her to her bed but she would no doubt consider herself too old for that kind of thing. Instead, he sat on the edge of the sofa.

"Hey," he whispered.

Her eyes flickered open and she looked at him, bleary-eyed and confused. For just an instant, she was his little girl again, the one who used to squeal with excitement after he would return from road trips and run to greet him with her arms out and her smile just about taking over her face.

She blinked away sleep and became the all-prickly adolescent again. "What time is it?" she asked.

He glanced at his watch. "Nearly one."

"I thought you were going to be in early." She narrowed her gaze. "Did you go to a bar or something?"

Though he had never been a drinker, Peyton was paranoid about that after Jade's party-hardy example.

"No. I stopped to visit an old friend, and we lost track of time." That was the truth, as far as it went. Maybe not the whole truth but she didn't need to know that.

"How did it go with Gretel tonight?" he asked.

"Fine. Boring. We streamed a really lame romantic comedy, and then she went to bed at like ten."

"She's nice, though, isn't she? You like her?"

She drew her legs up, the sharp bones of her knees jutting through her drawstring pajama bottoms. "I'll be thirteen in three weeks. I don't need a babysitter. But yeah. She's okay. She reminds me a little of Annie. We had her when I was like seven or eight, remember?"

"Didn't she have red hair?"

"Yeah. She wore it in braids a lot. I used to call her Pippi Longstocking."

He smiled, his heart full of love for his child. He certainly had to make amends to Charlotte for one terrible mistake, but he had twelve years' worth to make up for to Peyton.

She yawned and he wanted to tell her to head to bed. On the other hand, there was something comfortable about sitting here in the dark talking with her. They should try it more often. Maybe they could try cooking something together once in a while, too.

"How was the pizza?"

She lifted a thin shoulder. "Okay. A little too greasy for me. Gretel had three pieces, so she must have liked it. There's a ton left in the fridge if you're hungry. I know you love leftover pizza."

It warmed him that she remembered that about him. "Yeah, I do. Maybe I'll have it for breakfast. Meanwhile, you need to get to bed. I was going to carry you up but I didn't think you would appreciate it."

"Good guess."

She rose and started padding in her big fluffy slippers toward the stairs. He followed along. "Charlotte told me you were going to a bead class this week. That should be fun. She's taking you?"

"Yeah. I asked her. She said she didn't mind."

"Knowing Charlotte, she's probably thrilled at the chance to help."

She smiled a little and headed for the stairs. With one foot on the bottom step, she turned back. "An old friend, huh? Is that what Charlotte is?" she asked, a knowing gleam in her eye.

Unbelievably, his face suddenly felt hot. He didn't quite know how to respond to this sort of teasing from his daughter but found he didn't mind it.

How would she feel if he started dating Charlotte? he wondered. Her mother had been gone a year and before that, Peyton must have known they hadn't had any sort of marriage.

"I've known Charlotte since she was younger than you are. I'd say that puts her squarely in the category of an old friend, wouldn't you?"

"I guess," she answered. "But I don't go visit my old friends at midnight."

He snorted and shook his head. "Go to bed, Peyton."

"I'm going. I'm going."

As she headed up the stairs, he had to face the truth. Charlotte *was* certainly an old friend. But she was rapidly becoming something much, much more.

"NOW THAT YOU'VE picked the beads you want to use for the first pair of earrings you'll make, I'm going to teach you a few basics."

Charlotte watched Macy Bradford give a reassuring smile to the group of four girls around Peyton's age at the worktable. "I know it can be scary at first but, I promise, it's easy once you get the hang of it."

She went on to explain how to make a simple loop out of a headpin and Charlotte, sitting at another worktable nearby, beamed at Claire.

"Listen to her. She's a natural."

"I know, right?" Claire couldn't have been more proud. "I should have thought of this a long time ago. Girls that age don't want to sit and listen to an old lady like me tell them what looks cute, but from Macy or Taryn, it's a completely different story."

"She's doing great. They all look like they're having a wonderful time."

Charlotte was still a little worried about Peyton. Though she had smiled a few times, she seemed pale and more quiet than usual, while the other girls had been very welcoming to her.

"It was sweet of you guys to come and give her moral support," Claire said to Katherine, Evie, Charlotte and her sister-in-law, Angie.

"She doesn't need our moral support." Angie smiled. "She's a natural."

"I'm not here for moral support anyway," Charlotte insisted. "I've been desperate for new beaded hoop earrings and a necklace to go with the blouse I bought last week."

"I love those colors together," Claire said.

As she worked, Charlotte tried to shed her worry about Peyton. It really was relaxing to sit here working while she listened to her friends talk and the chatter of the girls next to them.

"There are so many cool beads in here," Peyton said

at one point. "How do you ever pick the ones you want to use?"

"That's the hardest thing about working here." Taryn Thorne, Evie's stepdaughter, walked over to check on Macy's class. "I can find something to make out of everything we have in the store."

Taryn was older than the girls in the beading class. She had just finished her senior year and was heading to college in the fall. Everybody loved Taryn. A few years earlier, she had survived a terrible accident that nearly killed her and had emerged from it with a strength and compassion amazing in one so young.

The younger girls in Macy's class probably just admired her because she was pretty and stylish and always sweet to everybody.

"Look at that, Peyton. You did it," Taryn exclaimed. "Your first pair of earrings!"

"Awesome," Peyton confirmed. "That was so easy. I want to do another pair."

Macy laughed. "Watch out. Now you're hooked, just like the rest of us."

Macy and Peyton rose to pick out more bead combinations that might work for earrings. They had only walked a few steps when Peyton stopped in front of a glass display case near both worktables.

"Wow. What a pretty dress," Peyton stated.

The crystals handsewn to the wedding dress caught the light and reflected it back around the room.

"It is, isn't it?" Claire said, a rueful sort of pride in her voice. "Too bad nobody has ever worn it."

"Why do you still have Gen Beaumont's wedding dress hanging in your store?" Angie asked. "It's been over a year since her wedding plans imploded, for heaven's sake."

Claire sighed. "I've tried to give it back to her a dozen times, but she won't take it. She claims she never wants to see the thing again. Laura wouldn't take it, either. Anyway, none of the Beaumonts have paid me the final amount for the beadwork. Until they do, I'll keep it on display here. It is some of my best work."

Charlotte fought down a laugh. Claire could be sweetly generous most of the time, but when it came to business, she could also be feisty and pragmatic.

"That girl is going to end up in some serious trouble if she's not careful," Taryn said grimly. "Charlie tells me all kinds of stories about her. Apparently, she's running wild in Europe, dating any playboy she can find, spending all kinds of money. I guess Mayor Beaumont has just about had enough. He's ready to yank her back home."

"Watch out, Hope's Crossing," Katherine murmured.

"How is Charlie these days?" Charlotte asked. "He used to ride his mountain bike to Sugar Rush all the time, but I haven't seen him in a long time."

Taryn's smile was soft and rather dreamy. Charlotte didn't miss the worried look both her grandmother Katherine and her stepmother sent her way. "He's good. Really great. We talked via Skype last night, as a matter of fact. He's going to summer semester, trying to hurry through his generals. He likes UCLA a lot, though he misses the Rockies."

"What's he studying?" Charlotte asked.

"He wants to go into criminal law. He's got two more years left of his undergrad."

"Criminal law? Really?"

"His time in youth corrections really changed his life," Taryn said. "He wants to make a difference."

Charlie Beaumont, Genevieve's younger brother, had been driving the vehicle that crashed, injuring Taryn and killing another teen, Charlotte's friend Maura's daughter Layla. Charlie had spent eight months in juvenile detention for driving under the influence, a sentence many people in town still considered too lenient.

"Hey, Taryn," Macy called. "Can you help me show them how to make a beaded hoop? You have such a better eye for color than I do."

"Sure." Taryn walked back over to the girls' table with that slightly lopsided smile, one of the few lingering effects of the months and months of rehabilitation therapy she had endured.

After she left and the attention of the younger class was fixed on Taryn, Claire turned to Charlotte. "How is Peyton settling in?" she asked in an undertone. "Do you think she's enjoying the class?"

"She's really hard to read," Charlotte answered, concerned a little at how pale Peyton still seemed. She wanted to ask if the girl felt ill but she had a feeling Peyton wouldn't appreciate being the center of attention.

"She's a funny little thing," Charlotte said. "My heart really breaks for her. She's trying so hard to hate it here but I think it's not working out as well as she would like."

"How about her dad?" Katherine asked. "How is Spencer settling in?"

An image of her wild response to his kiss the other night flashed in her head, and she could feel her face heat. "Um, fine, I guess."

Why did every conversation around town seemed to circle back to him? A person might think nothing else of interest ever happened inside the city limits.

"I hear Harry donated a bunch of money to A Warrior's Hope," Katherine said.

"So I understand," Charlotte answered.

"The word is, Harry isn't the only one putting up the big bucks. Mary Ella told me Harry's pledge was dependent on Spencer matching the same amount."

Charlotte looked up, shocked. "Really?"

"You didn't know? Mary Ella said the only reason Harry is so willing to open his wallet is because Spence is so committed to A Warrior's Hope. He doesn't think it has a chance of failing."

Spence had said nothing of making a big donation to the organization on Saturday night. The colors of beads seemed to merge in front of her in a shimmery rainbow. Why hadn't he mentioned it? Oh, it was difficult to protect her heart when he continued to sweep her legs out from under her like this.

"He's not quite the villain we all want to think, is he?" Angie asked.

"No," Charlotte answered softly, eyes burning with emotion. She looked back down at her beads, unable to bear the scrutiny of their gazes.

When the chimes on the door rang out, she was grateful—an emotion that turned to surprise when she saw the beloved figure who walked in.

"Pop!" she exclaimed. "What are you doing here?"

Dermot gave a hearty smile. "I brought you all a bit of pie. We made too many blackberry and chocolate cream today and I was trying to think what to do with them when I remembered you had this class today. Thought you ladies might be able to help me get rid of it."

He turned his considerable Irish charm on the girls, who giggled. Charlotte was amused to see her father looked anywhere but at Katherine, who was concentrating quite fiercely on the intricate braided seed-bead necklace she was making.

Charlotte didn't understand why the two of them didn't just get it over with and go on a date. Theirs had to be the slowest courtship in Colorado.

She had to wonder how her mother and father had ever gotten together and managed to conceive seven children if Pop could be this shy and awkward around a woman he was interested in, but she found it endearingly sweet, too.

"What an unexpected surprise," Charlotte said with a grin. "I can't imagine why you would think of *us,* completely out of the blue like that."

He gave a stern look, fully cognizant of the reason for her teasing. "If you don't want them, I'll take them back to the café."

"You will not," Claire said. "You wouldn't deny a pregnant woman, would you? I've had a craving for a piece of your blackberry pie for weeks. How did you know?"

Dermot gave his charmer of a smile. "Just a guess, my dear. Would you like me to cut them now or just leave them for you when you've got a moment?"

"Now works for me," Claire said. "Macy, what about your group?"

"We could all use a little break, I think," Macy said.

For the next few minutes, String Fever was busy with the sound of chatter as everyone filled their plates. Peyton didn't take a piece, Charlotte noticed with concern, and wondered again if the girl was feeling ill.

"I'll have just a sliver of the blackberry," Charlotte said to Dermot. "No whipped cream."

She had learned she could eat anything in moderation, as long as she didn't overindulge. Another lesson of the past eighteen months was that she stuck to her new healthy eating efforts much better if she didn't deprive herself of anything she really craved and Pop's pie was close to the top of her list.

"Mmm. Dermot. This is fantastic. How do you always get that crust so perfect every time?" Angie asked.

He and Alex's oldest sister talked for a few moments about high-quality ingredients and dough temperatures.

When their conversation lapsed, Katherine finally spoke to Pop. "How is Dylan doing after his surgery in Denver?"

He glanced at her, eyes wide. "How did you know about that?"

She shrugged her elegant shoulders. "I bumped into him at the grocery store."

"And he told you he had a procedure?" Dermot looked shocked and Charlotte didn't blame him. Dylan was notoriously closemouthed, even with his family.

"He didn't want to, but I can be…persuasive."

For the life of her, Charlotte couldn't figure out why Katherine didn't turn her skills of persuasion to convincing Pop they should take their relationship a step further.

"I noticed he was favoring the prosthetic," she went on. "He was trying to lift a big bag of dog food, and I stepped in to help him."

Oh, Charlotte would bet Dylan loved that, having the very elegant city council member—and senior citizen— help him with his dog food.

Charlotte had been trying to back off and give her brother space since his return from Denver but perhaps she needed to take a drive up Snowflake Canyon after they finished here to check on him.

"He's holding up," Dermot said. "Of course, it's not been easy for him but he's tough. He's a Caine, isn't he?"

Charlotte's mouth tightened. She adored her father but he sometimes saw what he wanted to see. He hadn't seen anything wrong with making a thirteen-year-old girl a four-scoop ice cream sundae after school or a big batch of buttered popcorn every time they watched a movie. To him, seeing her eat a hearty meal had meant he was doing his job as a parent.

She wondered if he really couldn't see how Dylan spent his days drinking and feeling sorry for himself.

"Well, I suppose I've done my duty to the lovely beaders of Hope's Crossing and should be on my way."

"Thanks a million for the pie. It was divine," Claire said. She got up and kissed Dermot's cheek, earning a blush.

"You're very welcome, my dear. Next time you get the craving, come into the café. I'll make sure we've always got a slice of blackberry just for you."

He said his goodbyes to everyone and hugged Charlotte. She smelled the familiar scent of Old Spice and his particular kind of laundry soap and felt a wave of love for her father, who had done his best after raising six sons to comfort a grieving daughter the best way he knew how.

"The pie was a nice touch," she whispered in his ear. "Maybe next time, you should think about flowers. She's particularly fond of white roses."

"Oh, hush," he said with another stern look, then picked up his pie tins and the leftover paper plates he'd brought along and headed out of the bead store.

"Well, that was a fun break," Angie said. "But I'm afraid I'm never going to finish this tonight if I don't hurry."

They all returned to their beading. About a half hour after Pop left, Charlotte was nearly done with her necklace and was holding it up to show Claire her progress when she heard Peyton ask where the bathroom was.

"Through that door, on the other side of the office," Macy told her.

"Thanks," Peyton said.

Something was wrong, Charlotte thought with concern as the girl walked past their table. She reached a hand out, intending to touch her arm and ask if she was ill, but before she could make contact, Peyton's steps faltered, her eyes rolled back in her head and she toppled to the floor.

CHAPTER SIXTEEN

IT WAS A STRANGE, surreal moment. Time seemed to grind to a halt and nobody moved for perhaps half a second, then Charlotte slid her chair back so hard it toppled over. She rushed to Peyton, whose eyes were now closed, long lashes fanning her cheeks.

"Peyton? Honey, are you okay?"

It was one of those lame questions people asked in moments of crisis. The girl was obviously *so* not okay. She was pale and appeared limp and lifeless, though Charlotte could see the rise and fall of her thin chest under her T-shirt.

She felt paralyzed by shock.

"What happened?" Claire asked. "Do I need to call the paramedics?"

Charlotte's medical background was limited to the Red Cross babysitting class she took in junior high school. Panicked fear and a vast sense of inadequacy overwhelmed her at the sight of the pale, deathly still girl on the ground. What should they do?

"Let's check out the situation first."

Relief surged through her at Evie's calm voice taking charge of the situation. Evie would know what to do. She *did* have a medical background, had spent years in California as a rehab therapist.

Evie knelt beside her and picked up Peyton's hand to

feel her pulse. "Steady," she murmured. "A little slow but steady."

"What happened?" Charlotte asked. "She was fine one moment, the next she just…fell."

"She apparently passed out," Evie said. "The question is, why. Peyton, can you hear me? Peyton? Look. She's starting to come around."

Peyton's lashes started to flutter and after a moment, she opened her eyes all the way. Her brow furrowed as she took in the ring of faces around her. She didn't seem to know why everyone was huddled around her.

"What…what happened?" she asked, a little color beginning to seep into her cheeks.

"Good question," Charlotte said, striving for calm. "You passed out, my dear."

"I…fainted? Oh." She scrambled to sit up but seemed too light-headed.

"Just wait for a moment, until you catch your bearings," Evie said.

The girl looked more embarrassed than concerned to find herself flat on the ground, which Charlotte thought an odd reaction.

"I'll be okay in a minute," she said. "Could I have a drink of water?"

"Of course," Claire said quickly. She hurried to the water cooler she had recently installed for her employees and customers.

She brought a cup to Peyton, who drank it slowly. When the girl lowered the cup, she gave a hesitant smile.

"I should be okay. Usually, I only need a minute or two to sit down and catch my breath and then I'm fine."

"Usually?" Charlotte seized on the word. "Has this happened before?"

"A few times. It's no big deal."

"I noticed you didn't have any pie. When was the last time you ate anything?" Evie asked.

A curiously guilty expression crossed Peyton's thin features. "I don't know. I had some toast for breakfast, I think. Oh, and some crackers for lunch."

A terrible suspicion grabbed hold of Charlotte's mind and wouldn't let go.

"You probably need something to eat," Evie said.

"I've got a protein bar," Charlotte offered. She grabbed her purse off the back of her chair and rifled through, grateful she never went anywhere without something to snack on. She had learned early that her worst binges came when her blood sugar dipped.

She handed the bar over, and Peyton nibbled one corner of it then closed the wrapper again. Charlotte studied her, trying to think if she had ever seen her eat anything. She remembered that day at the café, right after Spence and his daughter had moved to Hope's Crossing. Peyton had eaten a big hamburger—and then had gone into the bathroom and thrown up, claiming illness.

She was so very skinny. And when they had gone on a bike ride, she had been too weak to go very far. That must have been why she turned back.

Charlotte had worried about the girl's weight but had assumed she took after her supermodel mother's angular shape. She had never considered Peyton might have an eating disorder.

She had no proof now, she reminded herself. Only speculation and worry.

Nevertheless, she pulled her phone out. "What's your dad's cell number?" she asked, trying to keep her voice calm.

Horror sent more color seeping into Peyton's features. "Why do you need that? He doesn't need to hear about this. I just fell down."

"You didn't fall down," Evie corrected gently. "You passed out. And it sounds like this isn't the first time, is it?"

"It's nothing."

"Probably not. But whatever the reason, you really need to be checked out by a doctor. Your dad needs to know about this."

She looked around at the other girls, who were watching her with worried eyes. Tears filled Peyton's eyes and she scrubbed at them sharply. "Don't call him! This is so stupid. I'm fine now. See?"

She rose a little unsteadily and walked to the worktable and back. All of them could see she was shaky and weak.

"I'm sorry, Peyton. I am," Charlotte said. "But your dad has to know. He can then make the decision about taking you to a doctor. What's his number?"

She remained stubbornly quiet. Charlotte was thinking she would just call the recreation center and have them track him down when Taryn handed her a phone.

"This is Peyton's phone. She left it on the table. Her dad's number is probably in there."

"This is stupid! Oh, I hate it here. Why can't you all just leave me alone?" Peyton said. She sank into a chair and buried her face in her hands. Charlotte wanted to pull her into her arms but Macy and Taryn and the other girls stepped in before she could.

She had a feeling Peyton would appreciate comfort from her peers more than Charlotte anyway right now.

She grabbed Peyton's phone and took it to Claire's office. She quickly found Spence's number and made the call.

He answered after three rings. "Hi, hon. How's the bead class? Are you ready for me to come get you?"

She shoved down the heat fluttering through her at his voice. "This isn't Peyton. It's Charlotte. I'm using her phone."

"Charlotte! I was just thinking about you. What a surprise." And not an unwelcome one, she could tell by the warm tone of his voice.

She wanted to just close her eyes and savor that, but she pushed it away, focusing on what was far more important right now.

"I'm at the bead store, Spence. With Peyton. She's had an...incident."

He paused for only a heartbeat. "What's wrong?"

"I don't know. Maybe nothing but...she just passed out. She was unconscious for maybe a minute, maybe two."

Time had been such a blur in the craziness of the moment, she really wasn't sure.

"She fainted? Seriously? She's okay now, though, isn't she?"

He didn't seem to grasp this could be a major issue. She hoped she was wrong but all the signs seemed to point otherwise.

"She's awake and she's talking. She's angry that I'm calling you."

"Big surprise there."

"She wants to sweep it under the rug, Spence. I think she doesn't want you to worry about her."

"But you think I need to be worrying," he guessed astutely.

She sighed. "When she woke up, she didn't seem at all shocked to find she had passed out. She says it has happened before."

His voice sharpened. "What? When? She's never said a word!"

"She didn't elaborate, only said she had passed out a few other times but was usually fine after a moment or two."

"What the hell? Why wouldn't she think her father might want to know she's toppling at the drop of a hat?"

The hurt in his voice made her ache for him and their complicated relationship—and for the further complications she was very much afraid were in store.

"Spence. I have to ask. I want you to think about this carefully. Is there any chance Peyton might have an... eating disorder?"

Her words were met by a vast, awkward silence. "Why would you ask that?" he finally asked.

"I've just rarely seen her eat much more than a bite or two."

"She has a small frame and a small appetite to go with it," he answered, a hint of defensiveness in his words and his tone. "She eats, though. Once in a while, she eats like a horse. You've seen her, haven't you?"

"The one time I've seen her eat more than a smidgen of food was that night at the café. And then she immediately went into the bathroom and threw up."

"You think she's throwing up her food? Deliberately *starving* herself?"

"I have no idea. I doubt she would talk to me, and I'm not at all an expert anyway," she answered.

"No. You're not."

The words stung like a slap, and she wondered if she

should have kept her mouth shut. No. Not when a young girl's physical and mental health might be at stake.

"My friend Evie Thorne is here. She's a physical therapist, not a doctor, but she seems to think the fainting spells are concern enough that Peyton really should see a physician."

He was silent again for a long moment. "Okay. Okay. Whatever I need to do. I have no idea of any doctors around here but I'll figure something out."

"My general practitioner is wonderful. Susannah Harris. I've been going to her forever. I can call her clinic, see if she might be able to squeeze in Peyton tonight."

It was five-thirty, almost past office hours, but she knew Susannah would agree to see the girl, given the circumstances.

"I'm leaving the rec center right now. Give me fifteen minutes to make it down the canyon."

"Okay."

"Charlotte. Thank you for worrying about her."

"I really hope I'm wrong, Spence. I hope this is an anomaly. Maybe she's just got a virus or her blood sugar dipped or something."

"I'm going to hang on to that for now."

He hung up and she used her own phone to quickly call Susannah's office. When she explained the situation, Susannah's receptionist—a woman who had once dated her brother Jamie, as had half the women in town—patched her through to the doctor immediately.

Charlotte quickly went through the situation with the doctor. "I don't want to presuppose you toward any particular diagnosis, but can I share my concern?"

"Of course," Susannah said.

"I barely know the girl, really, so I might be completely off base here."

"Charlotte, just tell me your thoughts."

"She's painfully thin. I've rarely seen her eat anything and, when she does, it's either a very small amount or it's far more than a girl her age ought to need. Feast or famine, I guess you could say."

"You think she has an eating disorder."

"I don't know. It worries me."

"That's understandable, given your own issues with food. I should tell you, there could be any number of reasons for syncope—that's the medical term for fainting—in a young girl. Hypoglycemia, anemia. At the nasty end of the spectrum would be a cardiac issue. We can look at everything when I examine her."

"Thanks, Susannah. I owe you."

"A lovely box of that almond toffee fudge I love would probably cover it."

"Done," she said promptly and hung up.

When she walked back out, she saw the others had tried to return to some level of normalcy. Everyone was back at her table, though she intercepted several solicitous looks toward Peyton.

She handed Peyton her cell phone. The girl pocketed it and gave Charlotte a wary, resigned look that was blessedly free of resentment.

"Did you call him?" she asked.

"Yes. He's on his way from the recreation center. He's taking you to be seen by a doctor in town. Her name is Susannah Harris and she's very nice."

"I don't need a doctor!" she said again, hands clenched on the pliers she had been using to close a jump ring. "Why is everybody making such a big deal? I just fainted."

"You'll like Dr. Harris," Taryn said. "She's pretty awesome."

"Really?"

If the very cool Taryn Thorne gave someone the stamp of approval, apparently that was enough for Peyton.

"Yeah. That's who I go to for most of my follow-up stuff now, though I still have a neurologist in Denver."

"Why do you have to go to a neurologist?" Peyton asked, curious.

"That's a super long story," Taryn said. "I'll tell you about it while we wait for your dad. If we hurry, you can finish that cool bracelet you were working on."

"If you want," Charlotte offered, "I can make some matching earrings, then you can wear everything to the doctor's office."

"Thanks," Peyton said. She gave a tiny tentative smile of gratitude, but it was enough for Charlotte.

WHEN SPENCE PUSHED open the door to the bead store, he was met with an immediate assault to his senses. Color and light, the soft murmur of female voices, awash in mingled feminine scents of lavender and vanilla. Under other circumstances he might have found it appealing in a funny sort of way but right now he couldn't think of anything but his daughter.

His gaze found her instantly, her dark-haired head bent toward a silky golden-blond head he recognized as Charlotte's. Something tugged inside him at seeing them together. It just felt…right, in a way he couldn't have explained.

Nobody noticed him until the door closed behind him and chimes rippled through the room.

About ten female faces turned toward him but he barely registered anyone else except Peyton and Charlotte.

His baby girl looked a little pale but otherwise normal. Why the hell had she fainted?

"Oh. You're here." Charlotte was the first to speak. "That was fast. Hang on. Can you give us one quick minute? We're almost done."

He didn't quite know how to respond to that, especially after he had quite possibly broken several traffic laws in order to rush here as fast as he could.

"Never get in the way of a girl and her beads." Katherine Thorne stood up and he dutifully kissed her cheek. He had hung out with her son, Brodie, a bit back in the day, though Brodie had been a killer skier and Spence could rarely afford a lift ticket unless somebody else paid for it.

Katherine had always been kind to him and Billie. Katherine had paid for their groceries once, he remembered, when Billie had tried to use expired food stamps at the grocery store and then had started to get belligerent when the checker had refused them.

He had thought more than once when he was a kid that if he could have picked a different life, he would have wanted Katherine for a mother, then had cursed himself for the disloyalty.

"Isn't the doctor waiting for us?" He aimed the question at Charlotte.

"Yes. We're almost done. Peyton's making a bracelet, and we wanted her to finish it before she goes to the doctor. Can I get you a drink of water?"

He was about to say no, he didn't need a damn drink,

but he suddenly noted Charlotte was trying to send him the kind of nonverbal message that always baffled him.

"Uh, sure," he said, hoping he had guessed right.

She smiled a little and gestured for him to follow her to the water cooler in one corner, away from the tables.

"Sorry. She really is almost done," she said in an undertone. "The beading seemed to help distract her a little. It was Taryn's idea. Peyton was...agitated about having to go to the doctor."

"Tell me again what happened?" He pitched his voice low to match hers.

"It was so strange. She got up to use the ladies' room and one minute she was walking, the next she was on the floor, completely unresponsive. I don't know how long she was out, to tell the truth. Claire thought it was less than a minute. I thought it had to be much longer. Regardless, when she woke up, she wasn't particularly surprised and said it had happened before, more than once."

"This doesn't make any sense. If she's been passing out, why wouldn't she tell me?" He hated the gulf between him and his child. The hardest part for him was that he thought things were getting better.

The day before, they had gone for a hike and to the movies. She hadn't yelled at him all day, though she had seemed abnormally subdued—and she hadn't eaten popcorn, he remembered, only a couple of the Jolly Joes he liked.

"I'm sorry I don't know," Charlotte answered, blue eyes filled with compassion. He wanted to drown in her concern for his child, just hold her close and hang on.

"I can tell you that girls hit a certain age and it can sometimes be tough to talk to their fathers about...

female things," she went on. "I remember I got my first period a few months after my mother died. I can't even tell you how mortified I was when I had to tell Pop I needed certain supplies."

She understood, far better than he did, what his daughter was going through.

"Will you come with us to the doctor?" he asked on impulse.

She stared. "Me?"

"Peyton likes you. She trusts you. She might be willing to say things to you and the doctor she doesn't feel comfortable saying to me."

She glanced at the table where Peyton worked, and he saw concern mingled with a clear affection that warmed him. "She doesn't like me very much right now. Not after I insisted on calling you."

"I'm sure she understands deep down you were only looking out for her." He pushed his advantage. "I want you there. Peyton isn't the only one who needs you."

Her gaze flew to his. After a pause, she nodded.

"Yes. All right. Let me clean up my work project and grab my bag."

A few moments later he ushered Peyton, wearing her lovely new bracelet and earrings, to the car. Charlotte followed behind and Spence held the door open for both of them.

"You're coming with us?" Peyton said in surprise. "I thought you were just leaving at the same time."

"Do you mind? I think your dad needs the moral support."

Pure genius on her part, to put the onus on him. He was beginning to think he was crazy about Charlotte Caine.

"I don't want to make you uncomfortable, though," she went on. "If you don't want me there, I can always hang out in the waiting room. Or walk home, for that matter."

"No. It's fine. I'm glad you'll be there."

Charlotte sat in the front seat next to him and Peyton climbed into the back. After they pulled out of the parking space, his daughter leaned between the seats.

"Do you think the tests and stuff will hurt?" she asked Charlotte warily.

"Maybe. I hope not, but I honestly don't know. Dr. Harris will probably draw blood, at least, which can be just a little stick and then done. I *can* tell you Susannah is just about the most gentle person I know, if that helps."

A moment later, Spence pulled into the clinic parking lot, a low-slung building near the gleaming new hospital.

He opened Charlotte's door first and helped her out. "Thank you for being here," he murmured to her as he went to open Peyton's. "You were right. I'm the one who needs somebody to hold my hand."

She shook her head, fighting a smile, and he was overwhelmed by the calm peace she offered.

Susannah Harris was sitting behind a glass partition, talking to a woman he vaguely recognized as someone he had known when he had lived here before, though he couldn't have drummed up her name for the life of him.

Dr. Harris looked just as he remembered, lean and athletic, with short-cropped gray hair and snapping brown eyes.

She didn't wear a lab coat, just jeans and a T-shirt, with a stethoscope around her neck.

She was someone else who had been kind to him.

It was another of those humbling moments. All this time, he had been thinking he hated Hope's Crossing and couldn't wait to leave and make something of his life. Now that he was back, he was confronted everywhere he went by people who had done nothing but try to reach out to an angry lost young man.

He kissed her cheek. "Susannah. You're looking as lovely as ever."

Her weather-etched face creased into a smile. "And you're just as full of B.S. as ever."

She stepped away. "Hi. You must be Peyton. I'm Dr. Harris."

Peyton seemed to find the low pile of the commercial-grade blue carpet fascinating. "I told everybody, I don't need a stupid doctor," she muttered.

"Then it's good you've got me, isn't it? I don't mean to brag but I'm a pretty *smart* doctor."

Spence saw surprise and even a little amusement in the quick glance Peyton flashed the doctor.

"Come on into an exam room. We'll try to get you out of here quick."

"I can wait out here," Charlotte said, hanging back a little, obviously reluctant to intrude.

Peyton shook her head. "No. It's okay. You can stay. I would...like you to stay."

After a pause, Charlotte smiled and gave Peyton a little hug and the sight of them together made his chest ache, for reasons he couldn't have explained.

CHAPTER SEVENTEEN

FORTY-FIVE MINUTES—and several vials of blood, an intensive physical exam and a lengthy interrogation of Peyton—later, Spence stared at Dr. Harris.

"You want to keep her overnight? Are you serious?"

"Her electrolyte level is low. Dangerously low. We need to get this young lady hydrated and the fastest method to do that is through an IV. This way we can keep an eye on her, run an EKG and bring in a couple specialists."

Peyton's panicked gaze flashed among him and the doctor and she gripped Charlotte's hand tightly. "I'm not sick. I just passed out."

He put aside his own dismay at the news and ran a hand over her hair, aware she needed comfort and support right now. "It's only for a night, kiddo. I'll stay with you the whole time, I promise."

"They won't let you do that, will they?"

The disbelief in her voice burned. Did she really think he didn't care enough to help her through this? He had so much ground to make up, a dozen years of mistakes.

"I'll sleep on the floor of your hospital room, if I have to," he promised her.

"It won't come to that," Susannah said, her tone dry. "All the rooms at Hope's Crossing Hospital have a convenient couch that folds down into a bed. I can't promise it will be comfortable but at least it's better than the floor."

Peyton glowered at all of them. "I hate this. I'm not sick."

Dr. Harris gave her a long, steady look that was firm but not without compassion. "You might not be sick, but you haven't been eating the way you should, have you?"

His daughter's gaze fell and she shrugged. "I don't know. I guess not."

Dr. Harris touched her hand gently. "Your body needs the right kind of food to survive. Now I need to talk to your father out in the hall for a moment while we make some arrangements. Will you be okay in here?"

"Does Charlotte have to leave, too?"

"I'll stay right here," Charlotte promised.

"Thanks," Peyton said.

Deeply grateful for Charlotte's presence, Spence followed the doctor out into the hall.

"In addition to the dehydration," Susannah said bluntly, "I believe Peyton is on her way to being malnourished."

He stared at her. "How can she be malnourished? This isn't some third-world country. I feed her. The housekeeper feeds her. I can't believe this."

"Spence, she's about fifteen pounds underweight for her demographic and her teeth are already showing signs of enamel breakdown."

Everything inside him went still.

"So she does have an eating disorder?" He couldn't even comprehend how they had come to this grim pass in the space of only a few hours.

"That's a tough thing to diagnose in a forty-five-minute office visit. Let's start with getting her hydrated and go from there. You're lucky. We've got an excellent psychiatrist here in Hope's Crossing who specializes in eating disorders. I'll have her do an assessment in the morning, while Peyton is an inpatient, and we can get more information," Dr. Harris said.

"Forget about the tests and assessments and specialists. What do you think?"

"The signs are there," she admitted, after a moment's hesitation.

"Why the hell didn't I see them?"

She touched his shoulder. "To use familiar terminology to you, you had several strikes against you in that department. I'm speaking in generalizations here. Forgive me. But fathers as a rule aren't as observant when it comes to their daughters' eating habits and any physical changes. Add in a move to another state and a new job and I think it's completely understandable if you overlooked this."

He shouldn't be at all surprised, he thought on reflection. If Peyton did suffer from an eating disorder, the seeds for it may have been sown early. Jade had always been a control freak when it came to her food, dieting, weighing each mouthful, obsessing about calories.

He remembered now that she had made more than a few derogatory comments about Peyton's eating habits. He should have said something, damn it, but by that point everything he said that could remotely be considered criticism, constructive or otherwise, set Jade off into a screaming fit.

He should have stepped up anyway. Instead, he had chosen avoidance, thinking he was keeping the situation from escalating.

Regrets did him no good, not when he had a troubled daughter to help.

"This is completely new territory for me. Can we... fix it?"

"*We* can't. *We* are pretty helpless, except when it comes to making sure she receives the tools she needs to understand the problem. This one is up to Peyton."

He didn't know when he had ever felt so powerless. Susannah must have sensed it. She placed a hand on his arm again. "Spencer, your daughter strikes me as a very smart girl. When she understands the harm she's doing to herself, I hope she'll see how important it is to take care of herself. She's going to need ongoing counseling. In some cases, parents opt for intensive in-patient counseling, but let's tackle one thing at a time. As I said, we'll start by hydrating her and getting some decent nutrition in and go from there."

When they returned to the exam room, they found Peyton and Charlotte huddled over Peyton's cell phone, looking at photographs of her friends in Portland.

"It's going to take me a few moments to set things up with the hospital and find you a room. Meanwhile, you can hang out in here or in the waiting room. Whatever is more comfortable."

"This is fine." Spence made the decision for all three of them.

"Peyton, can I get you anything?" Dr. Harris asked.

"Maybe a blanket. I'm a little cold," she answered.

"I have just what you need. Give me a second."

The doctor returned a short time later with a white blanket. "This is my favorite thing about feeling under the weather. We have a blanket warmer here in the office. I'll tell you a secret. Sometimes I take one out just to sit and do paperwork. Don't get too comfortable, though. I'll be back in just a moment."

She left again and Peyton wrapped in a blanket and curled up on the exam bench. She had dark circles under her eyes, Spence saw, and her skin looked so translucent, he could see the pulse of blood beneath it.

He became aware that Charlotte was also gazing down at his daughter, and he felt as if a few more strands braided together in the subtle connection between them.

"Thank you for being here," he murmured to her. "I'm sorry we took up your whole evening. You probably had plans."

She shook her head. "Nothing concrete. I was thinking earlier that I would drive up to Snowflake Canyon to check on Dylan, but I can call him. He might even answer his phone. And I can always go up another night."

She had far more experience than he did with ill people. This was new to him. Before this, his hospital experiences had been limited to the terrifying but exciting period around Peyton's birth and his far more miserable shoulder surgery.

"It's going to take you time to settle into a hospital room," she said. "Can I get you anything? You're going to need dinner. Evie texted me a little while ago that she brought my SUV over. I can go pick something up for you."

She was worried about him. Her friends cared for her and she, in turn, wanted to take care of him. He didn't quite know how to handle that. Typically, only the people he paid bothered to worry much about his needs.

He glanced over and saw Peyton's eyes were closed, her breathing even.

"I'm not at all hungry right now but I probably will be.

I guess I should be modeling healthy eating—fueling my body when it needs it."

"I'll pick something up for you and be back as soon as I can."

She walked over to Peyton. When she saw his daughter was sleeping, she brushed a gentle, barely there hand over her hair, and Spence felt a lump rise in his throat.

"I don't want to wake her. Just tell her I'll meet you at the hospital once you're in a room."

"I will."

As she turned to leave, he couldn't help himself. He reached out and folded her into his arms and held on tightly, drawing all the comfort he had needed from the moment she had called him to come to the bead store.

"Charlotte. Thank you. The words are ridiculously inadequate. Just…thank you."

Her smile seemed a little strained but she hugged him back for a moment, then stepped away just as Susannah Harris bustled back in with an armload of papers.

THE SUN WAS beginning its gradual slide behind the mountains, sending long shadows across the parking lot when she walked outside the clinic to her car. Evie and Taryn were such sweethearts, to bring her car over for her. What a lucky stroke that she had thought to leave her keys with them before she had rushed out with Peyton and Spencer.

She stopped for a moment, lifting her face to the warmth of the August evening, staggered by all that had happened in such a short time.

Her heart ached for Peyton. Poor thing, to feel she had to starve herself in order to control a world that had become terrifying and tumultuous. Charlotte should have spoken up. She could kick herself for staying quiet when she first began to fret about the girl's thin bones and unnatural pallor.

Eating disorders could be debilitating, even deadly, if not addressed in time. She could only pray Peyton would be able to accept help, work through her demons and return to a much healthier attitude toward food.

She opened her car door and climbed inside. A small bag rested on the front seat and when she opened it, she found the necklace she had been working on, completed now, in addition to a matching bracelet and earrings.

Oh, her dear friends, probably putting aside their own work to finish her project. Emotions surged through her, hot and intense, and her chin wobbled. Tears began to seep out—tears of gratitude for the friends she loved, tears of worry for Peyton and for Spence…and a few for herself.

She was becoming entirely too enmeshed in Spence's life. She remembered that moment in Susannah's office when he had clung to her, and she had wanted to give him all the strength he would need to help his daughter over this tremendous hurdle.

What was she going to do when he didn't need her help anymore with A Warrior's Hope, with Peyton?

She couldn't bear to think about it.

HER ERRANDS TOOK longer than she intended. In Hope's Crossing, she could rarely just run into a store and pop back out. The relationships here were too intertwined for that, and usually she hated being rude to neighbors and friends by refusing to stop and chat.

Normally she loved the quiet pace, the friendly conversation, but this time she was filled with a sense of urgency.

She stopped first at her friend Madeline's clothing store and managed to squeeze inside just before closing.

Fortunately, Maddie had just what Peyton needed in the trendy teen section where Charlotte knew Taryn and her friends liked to shop.

Next up, she stopped at Sugar Rush and just narrowly avoided being tangled in a dispute her assistant manager was having with one of the seasonal workers.

Afterward, Charlotte was fortunate enough to find a parking spot halfway between the café and Dog-Eared Books & Brew. In the interest of conserving time, she called in her order to the café and headed for the bookstore while she waited for the food to be ready.

She was in the young adult section poring over her options when Maura spotted her and waved.

She headed over, her arms full of books to be shelved. The bookstore owner craned her neck to look into the basket, snugged into the crook of Charlotte's elbow. "Wow. Your reading tastes have taken a little eclectic detour lately. I like it."

Charlotte laughed. She supposed it would look odd to someone else. She had thrown in a couple teen-oriented magazines, a Jane Austen book she and Peyton had talked about once, a young adult romance novel she had heard the girls discussing over the beading, and copies of *Sports Illustrated* and *Outside* magazines for Spence.

"Not for me. I'm stocking up for a…friend." And said friend's father, she added silently.

"Oh, of course. These must be for Spencer Gregory's daughter. How is she? Claire stopped in a little while ago and told me there was an incident at the bead store.

She said you were going with her and Spence to see Su-sannah Harris."

"She's a little dehydrated," she answered, careful not to offer too many details that weren't hers to provide. "They're keeping her overnight to give her fluids and run a few tests. I'm sure she'll be fine."

She wasn't certain of any such thing but the words seemed just the banal sort people used in these circumstances.

"Is there anything I can do?" Maura asked.

Charlotte lifted her basket. "You've done it by keeping your bookstore so well stocked. I never doubt I can find what I need here."

Maura laughed. "I do what I can. Please let me know how she's doing. I hope it's nothing serious."

Worry was a heavy anchor on Charlotte's heart. An eating disorder was extremely serious in a young girl. She could struggle with it the rest of her life if she wasn't able to confront and overcome some of her emotional issues around food.

"I will. Thank you." She glanced at her basket and thought about everything else she had purchased. "You've always got cool tote bags in here. You wouldn't happen to have something an almost-thirteen-year-old girl might like, would you?"

"Oh, I've got the perfect thing!" she exclaimed.

She led Charlotte over to a display by one of the registers, where two slouchy, brightly colored fabric bags hung. The oversize bags were funky and cute, exactly what she needed, sewn out of strips of contrasting fabric and decorated with beads and embellishments.

"Gorgeous! Why haven't I seen these before?"

"They just came in. And don't ask me where I got them. I can't tell you that."

She raised an eyebrow at her friend. "Seriously, Maur? You think I'm going to go behind your back, steal your supplier and start selling cool handmade bags over at Sugar Rush?"

Maura laughed again. "That's not what I meant. I can't tell you because I have no idea. It's all very hush-hush. I received six of them in a delivery from an anonymous source, asking if I would put them in the store to see if they would sell. If they do, I'm supposed to send whatever portion of the profit I felt was right to a PO Box in Denver. I was also sent an anonymous email address to reorder."

Intriguing. Anonymous, nonsolicited consignment sales weren't exactly a traditional way of doing business. "What if they don't sell?"

"My instructions are to donate them to Goodwill, apparently. I don't think that will be an issue. I only put them out yesterday, and I've sold all but these two."

She thought the bags were cute already but the hint of mystery behind them only added to the appeal. "I'll take them both," she said promptly. She could always use another bag.

Maura grinned. "Guess I'm sending an email to the mysterious Madame X to order more."

Maura took her personally to an empty register to check out—and threw in a brownie and a couple of the huge wrapped oatmeal raisin cookies she sold at the coffee counter portion of her store.

"Take these to Spence. He came in earlier in the week and grabbed one with his coffee."

That was why Dog-Eared Books & Brew thrived

in an economy where so many other bookstores were struggling, Charlotte thought. That personal touch. Maura noticed those little details about her customers and cared enough to make sure they were happy.

After Maura rang her up—insisting on a store discount, despite Charlotte's objections—she helped Charlotte arrange the books and magazines in the bag.

"Oh, good. I was hoping there would be a little room leftover," Charlotte said. "I've got some cute pajamas and socks in the car for Peyton."

"Nice touch," Maura said. She came around the checkout counter and walked with Charlotte to the door. She handed over the bag, a little frown between her eyes. "Okay, I have to ask. I've bitten my tongue long enough. What's going on between you and Spence?"

Charlotte's stomach fluttered. She had been expecting this question from one—or *all*—of her friends for some time now.

"Nothing. Not really. We're…friends."

She thought of everything else: the tender, almost desperate way he had held on to her at the doctor's office; those wild, fiery kisses; that moment in her bedroom when she had experienced the most intense pleasure of her life.

She cleared her throat. "They live on Willowleaf Lane near me. Peyton and I have struck up a friendship. She's a sweet girl who has been through a very rough time."

"I can only imagine."

"I see something of myself in her," she admitted. "I lost my mom when I was about her age, too, and… well, I understand how it feels to lose somebody you care about."

Maura squeezed her shoulder. "If she needs anything

else, let me know. I understand that particular feeling myself."

She gave her friend a hug and headed out into the fading sunlight toward the café, where she knew her order should be ready by now.

She intended to simply grab the food and dash back to the hospital, but the first thing she heard when she walked through the door was her father's slight Irish drawl.

"Why, if it isn't my favorite girl. Twice in only a few hours."

Oh, fudge. She didn't have time to talk to him or endure an interrogation. Of all the people in town she didn't want wondering about her sudden involvement in the lives of Spence and Peyton, her father would have to top the list. She wasn't sure he would understand at all—especially when *she* still didn't quite fathom their complicated relationship.

"Hi, Pop." She kissed his cheek.

"Have you come to have dinner with me then? What a lovely surprise."

"No, I'm afraid I'm only picking up a take-out order."

"Ah, you've come to break my heart. You want my food but not my company."

She shook her head at his teasing. "I seem to recall we just had family dinner together last week."

It was tough to get all her brothers together when they were all going in different directions but Pop did his best.

"I suppose you're off. Where are you going tonight? Are you heading up to see our Dylan?"

She thought about making something up but Dermot had an uncanny ability to see through any prevarication.

"I had planned to but…things changed. You know Peyton Gregory, right?"

"Spencer's daughter? That wee little thing who wouldn't have any of my pie earlier today?"

That moment seemed like hours ago. Amazing how a life can change in just a short time. When Peyton wouldn't even touch any of Pop's delicious pie, Charlotte should have figured out something was up.

"Yes. After you left, she had a little incident and passed out. She's been to see Susannah Harris, who is admitting her to the hospital overnight, just for a few tests. I'm taking dinner back to Spence, along with a few little things to make the night more comfortable for Peyton."

Her father's handsome features twisted with worry. "Oh, the poor girl. How very thoughtful of you to worry over her. You would have made your mother so proud, my dear."

She wasn't sure her father would be giving her that approving look if he knew just how tangled her relationship with Spence had become.

"I should go. He's bound to be hungry."

"We can't have that." Pop grabbed the brown paper take-out bag. Before he handed it over, he slipped in a couple extra bags of chips. "Do you think Spencer would care for a piece of pie?"

"Maura gave me cookies and a brownie. He probably has all the sugar he needs for one night. Thanks, though."

She kissed her father on the cheek again and hurried out, the throbbing of her ankle reminding her she still wasn't wholly healed herself.

Spence would be astounded if he knew how many

people were concerned about him and his daughter, she thought. Too bad *he* hadn't been the one running around town receiving all these well-wishes.

Traffic was sparse as she drove back to the hospital. She loved this time of evening, when people were settling in for the night with their families or out having dinner together somewhere.

The brick and glass hospital gleamed in the summer sunset, looking modern and elegant surrounded by those timeless soaring mountains.

When she was a girl, the old redbrick three-story Miners Hospital had served the medical needs of Hope's Crossing but this new state-of-the-art facility had been built a few years earlier. It made a vast improvement.

She recognized the woman behind the information desk and smiled. "Hi, Tina."

"Hey, Charlotte. What can I help you with?"

Her clipped tone hurt. They used to be good friends in high school—fat girls tended to stick together—but they had lost track when Tina Butler had moved away after high school. The other woman had only been back in town about six months and seemed cold, almost resentful, every time Charlotte tried to make a friendly overture.

She didn't have any idea why. She really hoped it had nothing to do with the fact that Charlotte had fought so hard to lose weight while Tina, four children later, had gained at least a hundred pounds since high school.

"I'm looking for a patient's room. Peyton Gregory."

Tina typed something into the computer. "She's in room one-sixteen. Take a left."

"Thank you."

She didn't say *You're welcome.* "That's Smoke Gregory's daughter, isn't it?"

"Yes," Charlotte said warily. It wasn't exactly a secret.

"Oh, that must explain why she's in the behavioral unit then. Crazy mother kills herself, father is addicted to drugs. What else can you expect?"

The shock of the unnecessary cruelty slid under her skin like a filet knife. She straightened, as angry as she had been in a long time when she considered the pain Peyton had endured.

"I don't know. I guess I would expect common human decency, not to mention professional discretion. Or does the hospital condone its employees making out-of-line personal attacks on the people who come here for care? I'll have to ask the administrator next time he comes to dinner at Pop's."

She gripped her bag tighter and walked away, her heart pounding in her chest. She never lost her temper but she could feel it pulsing through her.

Coming after the care and concern everyone had showed this afternoon, Tina's attitude was a harsh reminder of what most of the world thought of Spence. How did he cope with that, day after day, especially when he wasn't guilty?

Why his silence? It was a maddening question that had haunted her all weekend. Why wouldn't he admit he hadn't been dealing drugs to his teammates? Who was he protecting?

Somehow she didn't think even Peyton knew the truth. If she did, perhaps she wouldn't have the same negative attitude toward her father.

The door to Peyton's room was slightly ajar. She peeked her head around and was grateful she hadn't knocked loudly or barged in with a cheery hello. Peyton was asleep, curled up in a ball on the bed, her dark hair a vivid contrast to the white sheets. Spence sat in a chair beside her, head back and eyes closed.

With some vague intention of dropping off the goodies then sneaking out again, she tiptoed into the room. She set the bag of food from the café and the funky tote beside what looked like a dinner tray on the little wheeled table beside the bed.

She turned to go then froze when a strong hand grasped her wrist.

A tiny shocked "Oh" escaped her before she could choke it back and her gaze flew to his features, where a corner of his mouth had lifted at the sound.

He pressed a finger to his mouth and uncoiled from the chair like a big cat stretching in the sunlight, with an athletic grace of which he was probably completely unaware.

He gestured back through the doorway and she followed him, grabbing the bag with his dinner as an afterthought.

She handed it to him out in the hall. "How is she?"

"Seems to be fine. You saw she dozed off again, which is a little concerning, but the floor pediatrician stopped by and seemed to think it was no big deal."

"That's a relief."

"We've mostly been settling in and having the IV hooked up." He held up the bag. "Thanks for the meal. It smells delicious."

"You're welcome. Pop sends his best wishes. And when I stopped at the bookstore to find some things to help Peyton pass the time, Maura was also concerned for you. She sent some treats and said something about how you particularly enjoyed the oatmeal cookies the last time you stopped for coffee."

"Really? That's...very kind."

He seemed taken aback and she wondered how long it had been since people had treated him with anything approaching kindness. "Everyone is very concerned for Peyton. People here worry about each other, Spence."

"I guess I'm finding that out." He held up the bag of food from the café.

"You should probably eat that sandwich while it's fresh."

"You know, I'm suddenly starving."

She knew that feeling from her time with Dylan at the hospital—long stretches of time when she couldn't even contemplate the idea of food, then random moments of famished hunger.

"I saw a dinner tray in the room. Did Peyton eat?"

He nodded, clearly troubled. "She didn't want to but I told her it beats a tube up her nose."

A small waiting area just outside Peyton's room had vast windows overlooking the mountains. Spence took one of the chairs and reached into the bag.

"Two wraps. I'm not *that* hungry. I hope one is for you."

She wasn't hungry, either, but was hesitant to leave him yet. "I'll have half of one," she said.

They ate in silence. She could only eat a few bites and noticed Spence finished about half a sandwich before wrapping it closed again.

"Do you think she'll be okay?"

The worry in his voice whispered its way into her heart. She could find no evidence of the cocky, arrogant

Major League baseball star, only a father concerned for his child. *Love made us all vulnerable,* she thought.

She covered his hand with hers. "I could answer you with platitudes, I suppose. *She's got you in her corner. She's tough enough to move past this. She's a fighter.* Those have their place, and all of them are true in their way. But it's really up to Peyton."

He turned his hand over and twisted his fingers through hers. "What the hell is a guy supposed to do in these circumstances? This is completely out of my range of experience."

She squeezed his fingers. "You move forward, step by step. What else is left?"

He sighed and seemed to take some small measure of peace from either her words or her touch. She wasn't sure which and it didn't matter anyway.

They sat that way for a long moment, alone and silent in the waiting room, their hands entwined. A subtle intimacy, dangerously sweet, seemed to weave around them, and she didn't want to move for fear of jostling away whatever comfort he might be finding.

Finally he sighed again. "I should probably get back in there," he said after a minute. "She might wake up and be afraid when I'm not there."

Their reappearance in the room was enough to startle Peyton awake. She gave them both a shaky smile, and her gaze landed immediately on the tote Charlotte had purchased at the bookstore.

"Wow. Great bag."

Charlotte had to chuckle. Peyton was in the hospital hooked to an IV and various monitors and still found room to be fashion-conscious.

"I hoped you would like it," she said with a smile.

"Me? You bought it for me?" Peyton looked thrilled and suddenly very, very young. "Thanks. Thanks a lot."

"You're welcome, honey." She leaned in and hugged Peyton. Out of the corner of her gaze, Charlotte was aware of Spence watching her with an odd expression that sent warmth all through her.

What was she doing here? she wondered as she straightened and moved away from the bed. She didn't have a place in their lives. They were only here for six months' penance, and then she had no doubt Spence would be back on his feet with other opportunities ahead of him.

She was going to make a complete fool of herself by falling in love with him all over again.

For an instant, she was once more fifteen and fat, standing in the crowded aisle at the hardware store, listening to him rip her dreams to shreds.

She did her best to compose her expression as Peyton started rooting around inside the bag Charlotte brought her.

She pulled out the pajamas first, cute and trendy, the fabric a pattern of rulers and boulders adorned with cartoon bubbles saying "You rock" and "You rule."

Peyton gave a sleepy sort of smile. "Wow. I love them! Can I put them on now? This thing is awful."

"You might want to wait until a nurse can help you with all the wires and tubes," Charlotte replied.

"What else?" Peyton asked, digging into the bag. She seemed delighted with everything, exclaiming over the books and the magazines, which Charlotte had struggled over to find a few that didn't show the typical emaciated teen girl images.

"Thanks. Thanks a lot for everything." Peyton clutched the pajamas to her chest.

"You're very welcome. I'm going to get out of your hair so you can rest."

"You don't have to," Peyton protested.

"I'm afraid I do."

If nothing else, she thought it was probably good for Spence and Peyton to spend this time together without her in the way.

"I'll see you later." She leaned in again and kissed the girl and then turned to go.

"I can walk you out," Spence offered.

"Not necessary. It's not a very big hospital. I don't think I'll get lost. Anyway, you should stay here with Peyton. She needs her dad right now."

"I can at least walk you off the unit," he said.

When she couldn't come up with a good argument to that, she merely shrugged and walked out of the room.

Back in the small waiting area, she wasn't prepared at all when Spence pulled her into another hug. She wrapped her arms around his waist, sensing it was as much for his own benefit as anything.

"I don't even know how to thank you for everything you did today," he murmured. "I would have been completely lost without you."

She mustered a smile. "It was nothing I wouldn't do for any friend," she said, placing just a tiny pointed emphasis on the last word.

Hazel eyes studied her intently and she thought she saw something there, a soft light that, quite ridiculously, made her want to cry. He tucked a stray lock of hair behind her ear. "I'm glad you still consider me that, after everything."

He leaned in and kissed her forehead, and at that moment, she knew it was too late. She was already in love with him, and her heart ached for the pain she knew was in store.

CHAPTER EIGHTEEN

SO MUCH FOR good intentions.

The next afternoon, Charlotte left work early to change her clothes after an accident with one of the copper pots she used to mix her fudge. A big chocolate smear dripped down the front of her Sugar Rush T-shirt, dried now, since she had ended up taking a call from a distributor that lasted another forty-five minutes.

Her plan was to slip into something clean before running over to the hospital to check on Peyton.

She pulled up to her house and walked back down the driveway to check the mailbox. Just as she pulled out what looked like a stack of bills and the latest *Eating Light* magazine, an SUV approached.

When she recognized Spence's Range Rover, she grew extremely cognizant of the smear of dried chocolate dripping across her right breast, blocking the *s* and *u* of Sugar Rush.

She subtly blocked it with the magazine and approached the passenger side, where she was pleased to see Peyton.

"Hello!" she said through the window Peyton opened. "I was just on my way to change my clothes so I could come to the hospital to see you. Looks like I would have been too late."

"Looks like," Peyton said, the words clipped and tight.

Charlotte frowned at the transitory mood and glanced through the vehicle's interior at Spence, who shrugged.

"How are you feeling today?" Charlotte asked.

"I don't think I have a stupid eating disorder," she burst out. Charlotte had the distinct impression that wasn't the first time the girl had uttered those words in the past twenty-four hours.

"The doctors say otherwise," Spence said mildly. "You're not eating and you've been making yourself throw up. You're severely anemic and in danger of being malnourished because of it. But we're going to work on it, aren't we?"

Peyton shrugged. "I guess."

To Charlotte's surprise, Spence turned off the engine and climbed out of the vehicle. Peyton put on earbuds as soon as he left, as if she had only been waiting for an excuse.

"So things aren't going that well?" Charlotte guessed.

"The eating disorders specialist spent almost two hours with her this morning. She's quite confident from the medical tests and her time with Peyton that she has anorexia. It's in its early stages, apparently stemming from a variety of things but especially the trauma of losing her mother suddenly and under such traumatic circumstances. I didn't help things, apparently, by uprooting her from everything comfortable and moving her here."

"I'm sorry," she murmured, saddened by the guilt ringing in his voice.

"We're starting an intensive therapy program. I say 'we' because apparently family therapy is part of the equation. So that should be fun."

He didn't look happy about it but she was confident

he would do whatever was necessary for his daughter. "You'll get through this," she said. "Just remember you're getting your daughter the help she needs to have a healthy, happy life."

"I know. But the process isn't necessarily pretty. Your care package was a lifesaver last night, for both of us."

"Good. I'm glad it helped."

He seemed to hesitate. "I hate to ask this, after you've already gone out of your way to help, but I could use another favor."

She would really have preferred to have this conversation in a clean shirt. "Of course. How can I help?"

His warm smile threatened to turn her insides as gooey as melted chocolate. "You might want to hear me out before you instantly agree."

"I figure I can always say no later," she said.

"True. Okay, I got a call today from Lisa, my assistant at the recreation center. I didn't have a chance to tell you in all the craziness yesterday but we're trying to arrange a media event in two weeks to introduce A Warrior's Hope project and break ground for the cabins."

She stared. "Already? Harry just agreed to donate the land a few days ago."

"He moves fast when he finds a cause he likes, apparently. If we want to finish by Christmas, we have to fast-track everything. I've managed to call in some favors with various old teammates to help generate a little more publicity. They've got one free Friday before the season ends, which is two weeks from today, so that's when we're going to do the ribbon-cutting."

She had no idea how he had moved so quickly but she couldn't deny she was impressed. "It sounds as if you've got everything under control. Why would you need me?"

Something flashed in his eyes for just a moment before he banked it.

"What do you think are the chances I could convince Dylan to show up at the ribbon-cutting?" he asked after a moment.

She let out a rough laugh. "About as likely as me winning the Boston Marathon. Actually, my odds are probably slightly better right now."

He sighed. "I was afraid of that."

"I'm sorry, but he thinks the whole thing is a big waste of time. I really thought he would be excited to have it here but I don't think he's in a place right now to see the possibilities in anything."

"I believe you. But I have to try, don't I? Having him there would be a very effective way to illustrate the need for A Warrior's Hope." He paused. "I was hoping that if the two of us teamed up to try convincing him, he might have a tougher time saying no."

"I doubt that would matter to him. He's very good at saying no to whomever he wants right now."

"How do we know if we don't ask, though? That's the advice I'm always giving Peyton. The only sure way to fail is not to try at all."

"Sounds like a locker room motivational poster to me."

"Little Miss Smarty Pants." His tired smile took away any sting from the words. "I'm going to ask him anyway, fully expecting him to say no. I would love to have you with me. You never know. He might surprise us both."

She sighed, absolutely certain Dylan would never agree to come be on display at some fund-raiser for a veterans program he thought was a waste of time in the first place. How could she refuse to help Spence, who was going to so much trouble for A Warrior's Hope, in large part because her brother's situation moved him?

The bigger question was, how could she possibly hope to protect her fragile heart from him? Every time she decided to extricate herself from his life, he tangled her right back up again.

"Yes. I'll go with you. When were you planning to speak with him?"

"As soon as we can. Time is ticking away here, obviously. I would have said tonight but I don't feel right about leaving Peyton with Gretel when she's only just been released from the hospital."

"Tomorrow?"

He hesitated. "I doubt I'll feel any better about leaving her tomorrow. Hell, I'm probably not going to want her out of my sight for months."

"Why don't you bring her along, then? Dylan won't bite and the drive up Snowflake Canyon is beautiful this time of year. The high-mountain wildflowers are finally blooming."

"That works. Let's plan on tomorrow night, depending on how Peyton's doing, naturally. I'll pick you up about six. Will you be done with work by then?"

"Yes. That should be fine."

With any luck, she thought as he climbed back in his SUV and headed for home, she wouldn't have a chocolate-covered chest.

"I STILL DON'T know why I have to go to therapy, but I guess Dr. Low is nice enough," Peyton said.

Spence shifted his gaze briefly from the mountainous road to Charlotte, leaning into the space between the two front seats in order to better hear Peyton from the backseat.

She smelled delicious, that flowery, spicy vanilla scent he found so intoxicating. He had a wild urge to reach across the space that divided them and press his mouth to that warm hollow at the base of her throat.

Her gaze shifted to him and he had to wonder what she could see in his expression that made her breath catch.

She quickly turned her attention back to Peyton but not before a tide of color soaked her cheekbones.

He couldn't remember ever finding himself this drawn to a woman.

Charlotte cleared her throat. "Yes. Well, you have to give them a chance to help you."

"I guess. I definitely don't want to go into an inpatient program. My friend Misha's cousin had to and she stayed for*ever.* That would totally suck."

Spence still wasn't convinced that inpatient wasn't the best route to go but the eating disorders specialist in Hope's Crossing seemed to think their current course of action was sufficient. He would trust her for now but keep all their options open.

"You'll have to tell me where I'm going," he said after a minute.

Charlotte gazed out the windshield. "Oh. Right. It's not far now. Shortly after you head around the next bend, there should be a turnoff on the left with a red mailbox."

He had forgotten how beautiful Snowflake Canyon could be. This high up, the wildflower season came late. Early August was apparently the perfect time to see their brilliant display. He recognized a few—Indian paint-brush, purple lupine, the multicolor hue of columbine.

He had come up here on fishing trips with Dermot and his sons, he remembered. That seemed another life-time ago.

"Thank you again for coming with us."

Charlotte sent him a sidelong glance. "I really hope you're not expecting much. Dylan barely wants to show his face at the grocery store in town. I just can't see him wanting to go on display for the cameras at a media event. Even before he was wounded, that prob-ably wouldn't have been his scene."

Spence fully expected to fail but stubbornly refused to give up.

"It's worth a shot, right? What have we got to lose, besides a few minutes spent enjoying a beautiful drive?"

She didn't answer, just pointed to the turnoff, where a dirt road wound through the trees. He turned off, grate-ful for the high suspension of the SUV on the bumpy track. The road was actually quite well maintained but a few good-size rocks gave them a solid jostle.

"What is he going to do up here in the winter?" he asked Charlotte.

She made a face. "Good question. The main road is plowed year-round these days because of all the new va-cation homes up this way, and Dylan bought an old trac-tor to clear his own driveway. He seems to think that's adequate but I'm not sure he remembers how much more snow they get up here than we have down in the valley. I have visions of him being socked in for weeks."

"I'm sure your father and brothers would come dig him out if need be."

"True."

On impulse, Spence rolled down the windows and the brisk mountain air blowing in was filled with hauntingly familiar scents from his childhood—sage and pine and the sweetness of the wildflowers.

"The house is just up there," Charlotte said. They turned around a cluster of bushy pine trees and he saw a sprawling log house with a couple outbuildings, but no neighbors that he could see in any direction.

He could imagine the stars up here at night would be incredible. There was something to be said for the isolation. At least a guy had room to stretch, to think. To heal.

Through the open window, they suddenly heard a loud, mournful baying.

"What is *that?*" Peyton exclaimed.

Charlotte smiled a little. "That's Tucker, my brother's dog. He's a great guy. I think you'll like him."

"He sounds like his heart is broken or something," Peyton said.

"He's a black and tan coonhound. They're known for their musical bark. Sometimes they actually sound like they're singing."

"You call that singing?"

"That's his way of saying hello," Charlotte said. "He's just happy to see me."

Spence noticed the hound's owner didn't look as thrilled. Dylan sat on the porch, his feet propped up on an overturned feed bucket and a beer can in his hand.

His repose was deceptively casual. On closer scrutiny, Spence noticed a wary alertness that only eased slightly when Charlotte climbed out of the passenger side of his SUV.

Dylan had been an Army Ranger. Spence imagined that wariness was second nature to him.

A couple chickens pecking at the dirt squawked at them and fluttered out of their way when Spence and Peyton climbed out of the SUV after Charlotte.

Dylan looked resigned as he watched the three of them approach the porch. Spence wondered briefly if he should have left Peyton home. She was still fragile, trying to come to terms with her condition and the new reality. She really didn't need the stress of a confrontation with Dylan if Charlotte's brother was in the mood to be recalcitrant.

"Well, hey. If it isn't our resident baseball star," he said, his voice only slightly slurred. Spence probably wouldn't even have noticed it if he hadn't had so much experience interpreting his mother's level of intoxication.

"Hey, Dylan. Nice place you've got here."

He wasn't being sarcastic. Despite its tumbledown appearance, the house had a certain rustic appeal.

"I like it." He sipped at his beer, looking menacing behind his eye patch, and Spence noticed several empty bottles piled up on the edge of the porch. Again, he wished he hadn't brought Pey.

"You remember my daughter, Peyton. I think you met her a few weeks ago at the café."

Peyton seemed to be having one of those shy moments. She stood close to him, which wasn't such a bad thing from a daughter who usually preferred to pretend he didn't exist.

To his relief, Dylan seemed to pull in a few of his prickly quills. "Hi, again, Peyton. Did I tell you I played ball with your dad, once upon a time? Never could get a hit off him in practice, even though I batted over .400 against everybody else."

He held up his empty sleeve and gestured to the eye patch with what was left of his arm. "I sure couldn't get a hit off him now."

"Yeah, well, I can't throw worth sh—er, *beans*—anymore so you never know," Spence said.

For some reason, Dylan offered up a rusty laugh at that. Charlotte, petting the grateful dog, looked startled.

"Have you had dinner?" she asked, holding up the bag she had carried on her lap all the way up the canyon. "Dad sent along lasagna tonight and some of the café's garlic bread sticks. Shall I put it in the refrigerator for you?"

He scratched just above his ear. "Sure."

When she went inside, the three of them seemed locked in that awkward tableau, with Dylan on the porch and Peyton and Spence standing just at the bottom of the stairs. Spence decided not to wait for an invitation to sit down. He walked up and pulled apart a couple stacking plastic chairs, positioning them near Dylan's spot.

The chairs were dirty but Peyton didn't seem to notice. She seemed fascinated by Dylan again and hadn't taken her gaze off him since they had climbed out of the car.

Jade hadn't tolerated imperfection so Peyton had been surrounded by physically ideal people all her life. It was good for her to see the gritty reality, Spence figured.

Dylan seemed aware of Pey's interest. To Spence's relief, he didn't take another swig of his beer, setting it down on the table beside him instead.

The dog came over to investigate the strangers. Pey seemed nervous at first but then relaxed a bit, petting the dog's long, droopy ears.

"What's his name again?" she asked Dylan.

"Tucker," he answered gruffly.

"Charlotte said he was a coonhound. Does that mean he hunts raccoons?"

"He'll tree any who dare come around, but I don't hunt. Not anymore."

Charlotte came out of the house before Peyton could ask another question. Since Dylan had three guests and two guest chairs, Spence rose to let her take his and leaned instead against the porch railing.

She sat down, her hands folded primly in her lap. She looked edgy and uncomfortable. Spence was sorry he had brought either of the females. He should have just come up here alone to talk to his old friend man-to-man.

"I'm going to take a wild guess that you've all obviously got some kind of agenda for driving up here." Dylan seemed to be sobering by the second. "What do you say we just skip the polite time-wasting chitchat and get straight to the point?"

Spencer had to appreciate the brusque, no-nonsense approach to life. Was that the sort of clarity that came from nearly dying on the battlefield?

Charlotte opened her mouth to say something but Spence gave his head a subtle shake. He decided to start things off with what she probably would consider a non sequitur.

"Do you remember that time we went hiking above the Piedras?"

Dylan stared at him for a second then gave that rusty-sounding laugh again. "Man. I forgot all about that. How old were we?"

"I don't know. Fourteen. Maybe fifteen."

"Even then you had a hell of an arm," Dylan said. He reached for his bottle but didn't drink it, only held the long neck loosely between his fingers.

"What happened?" Peyton asked. Spencer had to consider it a good sign that she was interested in something besides herself for a while.

"I used to go fishing once in a while with Dermot and his boys."

"I went, too, sometimes," Charlotte said.

He remembered now. She had been a tomboy in the years before her mom died. He had a flash of a memory of her tagging along on a couple fishing trips, chubby and cute with honey-gold braids sticking out of a baseball cap turned backward.

"I don't think you went on this one. Seems to me it was just Dermot, Aidan, Jamie and the two of us."

"Pop heard about some secret spot clear on the other side of the state and just had to drag us all there." Dylan wasn't quite smiling but he didn't look quite as dangerously grim, either.

Dermot Caine had been so good to include Spence on their family outings. It was astonishing, when he thought about it. What had Spence been to the man, really? Just the son of a drunkard employee he should have fired years earlier, but Dermot had always been kind to him.

When he thought of all the man had done for him, he burned with shame that he had moved away from Hope's Crossing without looking back. He hadn't made so much as a phone call or sent a Christmas card.

"What happened?" Charlotte asked, forcing him to push away that particular guilt for now.

"Well, after a morning of fishing near our campsite, Dylan and I decided to walk upriver a bit to check out this lake that was supposed to be full of German browns."

"Is that a fish?" Peyton asked.

He smiled. His daughter's education was sorely lacking. Before the summer ended, he would have to take her fishing. He could only imagine how she would love that.

"Yeah. Really tasty trout. Anyway, it was probably a mile hike from our campsite through the sagebrush. We headed out and had been gone maybe fifteen minutes when all of a sudden—"

Dylan cut him off before he could finish. "So there I was, walking along, minding my business, when suddenly Smoke yells, *Don't move!* Next thing I knew, this cantaloupe-size rock comes whistling toward me at about a hundred miles an hour."

"I couldn't throw a hundred miles an hour then. And I topped off at ninety-five, anyway," Spence said with a bit of a smile. "That particular rock was probably going no more than seventy-five."

"All I saw was a blur," Dylan said, one corner of his mouth lifted in a half smile. "You try having a rock catapulting toward you that fast and see if you can mentally clock it."

"I never heard this story," Charlotte said, gazing at her brother as if she couldn't quite believe he was actually interacting with them, and almost smiling in the process.

"I don't get it." Peyton frowned. "Why did you throw a rock at him?"

"I wasn't aiming at Dylan. I was going for the five-foot-long rattlesnake he was about two seconds from stepping on."

Charlotte's eyes widened with horror. "Did you hit it?"

"Bull's-eye," Dylan said. "Knocked him into another rock and popped the head clear off. As you can see, I lived to fish another day."

He said the words with an ironic twist and dangled his longneck over the armrest of his chair.

"Do you remember what you said? You said you owed me. Anything I wanted."

"I'd give you my left arm but I'm afraid it's already taken."

Charlotte drew in a sharp breath, and Spence fought the urge to say something harsh.

"I never took you up on that, remember?" he said instead.

"Something tells me my luck is about to run out." Dylan spoke again with that bitter irony.

Spence shouldn't have come here. Charlotte was right. Dylan would never help them. But they had driven all this way, so he plowed on.

"The week after next, we're having a media event to introduce our A Warrior's Hope program and break ground for the cabins we're building near the recreation center. Several athletes are flying in to help us draw attention to the program. Ty Jacobs. Jess Roman. Lucky Lucero. I would like you to come."

Dylan stared at him for a long moment then turned on his sister. "Did you put him up to this?"

"She didn't," Spence answered. "She thinks you won't want to help us."

"She's right." He looked as if he really wanted to take another drink but Peyton's presence seemed to stop him.

"This is a good project," Charlotte said, her voice vibrating with emotion. "Spence has worked really hard to make something worthwhile here. You, of all people, must see how important it is."

"Do you know what I see? I see a big waste of time and money. You'd be better off tossing your money into the Piedras."

"Why? You don't think we can help anybody?"

Dylan glared at all of them. "No. I don't. You have no idea what it's like. If you did, you'd never have come up with this dumbass plan. What the hell can a week in the mountains do for a guy who's had his legs shot off? Or somebody with a traumatic brain injury who can't remember his own frigging name anymore?"

Spence glanced down and saw Peyton's features had gone pale as Dylan's voice rose in intensity.

"Pey, why don't you go wait in the car?" he murmured.

"Why?"

"Just go," he answered sternly.

She looked reluctant but she obeyed. The dog trotted after her but turned away when she closed the door of the SUV.

"We don't have any idea what these guys have been through," Spence finally said. "You're absolutely right. That's my whole point. You do."

Something dark and haunted spasmed across Dylan's face. "You think everybody thinks the same, feels the same? No way. This isn't a one-size-fits-all situation. But, yeah, I know a hell of a lot more than you. Which is how I know you're not going to fix a damn thing with canoe rides and ski trips."

"Maybe the goal isn't *fixing* anything," Charlotte said softly. "Maybe we just would like to help these wounded soldiers come to terms with their new situation—help them see that no matter what has happened to them, what sorts of limitations or challenges, their lives aren't ending. They're just different."

"Which is your polite way of saying worthless."

Charlotte's mouth tightened, hurt drenching her blue eyes. She stared at her brother for a long moment, and Spence watched the heartbreak give way to a fiery, crackling anger.

"Oh, get over yourself, Dylan!" she finally snapped. "I'm so damn tired of you moping around up here, acting like you don't need anybody or anything, wrapping your pain around you like a hissing rattlesnake to keep everybody away. You lost an arm and an eye. That sucks. It really does. I wish it hadn't happened to you. But you're alive. Doesn't that count for anything with you? You're alive, and as far as I can see, you're wasting that miraculous gift of life you were handed by sitting around hating the world and feeding bits of yourself to that snake."

She rose to her feet and stood over her brother, looking fierce and passionate and wonderful.

"A Warrior's Hope is a wonderful thing for the soldiers Spence is trying to help, and it's a wonderful thing for Hope's Crossing. If you can't see that, I feel more sorry for you than I have since you were injured."

She was close to tears. Spence could see it in the tiny quiver of her chin, a certain watery sheen to her eyes.

She seemed to shove it away, though, and stomped

down the stairs and across the yard, pushing chickens away as she climbed into the car. An instant later, the slam of the car's door behind her echoed through the clearing.

CHAPTER NINETEEN

FOR A FEW SECONDS, he and Dylan gazed after her, the only sound in the clearing the squawk of one of the chickens and the distant sound of a creek tumbling over rocks somewhere nearby.

Finally Spence let out a long breath. "So let's be clear. What you're saying is, you're not going to help us."

Dylan gave him a gimlet stare out of the one clear blue eye not encumbered by a patch. "I think that's a safe bet, yeah."

"Does that also mean I can strike you off my list of motivational speakers once A Warrior's Hope is up and running?" he joked.

Dylan gazed at him for a long moment then actually laughed. "How did I forget what an annoying bastard you could be?"

Spence smiled, unoffended. He was actually feeling quite accomplished that he had made Dylan laugh.

Everybody who went through tough things had to take his own road back. Others could push and guide and help but nobody could chose another's journey for him.

Unlike Charlotte, he didn't blame Dylan for the route he had taken. There was definitely something healing up here in the trees, surrounded by mountains. If it took Dylan a while to find that, Spence completely understood.

He had thought the past two years of his life had been pretty close to hell—a career-ending injury, rehab, the grim reality of a failed marriage, then the charges against him. Having reporters camped out on his door-step had been horrible, not to mention the months and months of miserable press they had churned out.

Compared to what Dylan had seen, done, survived, Spence's life had been cake.

"I wouldn't worry too much about Charlotte. She'll get over being pissed at you. She loves you, you know. And she's worried sick about you."

"That's the thing about Charlotte," Dylan said with a rather pointed look. "She forgives too easily."

Spence let out a breath, wondering how *he* had ended up in the hot seat here. Yeah, he had been a jerk to her. The knowledge had been eating away at him since she had told him, especially since he had no real way to make amends for something that happened years ago.

"She does."

He caught a glimpse of her through the windshield of his SUV and felt a tremendous surge of emotion in his chest. Every time he was with her, he felt this kick in his gut and he didn't understand it.

"This may sound like a cliché," Dylan went on calmly, "but what the hell. It needs to be said. I might be a broken-down excuse for a soldier, but I still know a couple dozen ways to kill a man. Several of the bet-ter ones don't require more than one arm."

Spence raised an eyebrow, wondering just what Dylan had seen on his features. "Care to tell me why you feel the need to mention your interesting skill set right now?"

"We both know why." His friend took a long swig

out of his beer. "Charley isn't your average cleat chaser. She is vulnerable in ways you can't imagine. Before she lost all the weight, she never met anybody who could see beyond her appearance. Or if she did, it wasn't the kind of guy she deserved. I don't know if she's ever even been kissed."

Oh, she had. His mind was suddenly filled with images, especially that incredible moment in her bedroom when she had come apart with just a touch, the most erotic moment of his life to date.

Spence blinked it away. "Charlotte can take care of herself."

"No doubt. She doesn't have to, though. Here's something you might want to keep in mind. If you so much as *think* about hurting my baby sister, just remember that I'm a man who doesn't have anything left to lose."

His complete sincerity touched Spence, especially because he knew Charlotte had other brothers besides Dylan who would step up in a second to protect her. He envied her the steady assurance that the rest of the Caines would always be there to watch her back.

"Warning duly noted," he murmured. "If you change your mind about the event, you know how to find me."

Dylan sipped at his beer. "Don't hold your breath, Smoke. Or my sister, for that matter."

Spence laughed, shook his head and headed for his SUV.

CHARLOTTE SAT IN the passenger seat fighting tears of mingled anger and pain as she watched Dylan and Spence on the porch. What were they talking about so intently? she wondered. Dylan looked grim around the mouth, and

Spence no longer leaned casually against the porch railing but stood tense and still.

Drat her brother. She was so mad at him, she wanted to smack something. Why couldn't he see all the people who only wanted to help him?

"Are you okay?" Peyton asked in a small voice.

"Not really." She fumbled in her purse for a tissue. "My heart just hurts for my brother."

"Because he doesn't have an arm anymore?"

"I don't care about that. No, I'm sad because he's only focusing on what's gone instead of everything he has left."

Peyton was watching through the window at her father and Dylan, her slender features thoughtful. Charlotte thought she saw a hint of compassion there, as well.

The girl seemed genuinely interested in Dylan's situation, which Charlotte considered a positive sign that she was able to look outside herself.

"I guess I just wish he could see how much he has now and how many people care about him and want to help him through it."

Charlotte paused, compelled to press the point. She couldn't help her brother, apparently, but maybe she could give this troubled girl a nudge in the right direction. "Life is a precious thing, Peyton. Gone in a minute. I guess you know that, don't you?"

Peyton's mouth firmed into a line. "Yeah. I do. I still miss my mom."

"You always will. My mom has been gone since I was about your age, and I still miss her just about every day." She tilted her head. "I lost eighty pounds this past year and a half. Did you know that?"

Peyton's eyes went wide and she looked at her in

disbelief. "No," she exclaimed. "Eighty pounds? You must have been *huge*."

It stung but it was nothing less than the truth. "I had an eating disorder, too. It's called compulsive eating. It's different from what you might be dealing with, certainly. I ate everything I could. I ate to hide my pain, I ate to feel better, I ate because I was lonely. When my brother almost died, I realized I was doing more harm to myself than any enemy in war could do with a shoulder-fired missile."

Peyton appeared to mull this over. "My mom was always telling me I have to watch what I eat, that I have to cut calories if I want to be healthy."

"Your body needs food. Healthy food. I eat whenever I'm hungry and I never deprive myself. The difference is, I make smarter choices now. I've decided I want to embrace my life, not hide from it. I just wish Dylan would do the same."

She couldn't tell from Peyton's closed expression if any of her words made an impact. It didn't really matter, anyway. She felt better for having said them.

She watched Dylan take another drink of his beer, and then a moment later, Spence turned and walked toward them. Before her dad reached the SUV, Peyton put in her earbuds. Charlotte was quickly learning the gesture was the girl's own defense mechanism, like a turtle sucking its head back into its shell. For all she knew, Peyton wasn't even listening to music in there.

Spence gave Charlotte a regretful look as he climbed into the SUV. She cut him off before he could say anything.

"I'm sorry I stormed off like that. Apparently, my inner thirteen-year-old girl still surfaces sometimes, and I can't seem to help slamming doors and stomping around. Sad to say, my brothers all seem to be very good at pulling her out."

His soft laugh filled the SUV's interior as he pulled the vehicle around, carefully avoiding the chickens, and headed back down that rutted driveway. "I liked that thirteen-year-old girl. She was funny and...sweet."

"Except when she was slamming doors."

"I don't remember that part. I just remember how you used to review my English essays and write all these cute, apologetic little comments every time you wanted me to change something. 'I'm really sorry, but I think you meant *affect* here and not *effect*.' I still get those wrong, by the way."

She winced. Helping him with his essays had been an agonizing exercise in nuance. She had fought conflicting urges to make the work better yet not be so critical that he wouldn't want her to help him again.

"Well. Anyway, I'm sorry. I probably made things worse for you with Dylan."

He gave her a sideways look. "I don't think anything could have made it worse. He would never have agreed to help with the groundbreaking anyway. You knew that and tried to tell me but I insisted we come anyway."

"I hoped I might be wrong. Dylan *needs* to help with A Warrior's Hope. He just can't see that now, and I don't know how to convince him it would be healing for him."

"I think it's safe to say you've done all you can. From this point on, I guess he's just going to have to figure things out on his own."

"You've been talking to Pop, haven't you? That's what he always says."

"Your dad is a wise man. I've always said so. And

speaking of Dermot, which always makes me think of food… Have you had dinner yet? We're halfway up the canyon already. We could swing up to the ski resort and grab a bite at one of the restaurants there."

She was tempted, so tempted. At the same time, she knew she needed to exercise at least a modicum of caution here. She was in danger of losing all perspective when it came to Spence. She couldn't continue spending so much time with him and his daughter. She had no illusions that Spence would suddenly discover he loved living in a small Colorado ski town and throw down roots. He and Peyton wouldn't be here forever, and Charlotte needed to protect herself now.

"I'd better not. I have so much work to catch up on tonight. Anyway, Peyton seemed tired. I think she's still trying to adjust. Going out to eat might not be the best idea for her right now."

"You could be right," he said, a touch of dryness in his voice as he looked in the rearview mirror. She followed his gaze and found Peyton with her head nestled in the corner of the backseat. She was either asleep or doing a very good imitation of it.

Tenderness washed over her as she looked at those lovely, fragile features.

She already cared deeply for his daughter. When Spence decided to move on, how would she survive without either of them?

They rode in silence the rest of the drive to her house. When he turned onto Willowleaf Lane, she tried to summon the happiness that usually filled her at the sight of her little cottage with its kissing gate, lush English garden, the cute blue shutters.

It was hers. She had worked ferociously hard for it and had built a good life here, a comfortable one.

She had been happy before Spence came back into her life, and she would continue to be happy after he left, she told herself.

He pulled into the driveway and walked around the vehicle to open her door, something she had realized before was a habit for him. She found it a rather endearing one—not to mention surprising, especially when she considered the chaos of his uncertain upbringing and then the entitlement mentality that had likely been part of his life as a professional athlete.

He walked with her up to the front door. "I always liked this house," he surprised her by saying, almost as if he had read her mind earlier. "When I was a kid, I remember thinking it looked like something out of Beatrix Potter. English countryside, Wellies by the door, the whole thing."

She had to smile. "I always thought so, too. Do you remember the family that lived here when we were kids? The Lowells?"

"He worked at the butcher shop, didn't he?"

She nodded. "And she sold makeup to all the ladies in town. I used to love her visits to my mom when I was a kid because she always brought me lipstick samples in tiny little tubes to use for dress-up."

A priceless memory of her childhood, one she had completely forgotten until this moment. After six big strapping boys, her mom had been thrilled to have Charlotte. Despite Charlotte's natural instincts to follow after her older brothers, her mother had tried to mold her into a girlie-girl. She used to help Charlotte put on makeup and her too-big high heels and her oversize dresses.

They would have tea parties and play with dolls and tell silly stories.

She had to wonder if Peyton had known that kind of warm, fun relationship with her own mother. From what she had learned about Jade Gregory, she seriously doubted it. The knowledge made her want to tuck the girl against her heart.

"You're coming to the groundbreaking, right?" Spence asked as she unlocked her front door and walked inside. "A week from Friday. We'll have a small reception afterward. A couple of the guys I played with are coming. I think you'll like them. Lucky and Jess should be bringing their wives."

She certainly recognized the names he had mentioned earlier from all the years she had followed the Pioneers. They were heavy hitters, all of them—literally and figuratively—and it warmed her heart that they would still step in and help him with A Warrior's Hope, even after his downfall.

"I'll be there," she said, aware even as she spoke that, every time she tried to extricate herself from him and Peyton, the connection between them seemed to tighten. "I'll donate all the toffee and fudge you want. Once you approve the final logo for the organization, I can even have it printed on some chocolate gift boxes to hand out to the media. What else do you need from me?"

For one charged moment there in her entryway, she saw an answer she didn't expect—heat, hunger, tenderness. Her body instantly responded as if he had set a match to her, and she flushed at the same time she ached for all she knew she couldn't have.

"For the groundbreaking," she emphasized.

He looked regretfully out at the driveway and the SUV where his daughter waited.

"What you said to your brother tonight touched me. Would you be willing to say a few words Friday to help spread the word, from the perspective of a family member who understands just what we're trying to do?"

With several professional athletes and who knows how many members of the media present? Her stomach quailed at the thought. She hated speaking in front of people, wondering what they were thinking about her. It was silly, she knew, and really narcissistic, when she gave it any thought. Most people weren't nearly as judgmental as she had always assumed, eighty pounds ago.

"I'm not super comfortable in front of a lot of people, but, okay. If you think it would help A Warrior's Hope, I'll come up with something."

He said nothing for several moments, only gazed down at her with an odd light in those changeable hazel eyes, and then he slowly shook his head.

"What?" she asked when he remained silent.

"I just wonder if you have any idea how amazing you are."

With that, he gave her a quick kiss on the corner of her mouth and walked back to his SUV, leaving her to stare after him.

CHAPTER TWENTY

"WHAT THE HELL is he doing here?"

Fury crackled through him, hot and fierce, and Spence wanted to hit something. Preferably the man walking onto the vast terrace of the recreation center as if he owned the damned place.

"Sorry, man." Jess Roman, a close friend since their shared rookie year, gave him an apologetic look. "I didn't know he was coming until he and Kris showed up at the airport. Lucky's the one who chartered the plane. I tried to tell him you wouldn't want Mike to come but he wouldn't listen. I was going to call you from the airport to warn you but I didn't have a chance."

Spence could hardly breathe around his anger aimed at the man he had once respected as a mentor and trusted friend.

"How did he even know about A Warrior's Hope?"

"My fault there. Teresa mentioned it to Kris last week when they were shopping together. Krissy must have told Mike. Now that he's retired, I guess he's got all the time in the world."

Today, of all days, Spence couldn't let this bitterness eat away at him. It was too important that everything go off without a hitch.

"On the plane, Mike was going on and on to Lucky and Ty about a favorite cousin who lost a leg in Vietnam," Jess went on. "How the guy spent the rest of his life bitter and angry and ended up eating a bullet, and how he could have used something like what you're doing to yank him back to his senses."

Spence let out a breath. *Focus on what matters,* he told himself. The presence of Hall of Fame candidate Mike Broderick at the groundbreaking for A Warrior's Hope would only help raise awareness.

Yeah, Spence wanted to bash the guy's head against the wall. So what? He wouldn't. At least one of them still had a little decency left.

Or so he told himself, anyway.

In the mixed-bag category, while he despised Mike Broderick, he adored the man's wife. That was brought forcibly home to him when he spotted Kris Broderick heading in his direction.

"Spencer James Gregory. I suppose this proves you haven't actually dropped off the face of the earth, you've just been ignoring me."

That was true enough but he couldn't tell her that without going into all the reasons why. To avoid the subject, he picked her up in a sweeping hug, all four feet eleven inches of her.

"Put me down, you lunatic," she said with a laugh, even as she hugged him back and kissed his cheek.

Kris was one of his favorite people on the planet. Compact and a little round, with a firecracker of a personality, he suddenly realized she had always reminded him of Margaret Caine before she was diagnosed with cancer.

He set her down and was charmed when she adjusted his collar and smoothed out his jacket.

"I've been a little busy. As you can probably tell," he said.

"So I hear. Moving back to your hometown, taking a new job. All without a word to your friends. Why didn't you ever tell us what a charming place Hope's Crossing is? I feel like I've stepped back in time—and you know me and history."

"Right. This is the woman who keeps the History channel going at all hours of the day and night."

He pictured their house, brimming with antiques and warmth and welcome.

Not to mention her lying, son of a bitch of a husband.

"The antique streetlights—love them!" she gushed. "And our hotel is this fantastic little bed-and-breakfast in a huge old Victorian looking over the town."

"Yeah. Hope's Crossing definitely has its appeal," he answered.

"When Teresa told me last week what you were trying to do here for wounded veterans, I knew at once we had to help all we can. Mike has a check for you. Don't be shocked at all the zeros. I insisted."

He managed a smile, wondering how he could possibly take the man's money—and how he could break Kris's heart by refusing it.

"How are the kids?" he asked, to divert her attention.

"Good. Growing up. Can you believe Annemarie is nine now?"

"No. Wow, I remember when she was born." They had been on a road trip to Chicago, he remembered, a four-game series. Mike had flown back the minute Kris went into labor, and Spence had thrown his first no-hitter.

"They miss you. I wish you had come to see them

before you left town. Maybe we'll come back to ski when the weather changes."

"That would be great," he lied. His smile might just crack his face if he had to keep it there another minute. "Let me introduce you to Harry Lange. He knows more about the history of Hope's Crossing than anybody else in town."

He left the two of them engaged in an intense dialogue about striking miners in the 1920s and turned back to the milling crowd. As it seemed wont to do since she had arrived an hour earlier, his gaze sought out and found Charlotte. Wearing a flowery lavender dress, she was having what looked like an animated conversation with Ty Jacobs.

His mouth tightened. Somebody ought to warn her the guy had a reputation as a serious player—and not just in the outfield.

A sweet girl like Charlotte probably had no experience with a guy like him. She would think all the flirting and posturing meant something real.

With the vague idea of rescuing her—and perhaps subtly warning Jacobs off—he started to head in that direction but it immediately became clear that Charlotte was holding her own.

She seemed relaxed and comfortable with Jacobs, in marked contrast to the fine tension Spence sensed in her when she was around *him*. She laughed at something the outfielder said, the sound musical and light, and to his shock, he felt some of his anger escape.

How did she do that? He was so pissed about Mike showing up out of the blue he could barely focus around it, and Charlotte somehow managed to take the edge off with just a laugh—aimed at another man, no less.

He had to stop this. She wasn't *his* and he wasn't in any kind of position to change that particular circumstance, no matter how much he might wish differently.

"I'M SORRY. I can't tonight. I've got plans," Charlotte lied to the very smooth-tongued Ty Jacobs. He was even better looking in person than he appeared on ESPN, with tanned, rugged features and little crinkly laugh lines around dark blue eyes. Add to that the streaky blond hair and all those muscles and he was pretty irresistible.

Maybe for another woman who wasn't completely hung up on Spence Gregory.

She knew he was only flirting with her because he was bored but it was still a nice little boost to her morale.

"Come on. You can break your plans." He gave her a dazzling smile. "Have dinner with me. I'm only in town for one night. Are you really going to relegate me to a lonely hotel room—stuck alone with the remote control and the minibar?"

"You certainly paint a bleak picture."

"Have a little pity on a guy. Do you have any idea how many nights I spend on the road exactly like that?"

"Probably very few," she said drily.

"A shy, retiring guy like me? No way. Come on. If not dinner, how about at least a drink? You can show me where all the locals hang out."

She laughed. She couldn't help herself. He reminded her forcefully of a couple of her brothers, particularly Jamie and Aidan. "This local generally hangs out at the bead store, where the only drinks are bottled water. Oh, and hot chocolate in the winter. Here. Have some fudge."

She grabbed one of the etched silver platters off a pedestal table Spence's staff had set at convenient intervals around the terrace and held one out to him. "I'm particularly fond of the raspberry fudge. It was an excellent batch."

"Not crazy about raspberries. What's the white one?"

"White chocolate lemon. Also delicious, if I do say so myself."

"I'll try that one." He snagged a piece and took a bite. His face immediately went into paroxysms of delight. "Oh, man," he moaned. "Man, oh, man, oh, *man,* that's good."

"Yes. I know," she answered, laughing at his exaggerated reaction.

"What's the matter, Jacobs? You need the Heimlich or something?"

With a shiver, she realized Spence stood at her shoulder watching his former teammate.

"Fudge. Sooo good," he mumbled around another mouthful.

"I'll send a whole box of the lemon to your hotel room," she promised. "It pairs very well with one of those tiny eight-dollar bottles of wine from your minibar."

He grinned. "You are a cruel, cruel woman."

She managed to smile in response, not quite certain why Spence was glowering.

He should be celebrating. His staff had thrown together a beautiful event on extremely short notice. The terrace was adorned with baskets spilling over with lush Colorado wildflowers. In the late afternoon, it made the ideal venue, overlooking the splendor of the mountains and the site where the cabins would be constructed.

The media was out in force—one of the staff members told her giddily that at least a dozen different outlets had come.

So why was Spence looking so dour?

"Are you ready to say a few words?"

"Now?" Nerves fluttered wildly in her stomach.

"Sure. Why not? We'll give a brief welcome speech, I'll say a few words, you say a few words, then we'll walk down to the groundbreaking for the grip and grins, and afterward come back up here so Jacobs can eat more of your fudge."

She swallowed hard, her mouth suddenly bone-dry. "Okay. Yes. I'm ready."

Spence must have sensed some of her nerves. He leaned in and brushed his lips to her cheek, and she wanted to fall into his heat and his strength. "You'll be wonderful. Don't worry."

He walked away to arrange things and she stood frozen. She had a speech prepared but she had no idea if what she wanted to say would be worth listening to.

"Ah," Ty said suddenly. "Let me guess. The reason you have plans tonight is in some way connected to Smokin' Hot Spence."

"What? No! I— Why would you—" She let out a breath. "Am I that obvious?"

"No. Just something in your eyes when you looked at him tipped me off. That, and the way he came over here ready to bust my ass over a little hopeful flirtation."

"Spence isn't… We're not…together."

Ty looked as if he wanted to argue but the man in question took to the small podium before he had a chance.

"Welcome, everyone," Spence said. "I want to personally thank you all for coming to the groundbreaking for the first facilities of A Warrior's Hope."

How much longer did she need to stay?

An hour later—after all the speeches had been given, every ceremonial shovel had been turned and the group had moved back to the terrace for the cocktail party— Charlotte was physically and emotionally drained.

She had barely been able to speak after Spence's moving words about the reason behind A Warrior's Hope. Somehow she had managed to hold it together in order to speak unemotionally for only a few moments in general terms about what her family had suffered and how her brother was still coming to terms with his life, months after the injury.

She thought their combined words had made the point about the vast need for follow-up care for returning soldiers who had sacrificed so much. She had even seen one reporter surreptitiously wipe her eye, but that might have been allergies from all the wildflowers.

Now her ankle was throbbing from standing in heels for so long, and she had a headache blooming at her temples.

She didn't see any reason why she couldn't go. Her part was done, except for the Sugar Rush gift boxes that displayed the logo for A Warrior's Hope.

One of the staff had directed her to leave them in a room near the recreation center administrative offices. If she could escape through the crowd without too many diversionary conversations, she could set them out on the table for departing guests to take as a memento and then make her escape.

With that in mind, she wended her way through the

people, stopping here and there to talk briefly to people she knew. She pushed open the doors.

After the noise on the terrace, the cool quiet offices were a bastion of peace, one she didn't want to leave. Nobody would mind if she hung out in here to catch her breath, she decided.

She kicked her shoe off and rubbed at her ankle. Most of the time it didn't bother her anymore. She was back running every morning with only a trace of discomfort, but wearing the unaccustomed high heels must have irritated the tendons or something.

Had it really been a month since she had injured it? She couldn't fathom that Spence had been in town that long. Really, in the scheme of things, four weeks wasn't long at all, considering all that he had accomplished.

She rotated her ankle a little more and was just about to slip her foot back into her shoe and grab the fudge boxes when she heard raised voices coming from the reception area just outside the office where she was hiding out.

"I honestly can't believe you have the balls to show up here after everything."

Charlotte frowned. Who would Spence be speaking to with such leashed fury in his voice?

"Come on, man. Can't you let it go, after all this time?"

She instantly recognized the voice of one of Spence's former teammates, Mike Broderick, who had flown in for the media event with the others.

"I've changed. I cleaned up, just like I promised. You can urine test me if you want, right here, right now."

When Spence spoke, his fury hadn't lessened. "You threw me to the wolves, Mike. You were my best friend and you screwed me over. The drugs were the least of it."

Drugs. Mike Broderick. Her heart pumped in her chest. *This* was the core of all the secrets Spence had been keeping. She knew it.

She didn't know what to do. Should she go out there, show herself before this escalated into something even more ugly?

"I was so messed up," Mike said. She thought she heard a genuine note of regret in his voice. "You know how it is. You went through your own shit."

"Not like you," Spence growled. "The minute I woke up and realized I needed the pain meds to make it through each game, I walked away and went through a program. I didn't drag it out for years and destroy other people in the process. I just don't understand why. You didn't need the money. You had all the endorsements you wanted."

"It was never about the money. Things got out of control. I only meant to help a few guys out here and there with their game. You know, show them the ropes, like I helped you."

"You *never* helped me with 'roids or pills."

"You didn't need them. Not until later, anyway, and I would have helped you out there but your own doctor kept you supplied. But other guys weren't you. They needed that little extra boost and the team was better for it. We made it to the pennant race, didn't we? Because of me. It was just another way to play the game, you know? Then everything started falling apart. People started whispering. Rumors started flying. I knew it was only a matter of time until everything busted open."

"You needed a fall guy. Don't think I haven't figured it out. Everything you did, from sleeping with Jade to dragging her into the whole thing, was with the intention of boxing me in so I couldn't break free without implicating Jade and destroying Kris. You knew I would keep my mouth shut. You read me just like you could always read a batter's cues."

"Smoke, you have to believe me. I never thought things would go down like they did."

The note of sincerity in the other man's voice was chilling. Charlotte's chest ached, listening to Mike Broderick talk so casually about destroying Spence's life.

"I thought the club would sweep it under the rug, do a quick mock investigation and then let you go quietly. You were out anyway. Everybody knew you couldn't come back from that injury. But me, I was still on the fast track for the Hall of Fame. How was I supposed to know that asshole reporter from *Sports Illustrated* had sources who leaked the drug bust in your car?"

"You were willing to blacken my rep with everybody in the Pioneers' organization. What the hell did you care if it went wide?"

"I didn't want that. You had to know. Anyway, you never went to trial, right? Everything went away, just like I told you it would. No harm, no foul."

"You son of a bitch." Spence's voice was lethal and she wondered if Mike could hear it. "What about Jade?"

"What about her?"

"She loved you. In her own screwed-up way, she loved you and you used her to get to me, just so you could cover your ass. I know you gave her the pills she took that last day. Because of you, my daughter has to live without her mother the rest of her life."

"I never meant for things to go that far," he repeated. "I swear, I'm clean now and I'm here, right? That's got to count for something. I've got a big check for A Warrior's Hope."

"I don't want your money. Put your checkbook away." All the anger had trickled away from Spence's voice and now he only sounded exhausted—exhausted and un-utterably sad—and she had to clutch her strappy heel in her hand to keep from going to him, wrapping her arms around him and offering any comfort she could.

"Whatever you were going to give to the charity, I'll match it," he went on, "but I don't want anything from you. You can figure out what to tell Kris about it. Hell, you've been lying to her for twenty years. What's a few more?"

Charlotte loved Spence. In that moment, Charlotte realized she loved this man with all her heart.

"Come on. Don't be a prick. We came all this way. Take the check before I—"

His voice trailed off and she wondered for a moment if Spence had strangled him after all, and then she heard a new voice on the scene, a female voice she didn't recognize.

"Before you what, Mike? Don't let me stop you. By the way, you gentlemen might want to make sure no asshole reporters are within earshot before you start throwing juicy accusations around."

Charlotte had to see, to know what was going on. She peeked around the door frame and saw the reporter she thought had wiped a tear during Charlotte's follow-up to Spence's speech.

"Shit." At a glance, she saw Mike Broderick's face had turned an ugly red. "This was a private conversa-tion."

"A juicy one, for sure. Here I was all frustrated that I

can't seem to get cell service out there so I came inside to send an email with Wi-Fi and look what lands in my lap. It must be my birthday or something."

"Dina—" Spence began.

"This is quite a story, Smoke, you have to admit. Hall of Fame candidate Mike Broderick dealing drugs and steroids inside the Pioneers' locker room. And framing his own protégé to cover it up—not to mention sleeping with said protégé's wife in the bargain."

"You've got absolutely no proof," Mike blustered, a note of panic in his voice.

The reporter held up a phone. "Yeah. I do. When I heard the raised voices, I had a hunch and turned on my recording app."

"Illegally obtained recordings aren't admissible in court."

"Maybe not a court of law. But I think our friend Gregory here could tell you a little about how these things roll in the court of public opinion, couldn't you?"

SPENCE EASED A hip onto his assistant's desk, his mind racing. It would be so simple to let things play out this way. Dina could take the story and run with it. Mike would be vilified; Spence would be exonerated. The whole ugly truth would come out, as he had always expected it eventually would.

On the other hand, this would destroy Kris and their children, and Peyton would know Jade had framed him, had hidden the drugs in Spence's car, to help her lover make it to the Hall of Fame.

A disaster, all the way around.

What would Charlotte want him to do? She had to have heard everything through the open door of the darkened office where he knew she must be sitting. He wanted to go in and ask her how he should handle this.

"How much would it take to keep you quiet?" Mike asked urgently.

"More than you can possibly imagine," Dina snapped. "I was a huge fan of Smokin' Hot Spence Gregory. It hurt to watch his name dragged through the mud. You, on the other hand, I've always thought were an arrogant prick. Nice to know my instincts didn't let me down."

Mike quickly changed tactics and his expression took on a pleading note. "Let's think about this. Come on, Dina. Can't we come to some kind of arrangement?"

"Save your wheeling and dealing for the Portland district attorney. You're going to need it."

Spence didn't feel at all sorry for Mike, but he did worry for the innocents who would suffer if the whole sordid mess were aired in public.

"Let it go, Dina," he finally said quietly.

The reporter turned to him, black eyes wide. "No freaking way. Are you kidding me? This is a huge scoop. I won't just walk away."

Spence's life had been intentionally destroyed by Mike Broderick. He thought about the past year marked by bitterness and hatred. What the hell had those emotions accomplished? Nothing. Not one damn thing. Instead of moving on, he had drawn into himself and let his anger fester.

Until Charlotte.

She had helped him look outside himself at people with trials much bigger and life changing than his own.

He was a professional athlete who had been paid an obscene amount of money to throw a ball. When that had been taken away from him, first by injury then by scandal, he had spent far too much time feeling sorry for himself and hating the man in front of him, someone he now saw as rather pitiful.

It was past time to let go.

The people he wanted to help with A Warrior's Hope had volunteered to go into dangerous situations and now had to pay the price for it for the rest of their lives. Compared to their heroics, what he and Mike did made them little better than circus clowns.

Charlotte had taught him how to move forward and focus on the things that really mattered. Knowing she was in the other room listening added conviction to what he knew he needed to do.

"Let's think about this, Dina. What if Mike comes clean on his own terms? An exclusive interview with you. Instead of a scoop you're going to have to dig like hell for, especially because I'll deny everything, you get the full story."

"No way!" Mike exclaimed. He looked ready to explode.

"Mike. You don't have a choice here. You either let Dina take over the story and run with it her way or you control it. You make your apology, you express deep regret for your mistakes and all the people you hurt, you go into rehab. Real rehab. You can still fix this, as long as you're in the driver's seat. You might even still make it into the Hall of Fame."

Mike looked cornered and angry, and after a long moment, Spence set a hand on his shoulder, remembering the man he had once admired so much, who had tried his best to teach a naive nineteen-year-old kid how to handle sudden fame and all the pitfalls that came with it.

"Trust me, Mike. For Krissy's sake, trust me. You've got to go down swinging. That's the biggest mistake I made. I knew I was innocent and I figured justice would prevail. It eventually did, in a manner of speaking, but by then the damage had been done. This is going to come out, either way. You know it is. Give Dina an exclusive interview, laying out everything, then you can start rebuilding."

"You just want to clear your name," Mike said. "I wouldn't put it past the two of you to have planned this all along."

"Think about it. How could I have managed that? I didn't even know you were coming until you walked in. Beyond that, I'm not the master manipulator here. That would be you."

"You can't deny you're going to benefit, either way."

"You don't need to bring my name or Jade's into it. In fact, I would rather you didn't. My daughter has suffered enough. She doesn't need to know what you turned her mother into."

Dina looked at Spence as if he'd taken one too many line drives to the head. "He ruined your life. Why would you want to help him?"

Spence sighed. He couldn't explain it, even to himself; he just knew it was the right thing to do. "He was a good man, once upon a time. I'd like to think that man just got lost somewhere along the way. And he had the brains to marry far above him—Kris Broderick is one of the best people I know and she deserves better."

Mike scrubbed at his face, apparently realizing he didn't have any choice in the matter. "Damn it. I don't know what to do."

He looked like a weak, pitiful excuse for a man and

Spence felt sorry for him. It was an odd feeling after all the months of fury.

"In better days, you taught me that when the bases are loaded and you're facing a full count, your only chance is to listen to your gut and throw like hell. This is one of those times, Mike."

He could see the other man wavering, that it was sinking in hard that his life was about to change, and the only thing he had left was damage control. "I need to talk to Kris before anything happens. I can't just spring this on her. I'll...have to tell her everything."

"Why don't you take a day or two to come up with a plan?" Dina said. "You should talk to your wife, your agent, find a PR rep. I'm good with that."

All things considered, Dina was being surprisingly decent about the whole thing, for a reporter. Spence supposed either way, she was going to have a huge scoop.

"You two can use my office to figure out the details," he said.

Mike led the way and again Spence felt a little sorry for him, something he wouldn't have believed possible even fifteen minutes earlier.

When Dina closed the door behind her, still wearing a stunned expression, he headed over to the darkened office.

"You can come out now," he called softly.

After a pause, he heard a rustle of fabric and then she stood in the doorway, one strappy heel dangling from her hand. Her nose was red, her eyes watery.

"How did you know I was in here?" she whispered.

He debated what to tell her and finally decided on the truth. "You have a very distinct scent. Vanilla and something citrusy. It always makes me hungry."

"Pineapple," she murmured.

"Ah." He tilted his head. "Want to tell me why you're crying?"

She grabbed a tissue out of the little wooden box on his receptionist's desk. "You just… He ruined your life. You could have had payback and you helped him instead. I don't understand you."

He laughed softly. "Sometimes I don't get myself. Come here."

He pulled her into an embrace and, as her arms slid around his waist, he was filled with a vast sense of peace. He couldn't have explained it, he just soaked it in. She had believed in him even before she knew the truth. The wonder of that still astonished him.

She sniffled a little and just held on for a few moments then she pulled away, reaching for that tissue again. "This is going to change everything, you know. You told him to keep your name out of it, but we both know that reporter won't miss a chance to clear the name of Smokin' Hot Spence Gregory if she can."

Oh, how he hated that nickname. It had been a joke among his teammates early in his career, ostensibly referring to his fastball but really more of a dig after one of the women's magazines did a photo spread of him.

"We'll see," he answered.

For so long his goal had been to regain everything that had been taken away from him. But as he looked around this office, as he thought of all the people out on the terrace who were now working together to build something to help others, he wasn't sure what he wanted anymore.

After another few moments, Charlotte exhaled heavily and then stepped away. "I should, um, get this fudge out before people take off. My staff went to all the trouble to fix it up. I wouldn't want to have their work go to waste."

Before he could protest, she slipped her shoe on and picked up a couple boxes from the corner.

"Let me help you with that," he said.

"Thanks."

She gave him a smile that seemed a little forced and handed him one of the boxes. With one more look at that closed door, he headed back to the terrace and his guests.

CHAPTER TWENTY-ONE

AMAZING, HOW A man's situation could change in the blink of an eye.

Three days after Mike Broderick's shocking exclusive interview with Dina Hidalgo hit the media like a flash grenade, Spence's phone rang yet again as he was driving home from the recreation center.

He turned down the blaring rock music that helped him decompress after a day at work. "Yeah, Pete," he said to his agent.

What now? he almost said, but refrained.

"I predicted it. Didn't I predict it? Am I good or am I good?"

Pete sounded gleeful, which Spence considered fairly ironic. Four days ago, the guy had barely wanted to take Spence's calls.

"We're on the brink of a bidding war, son," he went on. "When the Pioneers heard Boston had talked to you about signing on with their coaching staff, they upped the ante. Started laying on all this guilt about how you're a local hero. They created you. The town loves you. They owe you and want to make it right. Blah, blah, blah. I'm still waiting to hear from Atlanta but right now you can basically pick your poison."

Though Mike hadn't given all the specifics while laying out everything he had done, with his wife by his side, he *had* singled out Spence and offered him a tearful, but highly effective, on-air apology. He had expressed regrets for letting Spence take the blame for something of which he had been innocent.

Spence wondered if Kris had forced it out of him. He hadn't spoken with her since the benefit, after one quick confrontation before she and Mike hurried back to Portland, when she had cried and hugged Spence and yelled at him for spending even a minute trying to protect her. His ears still hurt.

In the time it had taken for the capricious media to grab hold of the story and sports fans to begin responding, Spence had gone from pariah to a hotly sought-after commodity.

He couldn't believe it had all happened so quickly. Charlotte had been exactly right. Everything in his world had changed.

He still didn't quite know what to do with it.

"You're going to have to choose, and soon," Pete said.

He gazed out the windshield at the quiet streets of Hope's Crossing, the tidy houses, the well-kept lawns. He waved at Maura Lange, out pushing a stroller and walking a tiny little puff of a dog. She waved back and smiled at him.

Yes, some people had been warmer to him since the news broke but some, like Dermot and Katherine and Charlotte's friends, had been kind to him all along.

"Slow down, Pete. I told you, I haven't decided what I want to do yet."

"You can go where you want. The world is your oyster, and all that shit. But if you sit around with your thumb up your ass, you could miss this chance and end up stuck there in Snoozeville."

"If I remember correctly, you're the one who told me I didn't have any other options left for gainful employment except to come back to Hope's Crossing."

"Different time, different circumstance, man. You've got options now."

He had options. Did he want to take one of them? He desperately needed advice from somebody who didn't stand to make a profit from whatever he decided.

The person he automatically would have turned to was Charlotte. She had become his closest friend in the time he had been back home, someone whose judgment he trusted implicitly, but she seemed to have made herself scarce the past few days. He had tried to track her down at her house and her store but one of the employees had told him she had gone to stay in Denver for a few days.

He wondered if she was avoiding him and was more than a little disconcerted at how that idea hurt.

As if he conjured her up with his thoughts, when he turned onto Willowleaf Lane, he suddenly spied a very familiar figure mowing the lawn of a house that most definitely wasn't hers.

What in the world? He hit the brakes.

"I've got to go, Pete."

"Wait. What do you want me to tell Portland?"

"I'll let you know when I figure it out," he answered and disconnected the call.

Charlotte was wearing shorts and a Colorado State T-shirt. With her hair pulled back in a ponytail, she looked like a coed herself. When she spotted him, she turned off the mower and waited for him to walk across the grass toward her.

"You didn't tell me you were starting up a new lawn-mowing business."

"Ha. Very funny. The Walkers had a baby that was a month premature and has been in the NICU in Denver ever since. I stopped to visit them while I was there, and figured I would take care of this. That way Scott doesn't have to worry about it when they come home this week. I'm just about done."

If Spence left, he would miss that about Hope's Crossing—people stepping up to help whenever they could.

"Let me finish for you. It will take me all of five minutes."

She took in his Oxford shirt and slacks. "You're not exactly dressed for mowing the lawn."

"Humor me. I've been on the phone all day. I need to do something physical."

Without waiting for an answer, he took hold of the mower, started it up and took off, leaving her looking after him with a disgruntled expression.

How long had it been since he had mowed a lawn? He couldn't remember. That had been another of his jobs when he was a kid, mowing everybody's lawn who would pay him. He had vowed never to touch a mower again but right now he couldn't think of anywhere he would rather be than here on a lovely August Colorado evening surrounded by the intoxicating smell of fresh-cut grass.

When he returned the mower to the spot where he had left Charlotte, he found her kneeling down in front of a flower garden deadheading some daisies.

"There you go," he said.

She rose. "It wasn't necessary but thanks, I guess."

"Where do I put the mower?"

"They keep it in a shed in the backyard."

She headed in that direction, trowel in hand, and he followed after her with the lawn mower. The Walker's baby obviously wasn't their first. The backyard had a redwood swing set and a sandbox filled with toys. It was a pleasant space with trees perfect for climbing. The shed even had a little window box filled with flowers.

"How was Denver?" he asked.

She sent him a quick look. "Good. I needed a few things for the store and had to order more paper supplies. It's always easier to do it in person. Peyton stopped into the store this afternoon just as I got back. She looked great. She was excited for school to start. How's she doing?"

"She seems happier than she has in months."

She was starting to hang out with Macy Bradford and a few other girls; she wasn't complaining about going to therapy three times a week, and she was eating better. He thought she already looked much healthier, with better color and definitely more energy.

"I'm so glad her treatment plan is working." Charlotte brushed a little flying bug away from her face. "She told me you're getting all kinds of coaching offers, ever since Mike Broderick's interview."

"Yes."

She gave him a searching look. "You don't sound very happy about it. I should think you would be ecstatic. You've got options now beyond Hope's Crossing. This is everything you wanted, isn't it? To clear your name and return to the game you love?"

"A month ago, I would have agreed with you."

"But now?"

He studied her there in a patch of afternoon sunlight, bright and sweet, kind and lovely. A little wren flew into a gourd-shaped feeder hanging from a tree just behind her. He watched both it and Charlotte while that seductive peace—that sense of contented *rightness* he always found with her—curled through him.

"There are things here I'm not sure I want to do without anymore," he murmured.

"Like…what?" Her shoulders tightened and he thought he saw something that looked like panic flit through her eyes.

He wanted to say *her*. She was the most important thing he didn't want to leave. The word hovered inside him but something, perhaps her sudden fine-edged tension, convinced him the time wasn't quite right for that sort of admission.

He mentally shifted gears. "How can I walk away now, before A Warrior's Hope has even had its first session?"

She seemed to relax a little. "I suppose it would be a little like making a birthday cake, frosting it to perfection and then throwing it away before you even have a taste."

"Exactly. I want to see that first group of soldiers casting out a fishing line, hiking up the Woodrose Mountain trail, waterskiing on the reservoir."

"Understandable."

"And Peyton. She's finally starting to settle in here. What kind of father would just yank her right out again? Even if we go back to Portland, she would have to leave behind people she's started to care about. The therapy is working well and she likes her therapist. I hate the idea of moving somewhere else and having to start all that over again."

"Tough choices, all the way around."

"On the other hand, this is everything I hoped would happen. If I stay here and live quietly in Hope's Crossing, will people still think there was some truth to the accusations?"

"That's a possibility."

"You're not helping, Charlotte. I'm trying to make a decision here. What should I do?"

A mountain-scented breeze washed through the backyard, playing with the ends of her hair. She tucked a loose strand back behind her ear. "Why do you need my opinion?"

"I trust you. I..." *Care about you,* he almost said. The words caught in his throat.

"You've been a good friend to me. Possibly the best friend I've had since I've come back to Hope's Crossing. You believed in me even when, by all rights, you should have thought me an even bigger bastard than the rest of the world."

The little bird had been joined by a few friends. Charlotte shifted her attention to the feeder, but not before he caught an expression on her features that looked almost...wretched.

"I can't help you make this decision, Spencer," she said quietly. "I guess you have to weigh your options and figure out what's best for you and for Peyton."

"Why not? I want to hear your opinion. What do you think I should do?"

She didn't answer and he took a chance and stepped forward, brushing another of those errant strands away.

"What you think matters to me, Charlotte. *You* matter to me."

And then, because he couldn't help himself, because it had been far too long, because his chest ached with the need for it, he kissed her.

At the soft, immeasurably tender kiss, a whole host of terrifying emotions welled up inside him, so big he didn't know what to do with them.

She caught her breath, the sound a little ragged amid the twittering of the birds and the wind rustling the leaves of the tree overhead, then she kissed him back fiercely, her hands clutching his shirt almost desperately.

At the taste of her, the intoxicating scent of her, fire scorched through him, wild and hungry. He didn't care that he was standing in a stranger's backyard, he wanted to lower her to the grass, to kiss her until they were both senseless from it and ease into the warm, sweet welcome of her—

Abruptly, she wrenched out of his arms and stepped back so quickly she nearly stumbled. She was breathing hard, her hands trembling and her color high. She wrapped her arms around her waist, a clear signal that prevented him from reaching for her again.

"Okay," she said, her voice shaky, thin. "You want my opinion. Here it is. I think you should take one of the offers and go."

Pain sliced at him, raw and sharp. "Really? After that kiss?"

"*Especially* after that kiss." She turned away, her attention on the little birds now tossing seeds onto the ground for their fellows. "You broke my heart once, Spence. Before I ever even really knew what love was, you shattered me. I don't think I'll survive if…if I let you do it to me again."

He had been such an ass to her, but how could she give so much power to a cocky nineteen-year-old kid who should have known better?

"Why are you so certain I'm going to break your heart?" he demanded. "I hope you know by now I'm not that jerk anymore."

"I know. And you weren't a jerk. Not really. You were only being honest. But I'm not the fat, awkward girl in glasses correcting your English papers. I…I need more from you than your friendship and a few kisses when you feel like it."

"I can give you more. I care about you, Charlotte. I think…no, I *know* I'm falling in love with you."

He loved her. The truth of it washed over him like a healing rain. He loved Charlotte Caine. She was funny, she was sweet, she was lovely. She made him want to be better.

He wanted her to fall back into his arms, to kiss him and bring that precious sense of peace. Instead, she only stared at him, her eyes huge in her face, and said nothing for a long, long time.

His words hung out there like beach towels on the line, flapping hard in a brisk wind.

"I'm not sure that's enough," she finally whispered.

WHAT WAS WRONG with her? This was everything she wanted. Spence was standing in front of her, telling her he was falling in love with her. *She* should be doing cartwheels across the lawn.

Fear kept her feet rooted firmly in the grass, though.

How could she trust what he said? She had been hurt so many times before.

"What do you mean, it's not enough? What more do you need from me?"

She had no answer for him and hated herself for her cowardice.

The hard truth was, she didn't believe him. He said he was falling for her and, while some part of her wanted to burst with joy that he would even *think* the words, she just couldn't comprehend how it could be possible.

He couldn't really love her. He might think he did, but that was only because she had been kind to him since he'd come to Hope's Crossing when few others had accepted him. She had helped him with A Warrior's Hope and, she wanted to think, with Peyton.

He was confusing friendship and gratitude and maybe pent-up sexual desire for something deeper.

When he went back to the world where he belonged, he would see the ridiculousness of ever thinking he had feelings for someone like her.

The thought of him and Peyton leaving ripped across her like a sudden blizzard, leaving icy desolation in its wake.

How ridiculous she had been, to ever imagine she had loved him when she was fifteen. She hadn't known anything about love. Compared to how she felt now for this man, that was nothing, the difference between a pitcher's mound and the vast looming splendor of Woodrose Mountain.

She loved him more than she ever believed possible. How could he possibly share the same feelings?

"I believe you *think* you might...care for me," she said slowly. "That means the world to me. I'm flattered.

I am. But when you get back to Portland, I'm sure you'll quickly see you were mistaken. Now that everyone knows you didn't do anything wrong, you could have any woman you wanted. You're Smokin' Hot Spence Gregory, for heaven's sake. And I'm...me. Why would you pick the shy, quiet, *inexperienced* owner of a candy store when you could have anybody?"

He stared at her blankly. "I don't want anybody else. I want you. How could I not? You believed in me when nobody else did. You made me laugh when the world seemed a pretty miserable place. You were kind to my daughter even when *I* didn't like her very much. I love you, Charlotte."

The words tried to mend the broken cracks in her heart. She wanted so desperately to believe him but the fear was too huge. How could she ever endure the pain when he realized his mistake and left?

Her throat was thick with tears. They burned behind her eyes but she forced them back. She needed to go now before she lost the battle.

"Take the job, Spence. Go back to Portland. I'm sure Peyton's specialists can recommend an eating disorders program for her there. She can reconnect with her friends and you can return to the world you love."

It took every limited acting skill she might have ever possessed but she managed to summon a tiny smile that felt as if it might split her face apart. "Hope's Crossing will be a better place because you were here. We'll take what you've started with A Warrior's Hope and run with it. You know we will. Take the job. I wish you the very best with it."

Because she knew she couldn't stand here and talk to

him another moment without breaking down, she leaned on tiptoe, kissed the corner of his mouth with the last of her strength and walked away as quickly as she could.

CHAPTER TWENTY-TWO

"This is *so* not going to work," Spence stated.

Alex McKnight hung one last tea light lantern to go with about a hundred more that bobbed from the ceiling. She adjusted it a little and then climbed down the ladder with an amused look that made Spence grind his teeth.

"Will you just relax, oh, ye of little faith. Don't you trust us?"

He looked at the group of women scurrying here and there throughout the ballroom of the Silver Strike Lodge.

Katherine Thorne and Mary Ella McKnight were hanging yards of silver-spangled tulle, Maura Lange was primping one of the glorious flower arrangements that were probably costing him a fortune. Even the immensely pregnant Claire McKnight was there, directing Evie Thorne on the placement of one of the twenty or so little fairy-light-bedecked trees that lined the edges of the vast ballroom.

He couldn't believe how much effort they had put in today. The ballroom looked spectacular, he had to admit. Romantic and elegant. He had it on good authority all the decorations except the fresh flowers were the same ones used for the last Giving Hope Day gala and dragged out of storage for a good cause.

The string ensemble he hired, recommended by

Maura Lange, was warming up on the dais. There seemed nothing left for him to do but stand and fidget.

"What if she doesn't come?"

"She'll come. You really need to relax, Spencer." Claire McKnight gave him a warm smile, even as she stretched a little and pressed a hand low on her belly. He really hoped she didn't go into labor right now.

If not for Claire, none of this would be happening.

It had been a miserable week. Just about the worst of his life—and that was saying something from a man who had once been arrested and charged with multiple drug counts.

After Charlotte walked away from him in her neighbor's backyard, he had figured he would give her a little while to think about things but she refused to take his phone calls and wouldn't answer the door.

He felt as if he had been living in a weird state of limbo. He couldn't make any decision, despite the increasingly frantic phone calls from Pete. He knew he couldn't stay here under the current circumstances but he couldn't seem to generate any enthusiasm for taking a new coaching job somewhere else.

Finally, Peyton—probably in desperation—had asked him to take her to the bead store two nights earlier to pick out a couple things for the earrings she insisted she had to have to start school the next week.

He had gone with her on the vain hope that Charlotte might be there.

Claire McKnight had taken one look at him and dragged him into a little garden behind the store. He found himself telling her the whole story and asking if she had any advice to help him convince Charlotte he was in love with her.

Claire had made a quick phone call and, the next

thing he knew, the garden was filled with lovely chattering women filled with terrifying plans and schemes.

"She'll be here," Maura added her assurance now. "How could she refuse? Harry basically commanded her to come. I heard his end of the call and it was masterful as only Harry could be. You should have heard it. He told her he was so impressed by her speech at the ribbon-cutting that he insisted she come up to the lodge to help him wine and dine some potential big-money donors to A Warrior's Hope. Even I was half convinced he was sincere. She won't refuse, not if she thinks for a moment it would help the cause."

"Relax," Alex said again, giving him a peck on the cheek. "By the way, you look fantastic. Trust me, Smokin' Hot Spence Gregory looks much better in a tux than he ever did in those cute little tight pants you baseball players wear."

"Ex-baseball players," he corrected, ignoring the rest of what she said.

The title should have stung. Once, it would have, but he had come to accept that part of his life was over. He had finally called Pete this morning and told him he wasn't taking the Portland job or any other. He loved baseball, loved being part of the game. He always would. But he had other dreams now. Whatever came of tonight, he was committed to A Warrior's Hope. The first group of six veterans was coming in a few weeks, and they had events planned from now until Christmas. He couldn't wait to see all their plans come to fruition.

Anyway, he had heard through the grapevine that Hope's Crossing High School had a struggling baseball team. He figured they might be able to use him somehow.

"She's coming! The valet said she just parked her car." This announcement came from Maura's twenty-something daughter, Sage, whom he had just met this afternoon and who grinned broadly every time she looked at him.

Peyton and Macy let out little squeals, and Peyton even clapped her hands. He loved seeing her so excited about something, even what he was very much afraid would be his impending humiliation.

What if it didn't work? What if she took one look at him and walked away?

His heart wouldn't be the only one broken.

He felt a moment of sheer panic. He wanted to call the whole thing off, just tell everybody this had been a huge mistake. How could he, though? They had all gone to so much work. He was committed, whether he wanted to be or not.

"Okay, that's our cue." Alex made a grand sweeping gesture to the women still putting up decorations. "We'll have to leave it how it is. Sage, help me with this ladder. Come on, everybody. Let's get lost."

"Oh, come on," Peyton begged. "I want to stay. We could hide behind the curtains!"

Oh, man. Wouldn't that just add to his misery, to have all these women witness him falling on his face? Claire must have seen the moment of panic. She gave him a sympathetic look and made a shooing gesture to both girls. "Not this time. Your dad can tell you what happened later."

In that moment, he was filled with a vast rush of affection for her—for all of them. How had he been so lucky to count them as friends?

For a guy who had grown up with a poor excuse for

a mother and then married a troubled, lost soul, he was overwhelmed with affection for these strong, beautiful, wonderful women who had gone to so much trouble for something he was very afraid was a losing effort.

"Thank you all. I don't know what to say. Only thank you."

"Just don't screw this up!" Alex ordered.

"No pressure, right?"

She grinned at him and gave him another kiss on the cheek. Claire gave him one, too. Everybody else waved, except Peyton. She ran back and gave him a tight hug that just about made tears come to his eyes.

"Good luck, Daddy," she whispered and ran to catch up, leaving him standing alone in the ballroom with his heart pounding out of his chest.

CHARLOTTE PAUSED INSIDE the vast soaring lobby of the Silver Strike Lodge to quickly adjust her panty hose.

Was the dress too much? She hoped not but Harry had told her the last-minute cocktail party was a fancy affair. Anyway, it gave her a chance to wear the sleek midnight-blue waterfall of a dress she had worn exactly once, the last time she was here at the resort, for the Giving Hope Day gala.

Despite the undeniable fun of dressing in something that made her feel confident and pretty, she was in no mood to make nice with a bunch of moneybags. But when Harry Lange called and asked a favor—no, *demanded*—it was really hard to say no.

She looked around, realizing she had no idea where to go. She had assumed Harry would have someone to greet her and direct her to the penthouse apartment she knew he kept here at his hotel but no one readily stepped forward.

After a moment's hesitation, she headed to the concierge desk. "I'm sorry. I hope you can help me," she said to the twentysomething man seated there whose name tag read Jason.

"I'll do my best, ma'am."

"I'm supposed to be meeting Mr. Lange and his party for cocktails here at the hotel but I neglected to ask him where. Do you have any idea or could you contact someone to find out?"

The man's polite but impersonal expression instantly melted. "Oh! You must be Ms. Caine."

His broad smile took her aback. "Yes."

"I can help you. If you'll follow me, I'll be delighted to show you the way."

Okay, weird. Before she could protest, the guy jumped up and started heading through the lobby quickly, leaving her no choice but to hurry to catch up in her high heels.

"This really isn't necessary. I'm familiar with the lodge. I've been here many times. I'm sure if you give me directions, I can find the gathering myself."

"It's no problem at all, Miss Caine."

The lodge was renowned for its outstanding service but this seemed excessive. Perhaps the concierge thought she was one of the muckety-muck benefactors, ready to write a big check.

She didn't have a chance to ask as he led her down a long hallway. She knew this route. Strange. He was leading her to the ballroom, the site of the Giving Hope Day gala.

She couldn't help remembering the last time she

was here with Sam Delgado and her own ridiculously high hopes. She hadn't known at the time—how could she?—that Sam was already deeply in love with Alex.

What a lifetime ago that seemed. Her pride had been pricked a little when he had told her later that night about his feelings for Alex but her heart certainly hadn't been involved. She could barely remember that sting, compared to the vast aching pain that had come since.

"I think there's been a mistake," she finally said to the concierge. "I was told this was an intimate cocktail party."

Jason gave her a bright smile full of teeth and charm. "There's no mistake. This is exactly where you're supposed to be. I hope you have a lovely evening."

He opened one of the doors to the ballroom for her, and she frowned at the weirdness of this whole thing but walked through the door.

The first thing she registered was the ballroom decor. It was exactly as it had been two months ago for the gala. With a sense of déjà vu, she recognized the gauzy, glittery tulle, the lanterns she herself had hung with Alex and Maura, the little fake trees around the perimeter, lit up with twinkly lights.

Only the flower arrangements were different, roses instead of gardenias.

The moment she walked through the door, music rose to greet her, a soft, sweet ballad from a live string ensemble, and a man wearing an elegant tuxedo walked toward her.

She froze, trying to process what was happening. She couldn't seem to make her brain work as he moved closer.

"S-Spencer," she managed to squeak out. "What's

going on? Where's Harry? I'm supposed to be at a cocktail party."

"There's no cocktail party and no Harry. Only me."

Her pulse was so loud in her ears, she couldn't think over each beat of her heart. He looked wonderful in the tuxedo, big, muscled, gorgeous. She hadn't seen him in a week, and she suddenly realized how very much she had missed him. Every night had been worse than the one before. Ignoring his calls had been the hardest thing she had ever done.

She couldn't talk to him. Not yet. Afraid he would come to her house, she had even taken to staying with Dylan up in Snowflake Canyon. At least her brother didn't ask any questions, though she knew he wondered why he suddenly had a silent houseguest who cried herself to sleep every night.

"What is this?" she whispered. She would have gestured around to the ballroom except her hands were shaking, like the rest of her.

"You owe me a dance."

She stared at him. "Excuse me?"

He gazed at her with an intense expression that sent butterfly wings fluttering hard in her stomach. "A long time ago, I was an idiot and because of that I missed out on my one chance to go out with you. You asked me to a dance and it didn't happen. I'm more sorry for that than I can ever say, but the fact remains, you asked me to go with you to a dance and for various reasons, we didn't go. I'm taking you up on the invitation now."

She swallowed. "This is ridiculous."

She couldn't do this. She couldn't play these games, couldn't let him hold up her dreams for ridicule. She turned and ran to the door but the man she had seen snag an infield pop-up and turn it into a triple play moved far faster than she ever could.

He blocked her exit and she was forced to stop her momentum or crash into him.

"Charlotte. Dance with me. Please."

"This isn't going to change anything."

His mouth twisted into something that looked like sorrow. After a long charged moment, he nodded slowly. "Okay. I respect that. I don't understand where you're coming from, but I'm not going to be arrogant enough to tell you your feelings don't matter."

He gestured to the band. "I would still love it if you danced with me. I went to all this trouble, after all. Well, your friends went to all this trouble, anyway."

She should have known her friends had been up to something. When she stopped to think about it, everyone had been acting very strangely the past few days—whispered conversations that abruptly ended when she showed up, pointed looks exchanged behind her back but witnessed when she gave a nervous backward glance.

Darn their romantic little hearts.

She looked around at the ballroom, remembering well how long it had taken to set this up the first time around. And a band. He had brought in a band—a small string ensemble, four men and two women, playing something exceedingly romantic. She thought it might be Vivaldi.

Charlotte drew in a ragged breath. He had gone to all this work. For her. He said it was her friends' doing but she knew they wouldn't have hung the first lantern unless Spence had agreed.

And Harry. She remembered that strange phone call.

Harry Lange had apparently created the cover story that compelled her to show up here tonight. He wouldn't have done that either without Spence's knowledge and approval.

Why? Why would he go to so much trouble?

Because he loves you.

A tiny corner of her brain whispered the words to the rest of her but she still was afraid to believe.

"One dance. That's all. Please, Charlotte."

She knew it was a mistake but she couldn't resist this chance. With her heart racing, she stepped forward slowly, into his arms.

He clasped her right hand in his left, and she curled her other hand around his neck. He was warm and smelled delicious, that expensive aftershave he rarely used, probably because he knew his own pheromones were enough to make women swoon.

"I should warn you, I was a lousy dancer in high school, and I haven't gotten much better over the years," he murmured.

Amazingly, she was filled with the absurd urge to laugh. "That's okay. I'm probably good enough to carry both of us. Pop made each of my brothers practice with me before he let them go to any school dances. Six proms, six homecoming dances—you do the math."

He smiled down at her, and she wasn't sure her heart was big enough to hold all the emotions surging through her.

They danced through the empty ballroom while the tea lights twinkled and the orchestra played softly just for them. Contrary to his claim, Spence was a fine dancer. She should have known he would be, athletic and graceful, sure-footed.

It was a priceless, magical memory. Wanting to burn every instant into her mind, she closed her eyes and rested her cheek against his lapel, listening to each beat of his heart.

When he raised their clasped hands to his mouth and pressed his lips to her fingers, it was too much. Her feelings were too big, too terrifying. If he kissed her, she would be lost.

She slipped her hands free and jerked away, making a break again for the door. Again, he beat her to it.

"Charlotte, stop. Why are you running away? What did I do wrong now?"

"You didn't do anything." Tears began to trickle out, and she couldn't seem to stop them.

He looked stricken at the sight of them. "This was a stupid idea. I'm sorry. I just thought, I don't know, that maybe if I could go back and try to fix that one moment when I hurt you, we could get past it and move forward."

She shook her head, tears falling freely now. "It wasn't a stupid idea. Don't say that. It's the most romantic, wonderful thing anybody's ever done for me."

He stared at her. "So why the hell are you crying?"

She laughed and wiped at her eyes with shaky fingers. "I'm crying because I'm such an idiot." She had to say it, just push forward through the fear and get it out.

"I love you, Spence," she said in a rush. "I've loved you most of my life. Or I thought I did, anyway. When you came back, I fell in love all over again, and this time I knew it was no silly crush. This was the real thing. I love you so much I can't breathe around it but… I'm so scared I won't be enough for you. I'm terrified you'll never love me as much as I love you."

He continued staring at her without saying anything.

She had never felt so foolish, so horribly stupid, not even that moment when she had stood listening to him talk about her in the hardware store.

She fumbled in her clutch for the tissue she knew was in there, avoiding his gaze. Finally she found the darn thing and, as she pulled it out and wiped at her eyes, Spence started to laugh. It rippled through the ballroom, even over the soft music, and she heard relief and triumph in it.

He came over and took the tissue from her, wiping her eyes with a tenderness that made her cry all over again.

"You're right. You *are* an idiot—about this, anyway. This isn't some kind of competition about who loves the other one more."

He gave her that patented, devastating Smokin' Hot Spence Gregory smile. "Of course, if it were, I would remind you which of us made a pretty good living because of his fierce competitive streak. You have to know, there's no *way* I would ever let you win a contest like that. You'll just have to accept that I'm always going to love you more."

He did have a very well-developed sense of competition, she had to admit.

"Look around you," he went on. "How can you think for a second I don't love you enough? I'm so crazy about you, I put myself through all of this, for *you*."

She imagined the logistics that must have been involved in creating this wonderland, of her friends carting out all these decorations from the storage unit in town, hanging the lanterns, ordering the spectacular floral arrangements.

"For the past two days, I've had to endure all of your

friends giggling and smirking at me while they made plans for this. That's not even mentioning all the crap I've had to take from Peyton, who thinks this is the most hilarious thing she's ever heard. She's been completely insufferable."

He all but wagged his finger at her. "And just so you know, I had to personally approach Harry Lange. Do you have any idea how excruciating that was? He made me practically promise him our firstborn son in return for letting me use his ballroom and agreeing to make the call to order you to his imaginary cocktail party. Look at me, Charlotte. I'm wearing a damn tux. I *hate* wearing a tux."

She almost smiled at that. He likely had no idea how gorgeous he looked. Hearts had probably broken all across town as he drove up here.

She looked around at all he had done for her and a soft warmth began to beat back the icy fear, inch by inch.

"I don't know how much more proof you need," he murmured. "I love you, Charlotte. You're kind and loving and beautiful, inside and out. You're everything I never knew I needed."

He stood in front of her, Smokin' Hot Spencer Gregory, with his heart in his eyes. He was hers. She might be an idiot but she wasn't about to let him go because of some ridiculous fear.

In the next breath, she launched herself at him, wrapping her arms tightly around his neck and kissing him with every ounce of love she had stored up her whole life.

After one brief, shocked moment, he kissed her back with fierce emotion.

They stood that way for a long time, wrapped together

on the dance floor until gradually Charlotte realized something subtle had changed. The music had stopped.

A moment later, they heard a throat clearing over the sound system.

"Excuse me, sir."

Spence looked up at the violinist Charlotte had completely forgotten about—just as she had forgotten the other five members of the orchestra ensemble.

"Would you like us to keep playing?"

He glanced down at Charlotte, a question in his eyes. She smiled and took his hand, and they danced together there in the empty ballroom while the music played and the tea light lanterns flickered gently overhead and her happiness bubbled over.

* * * * *

HARLEQUIN
Reader Service

Enjoyed your book?

Try the perfect subscription for Romance readers and get more great books like this delivered right to your door.

See why over 10+ million readers have tried Harlequin Reader Service.

Start with a Free Welcome Collection with free books and a gift—valued over $20.

Choose any series in print or ebook. See website for details and order today:

TryReaderService.com/subscriptions